DEMON RISING

EMBERS DUOLOGY
BOOK ONE

Victoria Larque

BUTTERDRAGONS
PUBLISHING

Title: Demon Rising (Embers Duology Book One)
Series: Embers Duology
Author: Victoria Larque

Published by Butterdragons® Publishing
https://butterdragons.com

ISBN: 9789493229303 (ebook)
ISBN: 9789493229310 (paperback)
ISBN: 9789493287167 (trade paperback)
ISBN: 9789493229327 (audio book)

Cover Design by: Dazed Designs

Audio book narrated by MJ Webb and Joshua Schubart

For my mother, who reads everything I write.
I love you a thousand worlds.

He is my Maester
He wants to torture me
He wants to own me body and soul
To save my sanity
I must escape

The rumor of an Angel captured
Was a glowing bit of hope
I fought my way to him
And pleaded my case
With determination

****

They caught me
The Demons in the dark
They dragged me
To the fiery depths of Hell
To an eternity of pain and degradation

She came to me at my darkest
Offering a deal
A way to escape together
Forbidden possibility will free us
But bring Heaven and Hell upon us

by Helle Gade

Chapter One
Mihr
Somewhere along the Skeleton Coast,
Namibia

The air beneath my wings was cool and smelled of the sea. I dove low, gliding just above the frothing, green-gray waves, letting the spray catch on my face. The water glittered in the moonlight, as did the fine, white sand – I could almost feel it beneath my bare feet. The memory of walking along this very beach, at ease, free, and much younger, was brimming in my mind, almost coaxing a smile to my lips. For a split-second melancholy at what I'd lost since then spread through my chest, pulling me down with its heaviness, but I shook it off quickly. I could not afford to lose my focus.

I flapped my wings and rose higher, until I was next to Rapha – my assigned partner on this mission. He smirked, young idiot that he was, and winked at me, before flipping back into a looping effortlessly. His white wings made next to no sound and his well-trained body twisted in the air gracefully.

"Stop it, if we are attacked while you're peacocking around, you'll get killed," I told him, my voice distorted by the heavy wind.

"Come now, Mihr, I could finish a squadron of Demons off in my sleep." He whooped and twirled to the right in a precarious display of bodily control and flying skill.

Instead of letting him egg me on into topping his foolish aerial acrobatics – which was what he was after –

I scanned the area for any signs of enemies before following Rapha's course. We passed the beach and the small town nestled on it, then flew inland for a few minutes, until an old shipwreck came into view.

The mast pointed into the night sky like a broken black bone, sharp yet brittle. The ship itself was mostly covered by desert sand that had eaten away at the nautical carcass, smoothing over the wood, and breaking down the metal parts piece by piece. Bits of rust sprinkled the ground around the ship from where it had fallen. My younger self would have stood in awe before investigating the wreck, driven by a need for adventure, but I reigned in any foolishness this familiar atmosphere conjured. Apparently, it didn't matter how much time had passed – this favorite childhood place made me feel young again.

Without a sound, I landed on the soft ground, and immediately wanted to pull off my heavy boots and sink my toes into the sand. Curse this place and the way it spoke to my heart! I had no time for dallying, and no time to lose my shoes.

"Rapha, get back here," I ordered my charge, who was busy sticking his head into a porthole. "There have been Demon sightings around this wreck just a week prior. If you don't want to lose your head, I suggest not sticking it where it doesn't belong."

The young Angel laughed, his voice booming through the wreckage. Then he pulled his head free and grinned at me, "I heard you were a legend among the holy warriors, I did not know you were such a party-pooper."

"Party… pooper?"

Rapha wiggled his pinky around in his ear, pulled it out, and grimaced at his unearthings. "You know, a sour-puss, a downer. I thought flying with you would be fun and exciting." He wiped his pinky on his pants.

I stared him down for a few seconds. "You go that way. Keep your eyes open and be ready, the entrance has to be nearby."

He said nothing but made his way around the wreckage – in the direction I had indicated – hand on his sword-hilt.

Had I been younger, I would have acted on him goading me, but I had lived through enough young – recently turned – Angels to know that it didn't matter. Eventually, they learned and eventually, they lost that light in their eyes, that hunger for adventure and action. Hundreds of years of war could do that, if they lived long enough.

I rounded the ship, nearly drawing my sword as a gecko dashed past me and vanished in the net of succulents draped over a small dune to my left.

I breathed in the quiet night air, knowing it was too quiet. The creatures of the wild – even if no one would expect their density around these parts – were usually noisy. Geckos most of all. But there was no cackling from the males to lure a female to their hole. There was no jackal yowling, no hyena whooing and shrieking, not even a cricket chirping. We were definitely in the right place. The animals around us knew same as I did. There was danger afoot, unnatural danger, unholy danger.

My senses on high alert, I crept past the ship until I saw Rapha emerging from the other side. The wind picked up and I smelled them. Sulfur and ash, death and decay. Sweet rot and tangy roast.

As quietly as I was able, I pulled my sword from its sheath, motioning for Rapha to join me a few paces ahead, behind a large, white boulder. His eyes wild and excited, he dashed forward while pulling his own weapon. Biting his lower lip, Rapha spied around the corner of the limestone, his fingers flexing and grabbing his sword intermittently. "Where are they? Did you see them? How many?"

I held a finger to my lips to shut him up, then tipped it at my nose before pointing ahead.

Rapha's nostrils flared as he tried to sniff out what I smelled with absolute clarity. The odor grew thicker, more rancid – to the point of me twisting my lips in disgust. The Devil be damned, I hated the smell of Demons. The fact that their feet, hooves, and claws stomped through and defiled the very desert I had so loved as a child made me tighten the grip on my blade.

Foul beasts, unholy abominations. They had no right to walk this earth, no right to see the heavens above, not even from down here.

Slowly, I inched closer to the boulder's edge and peeked past its jagged rim. My breath left me in a rush – there was no way we could attack them and live.

Ten Demons strolled through the dunes, side by side, as if it was their place. The full, fat moon made their huge, dark bodies stand out like black paper cuttings against the near-white sand. It was fairly easy identifying the kinds of ilk coming toward us. The four Raiders – turned Humans that had entered Hell as sinners of various stages – were large and muscular, with numerous sets of horns twisting from their skulls. The four Wanderers – tall, slim figures, covered in layers of organza – seemed to float across the sand. And the two Incubi – breathtakingly seductive Demons who derived sustenance from intercourse – strutted through the night alluringly. The only upside was that neither of the Incubi had a Hellcat with them. Those large, winged beasts often accompanied their masters, who rode them into battle. But their absence was only a slight consolation.

I had fought and killed many Raiders and Wanderers, even though the former were incredibly strong and possessed various magical abilities, and the latter could make a Human burst just by shrieking. They didn't worry me, not even their numbers. The Incubi, however, did. Incubi were higher Demons, their thrall extremely powerful, and no match at all for Rapha, who'd surely never seen one up to this point. My charge didn't stand a chance against the two, and I couldn't take on the ten of them on my own.

We'd have to wait, watch, and then call for backup. "Stay low," I whispered to Rapha. "We will let them pass."

The young Angel's eyes lit up with anticipation. "Then we'll attack from behind, got it." He swiped some straying blond locks from his eyes, and his wings shivered with excitement as he turned from me.

I softly nudged him in the side until he looked at me again. "No," I mouthed, as the Demons got even closer. "No attack. Too many."

Rapha frowned, a crease appearing between his brows. He scrutinized me for a few seconds, his expression morphing into something close to disgust, and I had to restrain myself from making the idiot eat sand.

The Demons slowly passed us, and one of the Wanderers floated over the patch of succulents underneath which the gecko had taken shelter. The plants cracked and withered to black – dead in an instant. I knew the little reptile looked much the same and silently cursed. *Destruction without cause, like a child in an anthill.*

"We can take them," Rapha whispered when they were farther off.

"No," I insisted. "You have never fought Incubi. You're not ready yet."

His lip curled up aggressively, "You don't know that."

Typical hero complex. Typical former Human soldier. They were all the same. Rush into action without thought and without fear. "You are not fighting other Humans," I told him. "And if you die in this form, you are gone for good. No more second chances, no more Heaven, no more anything. You understand?"

His wings trembled so hard that his feathers rustled audibly. "I understand."

I was just about to release a pent-up breath when his scalding gaze found me. "And you should understand that living isn't everything. We are Angels, we protect, no matter the cost. I guess you have forgotten that over the countless years of being a coward. Legendary warrior, my ass." He pointed in the direction of the shore, "What happens when they reach the village? Who will protect the Humans from them?"

"Rapha," I said, the warning in my tone bordering on aggression. "Fly and get backup. We have enough time before they can do true damage to anyone. Go. Now."

He shot into the air with one flap of his white wings, where he hovered for a wingbeat. "I am not taking the chance of them being too fast," he said, before shooting off into the direction of the Demons.

I cursed, flinging myself into the air to follow him. There was no way I'd reach him before the Demons noticed, and no way we'd survive them. I bit my teeth together and raced on as fast as I was able – the wind blowing past my face, making my eyes sting – but I knew it was in vain. Still, I couldn't let the idiot get killed on my watch. Not so close to his first death.

****

I heard a yell – a war cry – from Rapha as he unsheathed his sword and cursed a bit more. Hadn't he learned anything during his training? What were they teaching these young things nowadays?

His premature psych-up alerted the Demons, and while he was close and fast enough to slice the first Wanderer's head clean off, two other Wanderers shot into the air ahead of him.

I strained my muscles, beating my wings at a break-neck speed to come to his aid. Right before the Wanderers could snatch Rapha, I barreled into them – eliciting screeches that had the calming quality of nails on a chalkboard. Dodging their claws by inches, I cut the wails short with two precise swipes of my blade. Black, oily blood sprayed through the night and burned on my skin where it landed. Having smelled and felt it countless times before, I still had to fight the urge to gag. The stench of Demon blood was like pressing your nose into roadkill – heated by the sun for hours on end.

Beating my wings to gain a little height, my eyes fell on Rapha, who engaged with three Raiders, while the one remaining Wanderer and Raider launched themselves at me. The Incubi stood together, clasping hands as they smiled, watching Rapha with a lustful gleam in their eyes.

"Shit!" I muttered, focusing on the two coming at me. I dove down, slicing through flesh and organza as I met the Wanderer, but a sharp pain tore through my upper left leg, where his claws mauled my skin and muscle. Using my sword like an axe, I hacked at his hand, and flapped my wings in a backward motion. A hair-raising cry erupted when his hand fell toward the ground, severed from both our bodies.

Twirling into a fast spin, I shot down toward the handless Wanderer and finished him off with a clean strike, just to come up against the Raider. With his curled horns aimed at me, he attacked. The Raider's black eyes gleamed like the pits of Hell itself, his sharp teeth revealed in a gruesome smile as he estimated my line of flight to catch me with his horns.

Pulling my right wing flush against my back, I left the other spread out wide and leaned all my weight into the turn. I dodged his horns and sliced him open with my blade from top to bottom. Right before my head hit the ground, I somersaulted and landed on my feet, catching my fall in a crouch.

"Well, well, well," a sensual voice rasped. "What have we here?"

I straightened and cursed some more. Rapha was up against one of the Incubi, who rubbed his shirtless upper body against the young Angel's back while snaking a clawed hand around his neck to grab his throat. Rapha gasped, his eyes dreamy as he let go of his sword. The sand caught the blade with next to no sound and I took a stance, gripping mine tightly with both hands.

Rapha had managed to kill one more Raider, but that still left two Wanderers to circle me. Along with the second Incubus. The Demon sauntered toward me, every step dripping with masculine sensuality that had me reciting prayers of protection. I had been trained against this kind of Demon, had even fought some through the ages, but it had never been easy, and took a lot of focus. I had to consciously tell my hands to stay closed around the grip of my sword, and my body to stay alert and ready.

Doing my damnedest to not make eye-contact with the Incubus and still watching his every move, I felt the reality of the situation catch up to me. This was it. This was how I died. There was no way out.

"Let go of your blade, Angel. Or my companion will rip the throat from your delicious little friend," the Incubus coming closer to me said.

"No. If I do that, you'll kill us both." I flexed my fingers, feeling a gust of wind blowing tiny grains of sand against and into the open wounds of my leg. "Like this, I'll take as many of you, abominations, with me as I can."

The Demon stopped and smiled, making me swallow and shake my head to clear it. No matter how much I hated his kind, his smile was speaking to parts of me I had not known I had. Dark and unholy parts. Parts that wanted to do unspeakable things. To ask unspeakable things, to command and submit at the same time. I bit my teeth together and did the only thing I could. I attacked the Demons circling me with all I had.

Seconds later, the remaining two Wanderers lay on the ground, their dead eyes collecting sand as their heads rolled through the dunes. With an angry roar, the Incubus launched himself at me. He was faster than I ever remembered an Incubus being. He littered my body with countless small and shallow cuts from his daggers and dodged each of my swipes. At least he wasn't smiling anymore, but that didn't really help as my wounded leg grew more tired of my weight with each passing second. When I started spreading my wings, the Incubus flashed past me, pulling his claws through my wounds in the process. Fresh golden blood flowed down and soaked the thirsty ground as a yell tore from my chest.

What felt like pure fire raced up my leg, spread through my wound, branching to my hip, and further up. Agony soon covered my entire body, and I felt my leg give out. *Poison.* He had to be a very rare Sumu-Incubus – a subspecies that had poisoned claws. A poison that would even stun an Archangel.

My other leg cramped, and I sank to my knees, still managing to hold my body upright and my sword tightly, but I felt my body weaken and prickle with every heartbeat. The Incubus danced away from each of my sloppy swings and laughed when an alarming numbness followed the pain. I fought it, fumbled with my sword and tried to get up, but my body didn't listen to me anymore.

I landed face-first in the sand. Rough hands pulled me up and lay me on my side, before taking my sword from me. The face of the Incubus came close to mine, wearing that dazzling smile. He licked my cheek once, winked and positioned my numb body so that I had a direct line of sight to Rapha and the Demon having him in his grasp.

There was no way to help as they stripped Rapha of his clothes, his face a mask of adoration. No way to stop the Demons from taking him right there in the open. I couldn't shield my ears from the cries of ecstasy, couldn't help but smell the sweat, lust, and sex in the night air. Couldn't get up as they started mutilating him in the throes of passion, couldn't do anything as his cries turned from lust-filled to the ones of utter terror and agony as they ripped off his wings.

I lay there, my eyes drying, prompting tears to stream down my face because I couldn't close my lids. Forced to watch Rapha losing his wings one by one, before his body was torn to shreds until he was truly gone. Grains of sand entered my nose and mouth with each breath, and I concentrated on the feel and taste of it. Coarse and salty. Round grains that tasted like childhood.

Mighty God, I have failed you, I thought as the Demons set their eyes on me, red with satisfied lust. Gruesomely beautiful, covered in Rapha's golden blood, they sauntered their naked bodies over to where I lay, leaving what was left of my young charge strewn across the dunes.

"Let's see," the one that had incapacitated me said, his voice guttural yet sharp. He bent over me, presenting me with a full view of his genitals as he swiped my shoulder-long hair to the side to view the nape of my neck. "No mark and four wings."

The other Demon smiled. "That means he's an original."

I was pushed back, and the Demon crouched lower to hover over me. "A born Angel." He smiled, "Hell hasn't had your kind as a guest in about five hundred years. I bet Lucifer would love to meet you." He kissed my sandy lips, biting my lower one till it bled into his mouth. "You are coming with us, pretty boy," he whispered against me. "Contrary to popular belief, we *love* sharing in Hell."

Chapter Two
Fane
Hell, First Ring

I watched my reddish skin turn black, the veins growing yellow, shining like a roadmap of fire, spreading down my forearms and into my fingers. The stone warmed when my palm met it, its texture like cracked crystal, but softening beneath my touch. I closed my eyes and breathed out, willing my fire to enter the stone. Onyx. The composition was flawless and malleable in almost every way I could imagine. The black wall of rock smoothed and heated as my fingers sunk in, and using my other hand I twisted and broke the stone from its form — exactly the way I needed it to. I pulled my hands free and slammed both fists as high up into the wall as I could, sending rock and debris flying everywhere.

I breathed in through my nose, relishing the smell of crushed rock. Cool and fresh in this otherwise hot and desolate place. I dug in, the stone crushing beneath my fingers, and once my hold was strong enough, I dragged my fists apart from each other, opening the wall to the next room in an arch. The critical part was getting the round shape at the top right, like drawing a circle freehand. Once I was happy with shape and size of the arch, I concentrated on the surface. The frame. This took the longest, and by the time I was done, I could tell from the strain in my back that I'd spent several hours on the form and decoration. Opening my eyes, I stepped back, admiring my handiwork, while shaking out my hands and rolling my shoulders, then watched my skin turn back to

21

its normal, reddish color. The arch shone and blinked in midnight black, polished by my fingers to perfection.

"Magnificent," a male voice said behind me, bringing a grimace to my face. "There really is no one who compares to you, Fane." He stepped closer, until I could feel his breath on my naked shoulder.

I shivered, not in a good way. The guy actually made my skin crawl. It really was a bummer that he owned me. "That's what they say, Lord Ragon," I mumbled.

He brushed past me, making sure his arm touched mine and the back of his hand grazed my hip. I had to force myself not to move, not to trip him so his leering face would plant into my decorated wall. That would bust up that pretty, behorned face good.

"Exquisite," Lord Ragon whispered, skimming the intricate arch decorations with his palm. The shiny black stone was twisted, looking like a black-barked tree, its edges ripped into sharp spikes. Molded around the arch was Lord Ragon's history, his battles won, and his prized possessions. All things I had to memorize and then eternalize here, in his newest palace. He palmed the stone as if he would a lover's body, while giving me suggestive glances.

I bit my teeth together to keep from cursing him to Heaven and back. He was goading me, as well as being his usual idiot self. If I gave in and reacted, it would seal my fate. Instead, I turned from him. "I'm done for today. My energy is sapped. I'll need to replenish myself before continuing with the furniture."

"Well, if it all turns out like this, I'm happy to let you go for now." He walked over to loom behind me again. "Oh, Fane, very soon you will be among my conquests, then you can etch your own likeness into the stone. You should give in and become part of my harem.

It would be easier than this… silly, little fight you're putting up."

My self-control – measly to begin with – snapped, and I spun to face him. "We have a contract, *Maester*, and it forbids you from touching me. The Hellcourt hasn't ruled in your favor yet, and I will do anything and everything in my power to win my freedom."

His red eyes narrowed, and fury flashed across his face for a second, but he reined it in and smiled indulgently. "You will never be free, little Ember, Demons with your powers might not be physically strong, but your talents will always be sought after. And it doesn't help that you look the way you do." His gaze roamed over my body, and I was a heartbeat away from head-butting him. "I will fully own you, Fane, and when I do, there will be no contract to save you from me. But rest assured… you'll enjoy every moment of it."

All I could do was turn and strut from the room with my head held as high as possible, no matter how much I wanted to kill him. Because he was right, my kind, Embers, were one of the physically weakest Demons in Hell, and I wouldn't last a second against him in a fight. Plus, if I did give in and harmed my Maester in any way, the Hellcourt was sure to lean his way. I stomped through a black hall, ignoring the still working builders around me, and snarled at nothing.

It wasn't like he was going to lose anyway. Lord Ragon was a Demon prince. Rich and powerful as he was, he could buy any verdict he wanted. And that right there was the bane of my existence, the one rule in Hell. *The strong rule over everyone else.* I was a weakling, with a big mouth and an even bigger talent when it came to my craft at shaping stone. So, various Maesters had owned me throughout my life, Ragon was just the latest in a row of stupid fuckfaces. In addition, he was bent on owning me in every sense of the word. No matter what, I'd find a way to avoid that outcome, but my time was running out.

Stepping outside the palace of said fuckface, I made my way through stony streets lined with black manors of varying grandeur and size. Just at the edge of the Waste, that was coming into view, these palaces marked the domain of the Demon lords who ruled over this ring. The very outer ring of Hell.

It felt like a weight lifted when I left the mansions behind me and entered the Waste. My naked feet sank into the dark, sparkling sand and I couldn't help a smidge of joy that entered my heart at the feeling. The sand was soft and warm, shifting beneath a lazy, hot wind.

If I ignored the lamenting ghostly souls coming my way to get into the deeper rings of Hell, I could almost relax a little. But their wailing was horrifying and their empty eyes the stuff of nightmares. Souls laden with sin on their arduous journey to the center, to Lucifer himself, where most would be born again as Demons. Fodder for the war, that everlasting shitshow that consumed countless of us. Thinking of the war nearly plunged me into an unwanted memory, but I stopped it before it could unfold.

"Not today, Lev," I muttered and walked on.

Sidestepping the damned souls as best I could, I hurried on. There was no time to mope or dally. Today was Saturday on the surface – the realm of Earth – the one day of the week I always looked forward to. And I still needed to change. Before the pull started.

My feet took me past the Hole, a bar amidst the Waste that was beginning to roar with life at this time. I spotted my roommate Maeve, a Fury, dancing through one of the coalbeds, her face alight with joy as she plucked some feathers from a set of Angelwings hanging from a pole. She blew the feathers she'd collected at a Raider, who accepted her invitation with a devilish grin.

I smirked when their lips met with abandon and walked on. *No time for glorious debauchery.* I needed to get away from this reality for a few hours, leave Ragon and his advances behind me, and I had counted down the days, longing for today.

Crossing the Waste took only a few minutes, and soon I climbed the jagged rocks to our little cave. Maeve had acquired this spot of mountain, overlooking the Sea of Despair, and I had carved a set of caves into it.

Once I'd reached my bedroom, I sank down next to my stony bed – a slab of granite – and focused my fire into my fingertips. The stone parted beneath my palms, a lot more brittle than the onyx from before, and I reached into the hole I'd created, taking out my clothes.

My stomach felt like bubbling lava as I pulled the shirt over my head and swapped my short shorts for yoga pants. Despite everything, excitement gripped me. Now, being excited by a boy of eleven summoning you to the midst of his bedroom might sound weird to downright creepy, and when it happened the first time, it was just that. Weird, and creepy.

I couldn't fight a smile as I recalled his dumb little face when I – a half-naked, reddish Demon – manifested in the pentagram he'd drawn on the floorboards in front of his bed. Hell only knew where he'd found the old tome containing spells and summoning rituals. Dax had even re-functioned a blanket into a hooded coat – said it felt like a magician's robes – looking amazingly stupid the way he stared at me while clutching his star-spotted makeshift-robe closer. Then he'd screamed, changing my life forever.

****

25

The pull started in the pit of my belly, and was –
in all fairness – a nauseating feeling, but I smiled through
it, nonetheless. The world around me twirled and danced,
the dark stone of my cave mixing with the red veins of
lava gleaming from the walls, until the only color I saw
was gray. I hunched over as I felt my body explode and
sighed once it reformed on the surface. *Finally.*

"Here she comes," were the first words I heard,
spoken by one of my two favorite Humans.

I opened my eyes, stemmed the tide of nausea,
and grinned at said two favorite Humans. Camille and
Daxter.

Cam pushed a button on her phone. "Four hours
left, starting now."

"Fane," Dax said, and used the tip of his shoe to
make a dent in the pentagram I was standing in so I could
exit. The boy rushed to me and I hugged him, my heart
warming as I kissed his messy, tightly curled hair.

"Good to see you, Daxter," I said.

Cam watched her son and me with a smirk,
waited until he'd untangled himself from me before she
threaded her arm through mine and gave me a kiss on the
cheek. "Welcome to movie night, you sleaze," she said,
her pale, green eyes filled to the brim with mirth. "How
was your week?"

"Same old, same old. Built a few things, roasted
a few sinners."

Cam laughed, making her curly black hair
bounce and revealing that cute gap between her front
teeth. She had a laugh that could rival the dirtiest
Demon's. It was one I would know and love anywhere.

"What are we watching?" I asked, drawing my
other arm around Dax's shoulders, strutting from the
room with one of them on either side.

"You liked the one with the dragon and the boy, right?" Dax asked.

"I sure did."

"Well, we got part two for you today," Dax piped.

"There is a part two?" I asked, my eyes wide. We made our way through the corridor and into the living room. When I'd been summoned here the first time, I had spent minutes examining the hardwood floor while Cam and Dax had cowered somewhere, completely shocked by my sudden – and very clearly non-human – appearance. Who did you call when your son accidentally summoned a Demon into his bedroom? The cops? An exorcist? Cam hadn't known what to do and after mustering all her courage, she had locked Dax into the bathroom, found me lying on her floor scraping and smelling at the wood – something I'd never seen before – and had demanded answers.

We ended up on her couch, eventually sharing a bottle of wine. We've been best friends ever since. And I visited my favorite Humans every Saturday since, for almost a year now.

"Of course, there is a part two," Camille said. "There is even a part three, and a series."

"What?" I picked up Dax and spun him until his feet lifted into the air and he whooped and giggled. "We shall watch all of them!" I declared, twirling us both in a circle. "One can never have enough of those two goofballs and their friends."

Only a few minutes later, the three of us sat on the couch, a huge bowl of popcorn in our midst, as we relaxed and enjoyed the movie. Once Dax left for a bathroom break, Camille took my hand and squeezed it. "How are you holding up?"

I squeezed back, allowing myself a moment of vulnerability. I knew I was safe here, if only for as long as my summoning lasted. "Ragon has petitioned the Hellcourt for a reversal of the clauses in my contract."

"He did *what*?"

I nodded, dread tightening my throat.

Her face scrunched up with incredulity. "But those clauses keep you safe from him, they protect you. He won't get through with it, right?"

"Yes, they do. And yes, I believe he will." I looked at our entwined hands. "Once he has complete control over me, I won't be able to come here anymore."

"You have to fight it, Fane! It's a court, they will have to rule fairly."

I chuckled, but it was a bitter sound, even to my own ears. "It's a court, yes, but it is beset with Demons. Demons who can be bought, intimidated, and swayed. I have no illusions that Ragon will do everything he can to annul *all* the clauses that grant me the small amount of freedom I got since..." I swallowed, knowing that even after all the times I had told Cam about him, it was still hard saying his name. "It's all I have left of him. Those damned clauses."

Cam threw an arm around me and pulled me close. "I know, love. I know."

I chuckled again, my voice thick with tears, "Thought I would be over it by now. I should be. I mean, it's not like he was a good guy."

"That doesn't mean you didn't love him," Cam said. "And your guilt will also not vanish overnight, sweety." She hugged me tightly.

"Damnation, I really didn't want to think of Lev today," I said. Swiping stray tears from my face, I cleared my throat. "And I'm not." Packing as much finality into my voice, I drew in a large breath.

"It's okay, you know I always got you," Cam squeezed my shoulder with one hand, and I lay my head on her shoulder, thanking the Devil that I had been summoned to this house a year ago. Without Cam, I would have lost it.

"I know. I just have to make sure Ragon won't reach his goal. Somehow."

Even the thought of knowing how powerless I truly was, made me both livid and frightened me to the core. It had taken a great deal of pain and suffering until I had those clauses added to my contract. Clauses that allowed me a modicum of freedom, and forbade my Maesters from abusing or even touching me against my will in any way. They were protection in a world where I should have had none. Lev's gift to me. To shield me from himself.

No, I was not giving up what I had found after all these years, a place I felt safe in and people I called family, even if it was only for one night a week. I had to find a way to stop Ragon.

"You'll get through this," Cam said and rocked us back and forth. "And thoughts of Lev will grow less over time. You know you did the right thing, even if it hurts."

Fighting past this moment of weakness became harder, enveloped in her warmth. "The only thing I really care about is not being able to see you guys. I don't think I could stomach it."

"Well, if you don't come back, I'll spend my life sinning, so we'll eventually see each other again." She kissed the top of my head, and I felt her smile against me.

I drew back, my sadness and guilt replaced by utter horror. "Don't even think that, Cam. Hell is not a nice place. I shouldn't even have to tell you that. You know some of the things I have seen, done, and experienced, but by Lucifer, I will not see you in that shithole. Do you know what a soul has to go through to even reach Lucifer, to become a Demon? No. And you don't want to. You have to promise me that you'll never, ever consider what you just said."

I palmed her face with both my hands, threading my fingers into her beautiful black locks. "Promise me, Cam."

She rolled her eyes and stuck out her tongue. "Okay, okay. I promise."

I sighed in relief and let my hands sink. I wouldn't wish my existence on anyone, least of all my best friend.

"But we'd take over the place, you and I," she said, wiggling her brows.

I snorted. "Sure, right after we'd charm old Lu from his throne. Do you even know how many circles of Hell we would have to cross?"

"Dante says nine," Dax said from the doorway as he strolled into the room.

I snagged him into a hug and ruffled his hair until he protested loudly. "You are way too young to be reading Dante."

"I didn't." He twisted from my hold and grinned at me, his brown eyes holding the same mirth his mother's always did. "I just looked at the schematics and theories. You know, since I met you, I have developed an interest in your home."

"Smartass," I mumbled. "But Dante was right, there are nine circles." I swallowed, knowing I could never explain the horrors of each one to him, no matter how old he got.

"On which one do you live? Are they the same as Dante says?"

I threw Camille a look, and she nodded for me to go on.

"Well, I live in the first one. Right between the Sea of Despair and the Waste is a granite mountain range. My buddy Maeve and I live in a cave in that mountain. And no, Dante was right about some things, but not all of them."

Picking up the remote, I un-paused and we settled back into our movie.

I didn't like talking about my home to them – especially Dax – and before now I'd avoided it. Even telling them felt like touching them with the ugliness I carried, and I never wanted that.

Cam knew about many things, but mostly personal stuff. I'd never tell them about Hell itself. For one, it wasn't a pleasant topic, and it was dangerous telling anyone about it. Even if I trusted Cam and Dax, one wrong word could attract the wrong kind of attention. Hellish as well as heavenly. And no Human should want either.

****

After my four hours were up, the summoning wore out and I was pulled back home. As always, the two had laden me with gifts. Chili chips, which I loved, and cushions for Maeve, who by now slept in a bed adorned by countless of them. I didn't care much for them as they interfered with my skin touching my stony bed and I needed to feel grounded to stone while sleeping. It calmed me and was my only means of defense, should I need it.

The moment I was whole again, I stalked out of my room and into Maeve's. The Fury was busy sending the Raider she'd brought home from the Hole packing.

"If you're not up for round five, get the fuck out," she snapped when I walked into the room.

The Raider snarled at her in between stepping into his shorts, tucking his junk from my view. "Greedy slut."

Maeve laughed, making her hair fan down her back in velvety-black waves, and her perfect breasts bounce. "Thanks, dearie. Now get out, you limp prick, we're not a hotel."

I stepped to one side when the Demon stormed past me, and threw Maeve a cushion. "Greetings from Cam and Dax."

She caught it and hugged it to her chest. "Damn. I have no idea why you spend so much time with these Humans, but I do love the pillows." Her blue eyes found mine. "Just got back?"

"Yup."

"Then you haven't heard, yet?"

"Heard what?" I asked.

"Horace and Valo brought an Angel with them from the surface."

I stared, my mouth open in shock. "An Angel?"

Maeve smirked evilly. "A born Angel. I can only imagine how much fun everyone is having with him in the Deep. Guess I'll see for myself when my shift starts tomorrow."

The name of Hell's dungeon sent a shiver down my skin. I hated that place, had spent some years there, carving cells, and being tortured. Some of the Maesters I'd had before Ragon and Lev had been pigs – even by Hell's standards.

"A born Angel," I whispered. An idea formed inside my head, it was both terrifying and making me grin like a maniac. "That is the best news in decades."

Chapter Three
Fane
Hell, The Waste,
close to the Second Ring

An Angel was a game changer. Provided I got to it before the rest of the Hellspawn had torn it to shreds, as they were bound to eventually. That very much depended on the winged fiend's constitution, and its capability to suffer. But there was nothing in Hell, on Earth, or anywhere in between that could suffer like an Angel. So noble, so righteous, so pure. Their suffering was certainly something to behold, they lost themselves to it completely, as only they could.

It gave me hope that it was still alive. But it being a born Angel meant I had to hurry, no doubt Lucifer himself would want a piece of it. I hoped that the Prince of Evil had too much to do right now, still, if I wanted to view the Angel intact – mostly – I had to beat feet. Plus, Ragon would be looking for me soon as I still had work to do on his mansion.

At the border between the first ring and the second, right behind the mansions where the higher Demon lords lived, was a steep ladder, adjacent to a chasm, leading to the Deep, the dungeons of Hell. It was the closest entrance to the Deep from where I lived and worked, and the one I would take. Granted, dangers lurked along the way, but I would be damned if I entered the deeper rings for a safer passage. Down there, danger was relative, and I would rather face monsters trolling my path than the Incubi and Succubi of the third ring.

I grimaced and shook the thought from my mind, weaving my way past the grand mansions next to the Waste. I knew my way around, had helped shape countless of these manors myself. The stone walls I had worked on warmed in recognition as I skimmed my palms over their smoothness. The memory of our touch, of me shaping them, ever present. It was a comforting warmth before descending the ladder, and I felt the loss as I stepped closer to the chasm.

My stomach rolled and clenched with nervousness and I told myself to get a grip. My way outside could be lying down there. In the Deep. I had to face it.

The ladder was rickety at best, and I cursed more than once working my way down. Never a fan of heights, I shook all over, trying hard to keep myself from looking past my feet. I kept my eyes firmly on the sandstone I was facing through the rungs of the ladder, taking comfort in the stone. Even if I slipped, I was close to a wall of stone, one touch was all I'd need to halt my fall.

After what seemed like hours, but could only have been a few minutes, I reached the bottom of the chasm and stepped from the ladder to look around. My eyes unable to pierce the utter darkness, I lifted my right hand and willed my skin to change. Heat gathered in my palm, wrist, and lower arm, until my veins glowed like lava, shining a dim light on my surroundings. It wasn't much, but I was able to see where I was going.

A narrow path led into cracked rock, barely high and wide enough for a Raider. I hiked up the little bag containing my clothes for the surface and slipped into the crack without problems, soon searching the wall with my fingers, finding my way as sure as if I'd travelled this path a thousand times. My instincts on high alert, I listened closely to what the stone told me. The smallest vibrations carried to my fingertips, thus enabling me to navigate past corridors and nooks that had inhabitants. Down here, countless critters dwelled, not as dangerous as the Demons above, but they'd take a bite out of you if you weren't careful.

The soft glow from my veins threw shadows past the jagged edges of the tunnel, praying on my fear and imagination. I saw movement where there was none, shadows that looked like dark forms darting away or toward me. I felt eyes watching me, heard soft growls when I got too close to occupied territory, and had to beat feet when heavy paws and sharp claws sounded not far away. The scraping of those claws on stony ground made me clench my jaw, the sound as unpleasant as screeching Wanderers. Not to mention that the sounds grew closer steadily. I was being tracked.

My heartbeat accelerated as I sped up even more, and promptly stumped my little toe on the edge of a wall. Cursing, I limped on and decided to make my whole body flare up so I could run. My presence was known. It made no sense to get caught now due to not being able to see shit.

A few seconds later, every vein I owned, shone from my skin and my hair threw bouncy, bright light all around me. Like a live flame, I flickered through the tunnel at a sprint.

My breath ragged and my heart hammering like mad, the tunnel expelled me near the Deep. All I had to do was pass a large flat space, littered with geysers… and a pack of Hellhounds lounging smack dab in the middle. There were pups. And they surrounded something small, yipping, and swiping at it.

"Just my luck," I wheezed, dimming my inner heat until my skin turned to its normal, non-glowing, red.

There was no way I could sneak past them. I would be dinner before I made half my way across. No, I had only one option, surprise. And the hope that the older hounds would flee, bringing their pups to safety. I took a bracing breath, then ran straight at the hounds and whatever they were circling.

My naked feet smacked the stone beneath me as a yell tore from my chest, rising to a roar. Sharp black ears rose, red-glowing eyes zeroed in on me, and growls answered my battle cry. Their sharp teeth glinted in the gloomy light as their flews rose to reveal them. I pushed off the ground, jumped into the air and closed my eyes with a smile when I barreled towards the cracked, stony floor. My feet sank deep into the stone, sending bits and pieces of it flying everywhere. Pressure reverberated through me, then punched into the ground with the force of my impact. The geysers around the hounds erupted with heat, the steamy air hissing and roaring like a beast come to life. Then lava shot from them, bubbling, orange heat sizzled though the air and soon yips and squeals sounded over it as the Hellhounds raced across the plateau, herding their pups away from the lava and me.

Already the lava had receded to lazily bubble from the geysers and I straightened. I smiled like an idiot, proud that my fireworks had worked. Truth be told, my show had not been dangerous at all. But the noise and heat had served its purpose. Thank the Devil that my audience had only been Hellhounds worried for their pups. Had it been different, I doubt my little trick would have worked. Well, Hellhounds and a Hellcat kitten. The small thing the hounds had surrounded spread its wings in warning and hissed at me.

"Pspspsps. No? How did you get here, kitty? You should be up in the pens of the third ring, choosing your Incubus or Succubus." Stepping from the hole I had created, I shook off bits of dust and sand before making my way over to the kitten slowly. It hissed once more, then zipped off, not yet able to fly, it flapped its wings and hovered every few steps. Soon it vanished from my sight and I frowned. Gosh, they were cute when small. But I didn't have time to bring it back where it belonged.

The fact that it would likely not survive made a small pang of guilt hit my chest, but there was nothing else I could do.

I sighed and headed for the entrance of the Deep. It was a side entrance, not prone to have anyone standing guard, still, I hoped it was early enough for the place to be empty. And if it wasn't, I hoped Maeve would be good on her word. My roommate was a fickle being and not really what you would call reliable, but she had promised to help me once I got inside. Her guard-shift inside should have already started.

To my utter delight, the corridor leading to the deeper cells was empty though, and I descended ever deeper without meeting anyone.

Low moans and rasped whispers haunted my way as I passed shackled – long forgotten – prisoners. Their beaten eyes followed me, the complete absence of hope in them a sign of how long they'd been here. A knot of anxiety started twisting in my gut. I knew that feeling, knew how hours, days, weeks, months, and years could turn into blinks, swallows, and the sound of a beating heart. Eventually, time became something unfathomable, measured differently. I knew. And because I knew, I would be damned if I let Ragon undo what Lev had granted me, just so I could possibly end up here again. The smell of Lillithium – Hellstone – entered my nose and I almost gagged. Bitter, acidic. *Blech.* I was careful not to graze the walls with my hands or I would feel it, too. The one metal I couldn't manipulate, the one thing that could keep even an Ember like me contained. It was all around the Deep, the feel of it constricting and dead. Not right.

My strides grew quicker, Ragon would not take away my scrap of freedom. A freedom that had nearly cost me everything.

This place still held so many of my fears, the smells, the sounds, even the stone I touched, it was all anchored into my very being, a maze I occasionally ran through in my nightmares. It had been long ago since I'd been here, tied up in my very own cell, and I had underestimated how much it would affect me to be back here.

"Get it, and get out," I whispered to myself as my heart hammered behind my ears and my hands shook uncontrollably. "Get the Angel and get out."

I passed a corner and stopped short. A line of demons came into view, leading to the very last cell across from me.

My skin bled to an oily black, so I could better hide in the shadows surrounding me, as I searched the corridor for Maeve.

"Damnation," I whispered when she was nowhere to be seen. Just then, a familiar burst of laughter to my right had me sigh in relief. The Fury strode past my hiding nook alongside a few other guards. I snuck behind them and tapped Maeve on the shoulder, she spun to me, a snarl on her full lips until she recognized me.

She fell back and followed me into the shadows. "Fane, this is crazy," she hissed, her tall frame shielding me from view. "There are too many people here already. How do you plan on getting inside unseen?"

I glanced around her, at the line of burly Raiders, sharp-featured and leathery-winged Cambions, Ifrits,

Gargoyles with stony faces – literally – and the one or other Demon prince.

"The only thing that would make them leave would be the news of Him coming."

Her blue eyes widened, and the brown feathers of her impressive wings rustled as she began shivering. "Are you out of you mind?" she snapped. "I can't announce Lucifer if he isn't coming."

I shrugged and smirked. "How would they ever know he didn't come, if they left?"

My roommate crossed her arms and bit into her lower lip, the light of nearby torches anchored to the walls throwing stark shadows over her beautiful face and curled horns. "I dunno, Fane. If anyone found out I helped you…"

A small smidge of guilt floated through my chest when I answered, "Come on, I only want to talk to it. Get it to cut my magical bond with Ragon. That's it." The guilt evaporated at the thought of my Maester. "You know what he wants to do to me, Mae. You're a Fury, no one will even *think* about messing with you, but me? If I don't have my clauses, I am fucking helpless. Please? Let me try and talk to it."

She shook her head, making her black tresses sway, but her face grew softer, "How would you even convince it to help you?"

"I have my ways." And just like that, the smidge of guilt was back. I had exactly one card to play and everything hinged on it, and it didn't involve talking to the Angel as much as springing him free. A fact that I couldn't tell Maeve, or she would never help me.

She would possibly take the fall for it, but Maeve was a Fury. She was able to look out for herself. "I only need a little time with it."

She gave me a stern nod and squeezed my shoulder once. "If you make it outside, good luck." Her lips pursed as she gave me a once over. "I'll miss you. A bit."

"Yeah," I whispered. "I'll miss you, too."

Letting her hand sink, Maeve turned on her heel and stomped off, squaring her shoulders with the sort of born authority I never had the luxury of knowing. "Okay, people, let's break it up," she shouted as she went.

Growls, yowls, yells, and angry voices followed.

Maeve walked on, shoving hardened warriors out of her way like they weighed nothing. "You can, of course, stay," her clear voice rang over the commotion she'd caused, "but then you'd have to explain to *Him* that you disobeyed his direct orders."

In the blink of an eye, silence rang through the corridor as though it were empty. Like one body, the line of Demons turned and headed past me, for the exit. Even the other guards followed suit at a nod from Maeve. The Fury winked in my direction when she and her peers passed me, and a breath escaped me. Nothing like dropping old Lu's name to empty a place out. The Devil was not to be fucked with, everyone knew that.

Heart in my throat, I traipsed down the empty corridor until I stood in front of the cell they had all wanted to get into.

I had seen – nay, dealt and received – my fair share of gore, hellfire, and violence, and usually kept my composure. Which is why I was miffed to discover that what I saw before me, made my stomach roll with unease and my heart speed up in wonder. I had never seen anything as breathtaking and upsetting before.

In the middle of the cell, spread-eagled and naked, lay a man – the Angel. It was badly beaten and bruised, its back a crisscross of whipping wounds so severe, parts of its skin were missing. Gray feathers covered the stone floor. Long feathers, tufty, small ones, and those that stuck to the floor, crippled and clumped together by blood, until they resembled spider legs. It didn't matter that the blood was golden, and not red or black. It also didn't matter that the nauseating reek of gore, meat and burnt hair, coupled with loads of other excrements, was overpowered by the smell of the creature. Clean, fresh, what I imagined spring and air smelled like. It wasn't like I knew as I'd never been able to leave Camille and Dax's house, because of the proximity laws of a summoning.

It didn't matter, because torture and pain always looked and felt the same. Its eyes – a clear pale-gray color, reminding me of the storm clouds forever hovering past the Sea of Despair – were filled with pain. And rage. And – it shouldn't technically know the feeling, but clearly did – hate. Its bloodstained face turned to look at me as I walked toward it, its hate-filled eyes blinking at me from between dirty-blond curls. The chains, it was bound by, clinked softly with each move it tried to make.

"And what do you want, demon filth?" it rumbled, its voice coarse and deep, too dark for such a being of light. And way too sensual. For the first time since hearing about it, I began thinking of it as he. It was a beautiful he. A bit worse for wear, of course, but beautiful, nonetheless. I probably wouldn't have thought of him as beautiful if he hadn't been bloody, bruised and plucked.

"Have you also come for some feathers? Or is it blood?" The handsome being of light spat on the ground. "Or do you want to whip me, as well? You'll have to look for a patch of skin still attached to me, so make it quick."

I smiled and placed my fists on my hips. He was snarky, I liked snark – was fluent in it. "Nope. None of the above."

The Angel frowned and narrowed his eyes. He even shook his head a bit, making the chains rattle. "What are you?"

The smile on my lips grew and I understood. My oily black skin hid me partially against the darkness. All he could see were my brown short shorts, and perhaps the amber of my eyes. I took a deep breath and let my skin change back to its original reddish-brown, and I heard him suck in a sharp breath.

What can I say? Hell is hot, literally, and I was wearing the standard attire. Brown short shorts. There was no such thing as gendered clothing down here.

But I had to remind myself that I was face to face with the one being down here that would take offence to my naked chest, because he likely wasn't used to it. And I doubted he cared much for the sinfulness of naked skin – he must've been horrified at being naked himself.

The Angel strained in his chains, and I could tell he tried hard not to look at my naked boobs, but his gaze slipped a few times. "What are you? And who sent you to tempt my conviction?"

"I am what my people call an Ember, and I wasn't sent." I hiked up my bag and crossed my arms over my chest before I gave the guy an aneurism from trying to decide where he should look – eyes or nipples – and failing. "Your conviction means as much to me as your pain and hatred does, namely nothing."

Now his hate filled scowl rested firmly on my face. "Then what do you want?"

"To get you out. And you'll do the same for me in return."

Chapter Four
Mihr
Hell, The Deep

The Demon was unusual in many ways. For one, I had no idea what kind of Demon she was supposed to be, which in itself was strange. During our training we learned about the countless kinds of their ilk, the layout of Hell as far as it was known to us, and the creatures that dwelled there, apart from them. The only reason I could think of, was that she had to be one of the lowlier kinds, the ones that never got out of here, or joined in the war.

But what really made me nervous – apart from her proud nakedness, paired with confidence and nonchalance – was her request.

"What did you mean with me doing the same for you?" I asked, straining my neck so I could keep my eyes on her.

She smiled and walked closer. "We don't have much time, so I'll make this quick." The Demon sank down next to me and placed both hands on the iron band encircling my neck. I hid the wince her touch caused, as my flesh was rubbed raw from the iron.

"I will free you, and help you get out of here," her unholy amber eyes held mine, "if you bless me and thus sever the bond to my Maester."

I stared at her, my mouth falling open, until I noticed how hot the iron was getting. A short, surprised yell escaped me, but with a soft *clang*, the band came loose.

The Demon shook what looked like red-hot metal droplets from her fingers. Her hands glowed in the same color, the veins snaking up her arms to her elbows a fiery yellow.

"Why?" I asked, my breath uneven, as she took hold of the chains fastened to my left hand, the glow from her veins growing brighter.

"Never you mind, Angel. I have my reasons. I'll free you and help your sorry beaten ass out of here. We got a deal, or not?"

Clang. My wrist was free, if a bit singed. Immediately, I wrapped it around her throat, snatching her down to me. The smell of burnt hair wafted around us as I sized her up, forcing her to kneel at my eye level. "You are Hellspawn, I can't bless you. It is forbidden."

She grabbed at my hand, not able to pull it off, even while using both of hers. Tears sprang to her eyes and her voice struggled past my fingers. "Would you rather die down here, after divulging all your secrets to Lucifer himself, or bend the rules a little and bless me?" she wheezed, trying to get air down her tightened throat. "He will get the information from you he wants, believe me. And then your kind will be in serious trouble."

As much as I didn't want her to be, she was right. Lucifer had ways of extracting information that didn't have to involve torture and manipulation, he just liked the torture to be a byproduct. This was my only option.

"How can I trust you?" I snarled.

"You can't," she choked. "You can either stay and suffer the wrath of Lucifer and his Hellspawn, or escape with me." Tears now ran down her reddish cheeks, but she kept glaring at me, not in the least intimidated by my chokehold. "Decide, Angel, before I pass out and we both end up as cell neighbors."

It wasn't a choice, not really. I didn't trust her for a second, but if there was even a *chance* she was telling me the truth, I had to try.

With a low growl I released her and sank back down, spots of black dancing in my vision. Even this small show of strength depleted me. My body felt like a broken shell, the poison still coursing through my veins, weakening me. The continuous torture had not helped. Even if she got me out of the dungeon, I very much doubted we'd get any further.

She wasted no time at all and went to work on the rest of the chains holding me, always burning me a bit in the process, but my body was thrumming with agony as it was, so those were just little jabs of added pain. Jabs I could live with if it meant getting out of here and not offering up the secrets of my kind.

The Demon pulled up one of my arms and ducked under it, then heaved me up. "Come on, you heavy fuck, help me a little."

I did, too weak to give any kind of comeback, suddenly standing had my head swimming awfully and I nearly vomited all over the cell. Not that it would have mattered, the floor was already covered in my blood, my feathers, bits of flesh and excrements left by my predecessor.

"Move!" the little Demon urged, and we stumbled towards the exit of the cell. She truly was small, compared to me – the top of her head barely reaching my shoulder – the perfect height to lean on. I shook my head to clear my thoughts. We needed to hurry.

I hobbled along the corridor I had been brought in, trying to go as fast as my broken left ankle let me. What was left of my wings hung limply down my back, the tips dragging behind me. Heavy. Useless.

We took a tunnel leading away from the entrance and the Demon hurried me on constantly, her breath ragged. The longer we took, the more frantic her voice grew.

The tunnel opened to a black plateau, peppered with geysers that shone slightly with half-cooled lava.

Escaping the dank air, even if traded for inexplicable heat, the kind that nearly burned my lungs to a crisp, gave me a shot of energy and we traversed the plateau fairly quickly.

We reached a wall of stone, with a crack that widened into a tunnel. Just as we entered it, a roar sounded from the dungeons. The Demon propped me against a wall and turned to the opening, and my heart sank. Had this all been a ruse? Was she to give me hope, then take it away? I wouldn't put it past a Demon to get some sick kick out of a game like that.

But to my utter amazement, she lit up her hands once more, and pulled the crack closed behind us, like a damned curtain. "That should keep them occupied for a while," she huffed. "Come on, we still have a long way to go." She ducked beneath my arm again, grabbed my hip with one hand and shone a light onto our path with the other.

The tunnel was rife with my huffs and grunts, and her colorful, whispered swearing accompanied us as she led me deeper into the mountain. If I'd had breath left, I would have told her that Michael's mother was definitely not a mix between a llama and a sideways-fucked heap of dung but had, in fact, been a very nice lady – if Human. Michael, being the oldest Angel who had been turned, had earned the status of Archangel millennia ago. Plus, he was my best friend, but I was not offended on his behalf, the rest of the Archangels didn't fare any better in her hissed rants.

"How are you so heavy?" she griped, giving my peers a rest. "Not to mention slow? The ones we slipped away from aren't idiots, you know. They will eventually think to look at what comes out the other side of this tunnel, and it would be very bad if we did them the favor of being slow enough for them to catch us. Not to mention, if my Maester finds out, he can summon me on the spot. You should bless me now and get it over with."

"Not a chance, Demon," I grumbled. "I'll bless you when we are nearly out, not before." She stared at me, a crease appearing between her brows. "Fine. But even as fucked up as you are, you should be healing by now. What is wrong with you?"

"Sumu-Incubus," was all I said.

That stopped her short and I nearly fell over without her support. "You are poisoned and only tell me this now? Do you miss your cell that bad already?" her voice was hard and sharp, yet there was an unsteady undertone that I interpreted as fear. "Stay right here, I'll be back."

A second later, the light she provided shrank away fast, as she sprinted off into another corridor, forking to the right. I leaned back against the wall and hissed when I discovered that the stone around me was even hotter than the air. Feeling like an idiot, I stood in the dark. Alone, naked, and waiting. Not knowing when, or even if, she'd come back, I had no choice but to stay put. I doubted that I would be able to navigate this labyrinth on my own.

I used the time to gulp in lungfuls of air, resting as much as I could. Strange place, how anything survived down here was a testimony of the evil nature of the creatures who did. Unnatural. *Unholy.*

The strangest sound I had ever heard, made me straighten to try and pierce the darkness around me with wide eyes. Sweat ran down my face and into my eyes, but I ignored the burning, looking around without seeing a devil-damned thing.

There it was again. A mewling hiss, followed by a rattling growl. A growl that sounded hollow and dry, going on for what felt like forever. It drew closer, coming from my right. I turned, still not seeing a thing in the inky blackness.

Balling my fists, I took a stance, drawing my wings up, making pangs of agony slice through them, which then radiated into my back and shoulders. But I didn't let it affect me, instead, I growled back.

The rattling stopped. Then another mewl echoed off the hot walls. It sounded strange, like a question. Whatever it was, I guessed an animal, and by the direction the sound came from, it was small. Following my instincts, praying that Hell's creatures were not that different from the ones above, I mimicked the mewl.

Silence. Then the same questioning sound floated my way again. A second later, pinpricks of pain prickled up my right calf as small talons sank into my skin. I hissed in surprise, but acted against my instinct to shake my leg. Whatever had latched onto me would rip open my leg if I shook it off.

I sank down, patting around my leg, hoping I could dislodge whatever had taken hold of me peacefully. To my utter surprise, I felt silky fur and a very small body. The questioning mewl sounded again as light flickered from an arm of the tunnel and I saw it. A black kitten with leathery wings. It sat on my foot, its minute claws buried into my calf. Red eyes stared up at me and when I lowered my hand to pluck it away, it leaned its face into my palm and a continuous purr vibrated through the air. I was stumped, ogling the creature on my foot, who snuggled into my hand.

"Ugh. Really? Him? I save you from a pack of hounds and you choose *him*? No loyalty left in this world," the Demon said, walking from the tunnel, her face grim as she looked at the cat. The cat she was clearly addressing. Then she focused on me. "Seriously, I leave for a second, and you go ahead and bond with a Hellcat cub? Inconvenient much?"

"Hellcat?" I stared at the tiny furball who stretched its black, leathery wings and flapped them once, making a small gust of wind billow over my legs. "This is a Hellcat? That can't be." I straightened and huffed from the effort. "Hellcats are huge, big enough to ride into battle."

She rolled her eyes, walked over to me, sank down and snatched the kitten from my leg. "Emphasis on cub. Duh. It looks to have been born only a few weeks ago." She picked the cat up earning that rattling growl from before.

"Oh, keep still, you drama queen," the Demon scolded. "I told you, you should be in the Incubi pens. How in Hell's name did you get down here?" She heaved out a sigh as the kitten bit into her fingers, drawing a drop of blood. "No matter, looks like we are three now."

"What are you even talking about?" I asked as she tucked the still fighting and hissing kitten into her side, propping me up with her other arm, so we could begin walking again.

"We can't take a Hellcat with us."

"It's your damned fault," she spat. "A Hellcat only bonds with one person in its entire life. See how it is looking at you?" She was right, the cat yowled pathetically, but its red eyes never strayed from me. "From now on, it will follow you anywhere. If we leave it, it dies."

"It is Hellspawn," I muttered. The statement sounded unconvincing, even to my own ears. As the creatures red gaze sank deeper into mine, I wasn't sure I would have been able to leave it behind. Strange…

"Well, we aren't leaving her on my watch," the Demon stated. "Besides, we can use this to our advantage." A shudder ran through her and she shook her head slightly. "Whoa. Got a real kick to it."

"What does?"

"The venom. A Hellcat's bite is poisonous. When it is fully grown, the poison is deadly, but as small as it is now… It has more of an adrenalin kick as a result." She blew out a breath, hiked my arm around her shoulder closer and dragged me down the corridor she had left into. Her steps were sure, and I was surprised at how much of my weight she took pressing on.

"We might just make it," she whispered.

I hoped to God she was right, but wrong where the kitten was concerned. I wanted out, but it wouldn't do having Hellspawn follow my every move once I escaped. The way the cat looked at me, though… Its large eyes trained on me while it was munching on the Demon's fingers, all the while snapping its wings and fighting her hold. The gaze was all consuming, an unblinking look that seemed to glance into my very essence. Something overwhelming tethered me to its gaze, and I was spellbound, tripping as we went.

"Stop looking at her," the Demon advised. "You'll have time to finish the bonding process once we are outside. Not now. It'll only slow us down."

"This is a process? I can stop this?" My head swiveled up so I could look at her.

A mirthless smirk flashed across her full lips. "Not likely. But there is more to this bond than the kitten sitting on your foot, clinging to you. But not now. Now we need to be vigilant, quick, and careful."

The tunnel opened up to a river of lava, framed by two steep stone-walls that shot up on either side of it. I craned my neck but couldn't see the ledges where the walls ended.

"What now?" I asked, meekly glancing at the bubbling lava a few feet away. Sweat ran down my face, drying uncomfortably fast. The heat was unbearably scalding, it felt like my entire skin was on fire.

"Chillax, man. I'm an Ember," she said as if that explained everything. The Demon thrust the kitten into my hands, and it stopped wriggling immediately, swapping the rattling growl to a purr in a matter of seconds.

I watched in awe as the Demon crouched down and sank her hands straight into the lava. Darkness bled from her arms into the liquid rock, spreading rapidly as what looked like a path cooled off. It stretched out and ran along our side of the wall, broad enough for one person to walk on.

The Demon drew her arms from the river, bits of rock cracking and crumbling around her hands as she did. "Come on, we still have to be fast."

She stepped from the crack and onto the path, holding out a hand to help me down. I placed the cat on my back, right where my wings poked past my neck, and the little beast nestled into the space, hanging around my neck like a tiny scarf.

I needed both hands to navigate the narrow path, the bubbling heat and burning stone didn't help, but I had to smile as I felt the last bit of lethargy from the Incubus poison leave me. Now, all I had to worry about was walking a path on a river of lava, following an unknown Demon, while carrying a Hellcat that had apparently bonded with me. Had anyone told me what situation I would be in a few days ago, I would have given them a rare laugh.

"Stop," the Demon hissed, reaching an arm toward me, pressing my back to the hot wall as she did the same.

The sound of wings rustled from above and all amusement I might have felt at my ridiculous situation left me like the poison had moments ago. On the other side of the wall, a group of Ifrits hung from the rock in clusters. Their reddish, burning wings cocooned them as they slept.

"Not a sound," the Demon whispered. Her back pressed to the stone she sidled on, her gaze glued to the sleeping Ifrits.

I did the same, concentrating on moving as silently as I could. We passed the first cluster without incident, my breath fast and my heart hammering almost painfully, all the while lava bubbled around us, small droplets shooting from the river sizzling on our path where it hit. The smell was abhorrent, and I wondered how I was even able to smell anything past my singed nose hair, but I did. Sulfur and roast, the telling scent of every Demon.

Dimly, I realized that if I could smell them so strongly it meant that my Demon didn't reek like Demons did. Then I realized I had called her 'my Demon' in my head and berated myself. I needed to concentrate if I wanted to get out of here.

Just as we passed the middle cluster of Ifrits a hollow howl sounded through the canyon.

"Fuck!" my Demon whispered. "The alarm." She bit her lower lip as the Ifrits shook their wings, screeching in response to the howl. The woman turned to me, took hold of me around my waist, and swung a leg around me.

Straddling me, one foot on either side of mine, she pressed her naked chest to my torso, hugging me close. "Don't move," she mouthed, her amber eyes boring into mine as a curtain of rock slid from the wall behind us, engulfing both of us in scalding darkness.

Chapter Five
Fane
Hell, The Chasm

I closed my eyes in the darkness I had just created, hoping against hope that the Ifrits hadn't glimpsed us in the seconds between the alarm went off and me cloaking myself and the Angel in a cocoon of rock.

Sweat ran down my face, my chest and my back in trickles of water. Somewhat shielded from the lava river, it didn't dry immediately, but rather had me slick like a snail in seconds. I kept a groan from slipping out of me as my nose started itching something fierce as a result. I fisted my hands inside the stone on either side of me, trying hard not to let go to relieve my plight.

The sound of mighty wings flapping, and roaring screeches passing us, sobered me up quickly. No matter how uncomfortable I was, I could not let go, lest the thin wall of the stone around us would crumble to reveal us and seal our fate.

Pressing my lids shut until spots danced in the black, I hoped we stayed hidden. We weren't nearly as far as I had hoped yet, still had quite a way to go, and my body was already straining. Soon, I would crash from the strength the cat-venom had provided and my powers would be sapped, similar to legs not working from running too hard for too long. I had used too much of it already. But I had to last until we got past the Ascent, where most of the Hellspawn couldn't follow.

The Angel moved from side to side a fraction and grunted softly, ripping me from my bleak thoughts.

"Still," I hissed when he shimmied once more.

"Too close," he mumbled back, sucking in his body as much as he was able.

When I noticed that my very naked upper body was pressed to his seamlessly, I nearly sniggered. The prude being of light had to be extremely uncomfortable by the proximity.

"Tough shit. Now, keep still."

Another grunt was all I got as an answer, but he stopped moving. The problem was, now that he'd gotten my focus on the subject of our positions, I noticed several things about it. His body was hard and unyielding, so much so, that I was the one molding to him. But there was no discomfort for me being so close. Though firm, his skin was soft. And what was more, I felt no sort of threat coming from him. His discomfort was amusing and slightly insulting, but it also meant he was harmless in a way.

His smell… It was amplified to a dizzying degree in this tight space. Fresh, clean, like a cool wind mixed with a scent I didn't know. The slickness of our bodies, sliding against each other when he breathed in, made images of sex flash before my eyes. This time, I almost burst into laughter. Hadn't I just been comfortable this close to him because he definitely *wasn't* interested? I blamed my visions on long abstinence and the adrenaline ratcheting through my veins. Adrenaline that wasn't in infinite supply.

I strained my ears but only heard the bubbling of lava behind me.

"I'll open the rock a fraction, let me know if they are gone," I whispered.

"Ready," he rasped.

Drawing my fists toward the wall, I felt the stone respond to my will and a crack open at my back. The Angel leaned forward, circling one arm around me to keep me from teetering off the path and taking a dip. Now completely squashed to his chest, I rubbed my nose against his pecs, happy when the itching vanished.

"They're gone," he said. "What are you doing?"

I stopped rubbing my face against him and drew the rock back further until it vanished as part of the wall once more. I winked at him and slipped onto the path ahead of him. "No time to chat, let's go."

His jaw tightened at my wink, but he said nothing and followed, the black kitten draped around his neck like a fluffy scarf. Had he known how flamboyant he looked, he might have become a tad self-conscious.

Irritated by the misplaced giddiness popping up since he was tagging along, I sank down and made another part of path appear so we could walk on.

Every few minutes I had to make more path, and my power began aching from use. A searing agony that started between my shoulder blades and worked its way up my neck to my temples, until my shoulders, neck, and head pounded. It got worse each time I used it.

When I felt the stone of the mountains Maeve and I called home, I nearly collapsed with relief. Only a little further now. Past these mountains and across the Sea of Despair, and we would be at the Ascent.

I sank to my knees, fashioning a second path that would take us across the river so we could climb the mountains to get to the Sea. Pain laced through me, and I kept from yelling as it pummeled into my back like an iron hammer.

When I got up again, I swayed, nearly vomiting from exertion. To mask it, I stumbled on, crossing the river.

I turned once across, seeing the Angel stare at the small path I'd made. "Come on, what are you waiting for?" I asked.

He glared at me. "This thing is as broad as one of my feet, and there is lava everywhere. Just give me a minute, I'm not a bloody gymnast."

The cat on his shoulder mewled as if to underline his comment and I rolled my eyes. Hellcats. Of all the creatures to run into, it had to be a Hellcat, who bonded with the strongest warrior in its vicinity. The irony of it being an Angel wasn't lost on me, but the kitten didn't know that.

I looked around, searching for a way onward while the Angel balanced across the ledge, arms and wings spread out to either side of him. A huff escaped me when I noticed that I would have to use more of my powers, a lot more. There was no way the both of us would cross this mountain by climbing. The walls were steep and angled over a bit, meaning we would be hanging over the lava river at one time. I had to tunnel through it.

But just thinking of using my power once more made pain erupt across my back.

I took deep breaths, tasting the fire and ash at the back of my tongue as I slid my fingers over the stone wall before me. Hard stone, high concentrations of iron, mixed with pockets of other stone. Volcanic stone. The worst kind to shape. Its brittle nature meant that it was nearly impossible to form a stable tunnel.

"Should have thought of this," I said with a defeated sigh.

"What?" The Angel had finally crossed the river and scrutinized me.

I straightened to hide my fatigue and looked at him. "Well, to be honest, this might be as far as we get. I can't tunnel through this mountain, my power is pretty much sapped, and the cat-venom is used up."

"Are you serious?" His brows shot up, then he frowned. "You got me out of the dungeons and chose a path that you didn't know we could brave? What kind of a plan is that supposed to be?"

"I didn't have much time to plan," I snapped. "Besides, had you been quicker on your feet we would have taken another way, but since I had to nearly carry you at first, we lost a lot of time. I didn't count on having to *pave* our fucking way on a river of lava." Crossing my arms, I glared at him. "I was improvising."

His pale-gray eyes narrowed. "This is great. The one creature in Hell who helps me is spontaneous of all things, as well as incompetent."

"Hey," I pointed a finger at him, "I could have let you rot in that cell."

"Then you'd be no closer to leaving yourself."

I opened and closed my mouth a couple of times.

"It doesn't matter either way," he said, drawing a palm through his dirty-blond hair that stuck to his neck and nipped at his shoulders in sweaty curls. "We have to think of a way to get up this mountain. How far after we cross it?"

"Just past the Sea of Despair. Then we are at the Ascent."

He stepped closer to the river and looked up the wall, his curls catching in the updrifting heat. The Angel turned and held a palm out over the bubbling lava.

"The updraft could help. My wings aren't healed fully yet, but we could… hover." He frowned looking up. "But the winds will be strong further up, we'd undoubtedly crash before we reach the top."

"I got it!" I shouted, feeling over the wall once more with my fingers. "If we work as one, we can clear this mountain. You hover and I anchor."

"What?"

"Open your wings," I said.

He still frowned, but tugged them open. The gray feathers looked magnificent, if still a bit frazzled, and missing bits and pieces. But an Angel with spread wings was a sight to behold, and not one I came by on a regular basis. Here, Angelwings were decorations, trophies, spoils of battle.

"You're not gonna like what comes next, though."

He snorted. "It's not as though I have liked your plan this far."

"You'll have to carry me." I stepped over, turned so my back was against his chest and wrapped his arms around me, "Like this."

A displeased grunt sounded from over my head.

"Yes, yes, I'm not exactly enjoying this either. But you wanted to 'hover,' didn't you?" I asked.

"Fine." He tightened his hold on me, pulling my back flush against him so I could let go. "Now what?"

"Open your wings further." I felt the updraft tug at our bodies and punched my hands into the wall before me, then my feet. I began scaling the wall with him and the pull he provided at my back. His feathers rustled as we climbed higher, the hot wind steadily pushing us upwards. I anchored us to the wall with my fists, steadily climbing higher.

"I'm not sure whether this is genius or crazy," the Angel yelled over the increasing wind. "The winds are unpredictable, we might fall."

"Then keep your damned wings steady," I grated out, the pain from using my power searing through me with every second. Seconds that turned into the spaces of rock I punched my fists into, until that was all I saw. That, and the agony in my back. It radiated further now, down into my legs, over my shoulders, pounding down my arms, until my whole body was an ache. Each new punch was accompanied by a yell, as I was unable to suffer this torture in silence.

My body trembled with cramps and exhaustion. Any minute now, I would let go and we would be subjected to the hot winds, either plummeting down, or spiraling into the walls around us. Just when I was sure I couldn't go on, my fingers met the ledge and I pulled us up and over. We landed in a tangled mess of limbs, feathers, grunts, and a squeak.

I rolled away from the Angel and onto my back, just breathing for a few minutes. The kitten had tumbled off to one side and now stalked back to her Angel, who picked her mewling fluffiness up and placed her back behind his neck. He then walked over to me and offered a palm. I looked at it, my breath ragged, before I grabbed hold and was heaved to my feet.

"Whoa. The poison seems to be out of your system," I observed.

"It is. My wings still don't work properly, but most of my body is healed."

He was right, his foot wasn't swollen and many of the cuts had vanished into long, thin scars. Even his nearly skinned back only had a few deep gashes left. Amazing. It took way longer for me to heal.

"Born Angel resilience, huh?"

He shrugged, "Something like that. Which way?"

I pointed at the Sea ahead, "We can round the water on the right side, but we have to be quick, it won't be long until they find us, now that we are out in the open."

He nodded once and we settled into a jog beside each other, drawing closer to the dark waters of the Sea of Despair.

The sea was poisonous, even to the dead, which was why they had to be ferried over. But the Demons fighting in the war had their own way to the Ascent. Like Lev. And he had once told me of the way he and his squadrons took. Granted, he'd probably never thought I'd use the knowledge, or the path itself, but he wasn't around anymore to care either way. I shook the thought of him from my mind and sped up my steps.

"The idea on how to scale the wall was pretty good," the Angel said, not sounding out of breath. "It nearly went sideways, though. I'm not sure how long you would have held out."

"I was fine." Truth be told, I hadn't been, and right now, the jogging was painful, as the overuse of my power had been so severe that my body felt like it was one big cramp. Every step was agony, but I had to hold on, I was so close to getting out.

"Get down," the Angel yelled and dashed to the side in a sprint.

I dropped to the ground in response, feeling something whoosh over me. My bag was ripped from my back and I yelled in fury as I sprang back up. A few feet away, the Angel dodged an Ifrit. The Demon missed him and swooped up in a deafening screech – my bag in his clutches, slowly starting to burn – hovering in the air, signaling his and our position to his peers.

"Run!" I hollered, barreling past the Angel, who followed suit. Together, we hauled ass alongside of the mushy, gray beach, heading for a huge rocky arch to our right.

A roar behind us signaled that the Ifrit had taken up chase. Sharp hissing was the only warning I got, then a ball of flame crashed into the ground to my left, sending sand and clumps of earth in the air. My hair whipped around my face in the blast, but I just kept on running, my heart pounding a mile a minute.

I could not let them catch us, not this close to freedom. A yelp tore from my mouth as the Ifrit dove down, scooping up the Angel running next to me. Skidding to a stop, I watched as the Angel twisted in the Ifrit's hold, snagged one of his huge wings and pulled. An ugly crack was followed by a sharp wail, and they both spiraled to the ground, impacting with a dull thump.

The Angel sprang up and dropped onto the Ifrit, pinning his healthy wing with one foot, he warded off his claws. I didn't think on it, but picked up the nearest rock I found, and ran over to the fighting men. Raising the rock over my head, I aimed for the Ifrit's head, but before I could strike, the Angel and the Demon twisted and rolled over in the sand. In a flash of movements, punches, and snarls, they battled for dominance, until the Angel lay on his back, having the Ifrit in a chokehold. Another ugly crunch sounded, and the Demon went lax in the Angel's arms.

I stared as the being of light shoved the Firedemon off him and scrambled to his feet. He was caked in dirt, black and gold blood, and he looked gloriously pissed off.

Next to him, the Hellcat swiped a paw at the motionless Ifrit, hissing with flat ears and flattened wings. The Angel swiped his face with a palm, which did nothing to get rid of the dirt, then bent down and scooped up the kitten once more.

"I'm sick of this place," he stated. "You say the cat-venom provides you with a rush of energy?"

I huffed and let the stone tumble to the ground. "Yeah." I rubbed my hurting arms. "But once you come down from it, it's not pretty." I grimaced at his knitted brows. "I feel similar to how you looked when I found you. I don't even know how much further I can keep running."

"You won't need to," he said, his face solemn.

For a split-second, I thought he meant to leave me behind, but then he pointed to where we'd come from. Glowing spots of light in the air told of the Ifrits heeding their comrade's call. A leaden heaviness dropped into my gut. They would be here soon.

A soft hiss had me look back at the Angel. He gently pulled the cat's mouth open and poked his index finger with one of her teeth. The creature yowled and growled in that signature rattling way and pulled back, but the Angel's skin had been pricked.

The being of light placed the kitten around his neck then stalked over to me. His pale-gray eyes glittered with determination, then changed into the dark gray of his wings. I was nearly unable to hold his gaze as it bore into me with the intensity of a branding.

"You'll show us the way," he rasped, his voice strangely echoey. Then he rounded me and wrapped both arms around me. His magnificent wings unfolded, and he bent his knees a bit.

"Oh, no," I said. "No, no, noooooooo!" But he had pushed off, launching us both high into the hot air. Each beat of his wings had us shooting up and my stomach lurched. I clawed at his arms, terrified of falling. The ground seemed so alarmingly far away, then it got worse, when we glided over the Sea itself. If I fell now, I was dead. All I could do was close my eyes and scream, so I did, wishing I'd never gone with this hairbrained plan.

"Which way?" his voice shouted from behind me.

I didn't answer and he shook me a bit. "Demon, which way?"

Prying my lids open, I noticed that we had crossed a good portion of the Sea already, the Angel was incredibly fast. But the Ifrits weren't far off, and they were gaining on us.

With shaking fingers, I indicated to the right, at a dark-clouded storm that always raged at the edge of the Sea. Bolts of red lightning struck, followed by thunder that got louder the closer we got.

"We have to get into the middle – the eye of the storm."

In response, his arms tightened around me firmly, then we almost doubled in speed, shooting straight at the ominous bank of clouds. In no time at all, we had reached them. All thoughts of the Ifrits following us were wiped from my mind as we entered the storm with the velocity of a bullet.

My eyes stung and burned from the wind, and tears gathered in my eyes, making the world blurry. I swiped them away and then wished I hadn't. Deafening thunder and flashing lighting boomed around us, but even worse were the fiery glowing bodies of the Ifrits who had caught up and surrounded us as we all barreled on.

"Hold on!" the Angel yelled, right before tugging his wings around us and leading us into a downward spiral.

I would have screamed my heart out, but the utter terror and surprise took my breath away. Then I saw something, and the terror ten folded. "Up!" I roared, glimpsing a cluster of rocks we were heading for.

His wings snapped open, jerking us back. With an embarrassing 'umph,' the air was slammed from my lungs. Three Ifrits shot past us, vanishing in the black clouds ahead, but the sounds didn't leave much room for interpretation. The slamming of flesh against rock, the cracks of breaking bones, and the screams of agony meant we most likely wouldn't see them again.

The Angel rose again at breakneck speed, until our climb was halted with jarring suddenness. An Ifrit had slammed its claws into the Angels right calf, and was trying to snag his wing while pulling us down.

A cry of pain and a thud had me looking to the other side, where another Firedemon was clamping onto the Angel's arm, ripping away his hold on me.

"Oh, you, fucking, will not!" I screamed, punching the snarling Demon with all I was worth.

It only made my fists hurt and the guy snarl at *me*. Quick as a flash, the kitten landed on his face, yowling something fierce, while scratching at his eyes. It must have struck true, because the Ifrit wailed and let go. I snatched the cat from his face right before he vanished.

The feline and I looked at one another, then at the last Demon hanging onto the Angel's leg. I wiggled around until I faced the Angel, his expression still gloriously pissed off, but his eyes were almost that pale gray from before. He didn't have much left.

"Hold my legs," I ordered, then bent backwards, placing the cat smack dab onto the Demon's face. "Kitten-Attack!" I yelled. Without fail, the cat found purchase, hacking at the Demon's eyeballs. It took three swipes, then the Demon let go, but he tried grabbing the cat as he went. I bared my teeth and tried the punching thing again. There was not much effect to speak of, but it derailed the Ifrit's focus long enough for the Angel to escape his immediate vicinity.

I pulled up again, the kitten safe in my arms. The Angel switched his hands from my legs to my back and I hooked my feet around his hips. The look we shared was short lived, as we broke from the black clouds and into the light.

"Now, we go up," I said. "Follow the tunnel."

The Angel did, and I watched with wonder as the black clouds turned to black rock, but no kind I had ever seen, felt, or manipulated. We rose up a perfect rock circle, with what looked like an endless spiral staircase cut into it. The way of our armies. This was the Ascent.

"Bless me," I said. "You have to do it now, or I won't be able to leave."

He looked at me, uncertainty clouding his tired features.

"Really, man? After what we just went through?"

"You are a Demon, you are Hellspawn."

"I saved your fucking ass, I dragged you up a cliff and made a path on lava for you, I was ready to kill one of my own. I kept my end of the bargain, now it's your turn."

He blew out a breath, a look of pure torture on his face, but he cradled my head against his chest and started talking in a language I had never heard. The words registered with a deeply buried part of me. Discomfort laced through my chest at hearing them, then lashes of stinging pain followed. His palm on my head grew warm, and not in a way I could accommodate. It was a warmth that jumbled my insides, a warmth that grew into an all-consuming fire. The fire spread through me, burning away my jumbled insides, my fear of being this high up, my thoughts, all that I was. All I felt was the roaring burn, and all I heard were the Angel's words. Those stinging, lashing words.

I screamed until no voice was left, then I heard him screaming as well. Something splintered off me, like the crust of a second skin, and the fire was gone. I looked up and saw that his face was covered in blood. It seeped from his eyes, his nose and his mouth, turning his face into a mask of glittering, pained, gold.

I palmed his cheeks as his lids fluttered closed and we dipped in altitude. "Hold on. Just a bit further. Just one more wingbeat. Hold on."

With a grunt, he beat his wings once more. One last time.

Chapter Six
Fane
The Surface,
Unknown Location

Something roared from below, then the Angel grunted as the roaring something slammed into his back, easily doubling our velocity. Air and rock rushed past us, a blur of sensation so stark, it made my head swim. The Angel's lids fluttered shut and his arms around me slipped away, just as we were flung from the Ascent like the cork of a champagne bottle.

My stomach lurched when our height peaked, and we fell down. All I could do was cradle the kitten to my chest and hope we landed on soft ground.

The ground wasn't soft. The air got knocked from my chest as I rolled over the dirt like a ragdoll, the fall separating the three of us.

Eventually, my tumbling journey stopped and I flopped to my back wheezing, trying to breathe. Panic set in when my lungs didn't inflate for precious seconds that felt like forever. Then sweet air streamed down my throat with rattling breaths, and I slowly sat up to take in my surroundings. A couple of feet away, the Angel lay sprawled on his side, his back and wings smoldering from whatever had hit him. Tentatively, the Hellcat mewled and dabbed his face with a paw. He didn't react. Seemed to be out cold.

Around us was nothing but coarse, pale sand, speckled with small dry bushes that looked utterly dead. But above us… above us, the night sky spanned into what looked like eternity and the stars winked at me as if in welcome. The cool wind kissed my skin and I marveled at the lack of ash and sulfur in the air. There was nothing but fresh, cool oxygen, and I felt my hurting ribcage expand with its sweetness.

A small smile spread across my lips before my gaze was drawn to the hole in the ground. The Ascent. I got up and stumbled over to look inside, but instead of a hole, there was a perfect circle of the same black stone I didn't know. While I looked on, hearing muffled crashes and bangs from below, the coarse sand drew over the stone like a curtain, obscuring everything from view. When the stone was gone, so were the sounds from our pursuers.

They couldn't follow, the number of ascending Demons for the day already met. Me and the Angel got through because he was an Angel and I had been blessed. The way for anyone else was closed.

I stuck a hand into the sand, but to my utter amazement anything resembling the stone I had just seen was gone. The sand went on and turned to dense limestone ways down. Keeping my palm dug into the sand, I felt for the magnetic field, getting my bearings as to where we had surfaced.

A snort escaped me, we had the right continent, at least. But Cam and Dax were far away still. Too far to walk. I pressed my lids shut in concentration, feeling for what was in our immediate surrounding. A sudden vibration tickled me from the far left, the earth sang from there. A road.

I pulled my palm free and dusted it off as good as I was able, caking my shorts and upper legs with the dusty sand in the form of handprints. For a second, I cursed myself for losing my bundle of clothes. It couldn't be helped. I had pants, that was more than the Angel had.

Speaking of which, I walked over and tilted my head, looking down at him. He was still unconscious, and when I rounded him to get a look at his wound, I nearly winced.

His wings had almost been burned away completely, worse than when I had met him. There was barely a feather left. And his back… a circular patch of flesh was burned away. To the point of his ribs glinting at me.

"Bummer," I mumbled. "I really wished you'd have survived. Welp, this also can't be helped." Straightening, I turned toward the road. Time to get to a small town called Emerald Falls.

A hiss made me look down. The kitten took up a stance, her back hunched, her wings spread and flapping aggressively, her ears flat on her head, all the while exposing her sharp little teeth in a snarl.

"Hey, it's not my fault he got hit at the last second," I told her. "Take a look around." I indicated at the nothingness we had landed in. "You expect me to drag an Angel through this desert by myself? I don't think so."

The cat meowed and sat down firmly, as if to counter my words.

"He weighs a ton, you know."

Another meow, this time ending on a small growl.

"You should come with me, leave him behind."

This elicited a hiss.

"Drama queen. He is an *Angel*, a being of light, his kind will kill you once they see you. It doesn't matter to them that you chose him, you – like me – are part of the Hellspawn." I pointed at him. "Feathery guys like him kill us. I only got this one to help me cause I got him out first."

A weak cough caught my ears and I cursed when his voice sounded behind me.

"Mi… might kill me now, too," he rasped. "Blessed a damned one, two actually." He coughed again and I pivoted to see him lying on his side, his beautiful face a mask of pain, golden blood still sticking to his skin.

"You leaving?" he asked.

"Yeah, there is a road not far away." I sighed and looked at him nodding slowly, coughing a bit more.

"Dying under the heavens is better than down there, so thank you for," he hacked and spat out blood, "for getting me out."

At my feet, that cat meowed once more, this time she rubbed her head against my calf. She would die alone out here, and she would never leave his side as long as he was alive. His corpse would draw Angels. She'd try to protect his lifeless body and they would kill her. I groaned and pursed my lips.

"By Lucifer's magnificent balls. Okay, I'll help you. But we go where I want and do things my way. Understood?"

"It would be better if you left me to my fate," he said.

"Yeah, yeah, I know. But I'm not doing this for you. Now, can you stand?"

He scrutinized his legs, one of which had been mauled by an Ifrit. "I think one leg will work."

Walking over, I offered him my palm. "Let's get you up, Angel."

"My name is Mihr," he said.

"Don't really care."

He grabbed my hand and with combined effort we got him to stand. The being of light – Mihr – gasped and groaned, while painting the sand around him golden with his blood. I wasn't sure he'd even make it to the road.

"You might not care," he pressed forth between clenched teeth, "But I do. What do they call you?"

I ducked under his arm, having flashes of *déjà vu*. "Fane."

****

The road could well have been unreachable. At least that was what it felt like as we hobbled through this desolate place together. We made next to no headway and the Angel was steadily weakening. His wound seemed to be too much for his holy resilience to help him bounce back. The arm I had wound around him slipped from the blood pooling down his back and made it even harder to steady him. Add all of the above to the fact that my body still felt like a steamroller had gone to town on it, and I was well and truly pissed.

Should have left the Angel back there, I thought. As if she could hear my thoughts, the kitten trotting ahead of us turned her black head and appraised me with a penetrating look. I raised a brow at her, and she returned to her scouting-ahead business.

"Is it true that Humans normally can't see your kind?" I asked, to keep from spiraling further into frustration and fury.

"Not our true selves, we –" He cleared his throat and spat out some more blood. "We can appear as Humans if we so choose. Or not at all. But to appear to them as we truly are, would take them either knowing what was before them, or the divine Lord's command."

"So basically, you could just tell a Human what you are, and he would see you? That isn't very well thought through."

He threw me a dirty look. "It is the decree of our Lord. He makes no mistakes."

73

Despite everything, I chuckled at that. "Oh deary, you are so fucking blind to the world and where you come from, it's not even funny."

"Stop it, Demon," he rasped. "I know there is evil in the world, I'm currently hobbling around with one such evil."

"Evil is in the eye of the beholder. Your Lord started all of this by kicking out old Lu – his favorite Angel no less. The rest is history."

He opened his mouth, his brows knotted in anger, but a coughing fit took hold of him and his retort was lost.

"Besides," I said when he started breathing normally again. "It won't do you any good pissing me off, or I'll just drop your holy ass and go on alone."

He pointed a bloody, golden finger at me, "Evil."

The way he said it and the look he gave me had me chortling once more. "Yeah, yeah. Keep telling yourself that. So, if your rules are so lax, why isn't the world overrun with true believers by now? It would give your Lord the power he needs to win the war."

"We *can* tell Humans about us, but we aren't *allowed* to. And even if we did, how many would actually believe? If they don't believe, they don't see."

"Not very fair, is it?" I asked, sighing with relief when I saw lights in the distance. The road had eventually appeared. About fucking time.

"It's not like your kind can even tell and be seen. You have no choice but to be invisible."

"Exactly, Sherlock," I grinned broadly at his surprised face. "Unless we are summoned… or blessed. Isn't it true that a Demon will become visible if it receives blessing? Exorcisms have proven that, haven't they?"

"Yes, but once without a host, or past the summoning time, the Demon must return to the depth."

I grinned even wider. "And I don't have either problem. I am a free Demon."

Saying those words out loud helped me understand that they, indeed, where true. What a trip. I was out. I was free. Free from Ragon and the Hellcourt. Never to be anyone's property ever again. A deeply rooted feeling of peace and euphoria overtook me, cancelling out my prior frustration completely, and not even having a hobbling Angel at my side could break through my bliss. I'd be with Cam and Dax soon.

"What I would like to know," I mused, "is whether or not Humans will see my and little kitten's true form."

That earned me a stricken sound from Mihr, along with his face paling.

I shrugged. "Well, no time like the present to find out. Stay here, will ya?" I slipped out from underneath his arm, leaving him standing on one leg. He snatched my wrist with surprising strength and pulled me back to face him. Bringing his face close to mine, he glared at me. "I'll not let you hurt anyone."

"Chillax, Theodora. I'm only asking for a ride. I hear topless hitchhikers have big chances of being picked up." I wiggled my brows. "We might have more problems with someone taking you along." I looked him up and down, his gaze following mine until he swallowed audibly. "You neckid, Mihr. But don't worry, I'll make it worth their while." I flicked his nose with my index finger, and he recoiled, letting go of me.

I turned toward the road once more and climbed the small hill of rubble it was built on. Smelling the fumes of the cars, and the cold tar, I placed one fist on my hip and stretched out the other, all the while proudly presenting my naked chest.

****

The effect was immediate. Even though the road wasn't full, the cars that did pass, slowed, their passengers gawking at me. A pickup truck full of men sent wolf whistles and very inviting comments my way, but they hit the gas when Mihr crawled up the hill next to me – naked as his Lord made him. The cars generally sped up now.

"You ruined it," I told him, pouting. "I was about to hitch a ride with fuck-willing gentlemen when you showed up."

His face was angry, no news there. "You had no way of knowing what their intentions where, and what is worse, neither did they concerning *your* intentions."

I tilted my head to the side. "I think I had a pretty good idea. And maybe I would have let them survive the night." His thunderstruck face had me laughing.

"You find this funny?"

"Absolutely." I had trouble getting air down between the hiccups of laughter. "I-If anyone had told me how thin-skinned you guys are, I would have won the war already. With boobs and hookers."

"You are a vile creature, Fane."

"And you are an impossible goody-two-shoes. Ah, look at that. Someone who is not afraid of you, it seems." I waved at the car slowing, throwing out their indicator before driving off the tar and onto the strip of grit beside it. "Can't say I trust someone halting for a naked dude, let's see who we have here." I picked up the kitten who had taken refuge between us during our talk, but Mihr took her from me and held out his arm for me to slip under.

"We go together," he said.

76

The cat purred up a storm at the fact that he held her to his chiseled chest, and I grimaced at the both of them. Weird combo, just weird.

Together, we hobbled over to the car, waiting for the window to slide down so we could peek inside.

An elderly man scrutinized us, his brown gaze hard as steel under his bushy brows. He seemed to like plaid, because he was dressed in it from stem to stern. Shirt, vest, and hat. Very stylish to be honest. If this guy smoked a pipe, I would lose my shit.

"What are you kids doing outside at this hour, without clothes?" He leaned over to get a better look at Mihr and gasped, "You need a hospital, boy. Get in." It was obvious that he could neither see my skin for the red it was, nor Mihr's wings, and I was delighted, if curious as to how I looked as a Human.

The locks of the doors clicked, and I wrenched open the back, heaved Mihr inside, who groaned and moaned the whole time, until he was positively ashen from exhaustion, then I placed the cat on his lap and slid into the front seat.

"Much obliged, lovely. But we won't be going to a hospital," I told him.

The old man glanced at me and blinked at my nakedness. "There are blankets in the backseat, I would be happy for you to use them as a cover against the cold. And..."

"As a cover in general?" I suggested.

He nodded.

"Mihr, be a dear and throw me a blanket from next to you."

A weak groan answered at first, but seconds later a scratchy blanket was thrust into my open palm. I grimaced as I pulled the thing around me. It smelled as musty as it was rough. This would give my tits a rash, for sure.

"If not the hospital, then where are you going?"

"Emerald Falls."

His hard brown eyes widened. "That is… far. Your friend needs medical attention. He doesn't look like he'll last long."

I waved him off. "He'll be fine. If you could get us as close as you can, that would be great. I will make it worth your while. Promise."

The old man grunted and put the car into gear. "I am Earl."

"Great meeting you, Earl. I'm Fane and the sour sack of bones in the back is Mihr. The cat has no name as of yet."

Chapter Seven
Mihr
The Surface,
The open Road

I woke to the sound of humming. Humming originating from numerous sources. The second thing I registered through the clouds of unconsciousness was the fire in my back and the right calf. The taste of blood, metallic in my mouth, had me swallow a few times and open my chapped lips.

Groaning, I shifted a bit to take the strain off my back, my bloody skin stuck to the surface I was lying on and made a ripping sound when I moved. Hurt like Hell, too. I gave up shifting around and just accepted my position. Half sitting, half lying. The sensation of moving at high speed wormed through my consciousness and with it memories slammed into me.

Hell, Fane, the Demon who had fled with me and whom I had blessed. Cat? Being blasted in the back by a ball of fire, walking, and an old man.

I ripped my eyes open and hissed as blinding daylight assaulted my retinas. My arm felt like it weighed a ton when I raised it to rub over my lids.

One of the hummings stopped. "Ah, you're finally awake. Welcome to the living, Georgina. I wasn't sure you'd make it."

I sat up, careful not to let my back touch anything. We were in a different car than I last remembered. I was propped into the backseat, covered with a rough blanket. Fane was driving. Blinking, I looked around. The Hellcat had rolled up into a ball of fluff and leather next to me on the far end of the dark-red, leather bench. It seemed to be asleep, its wings tucked to either side neatly, but shivering slightly with each deep breath it took. Another problem I faced now.

"Where are we?" I asked, my throat feeling like it was rubbed down with sandpaper. I coughed, trying to clear it and wound up with a fresh bout of blood-taste. *Spectacular.*

"Not far from our destination now." Her amber eyes flashed to me in the rearview mirror for a second. "You passed out during our trip with Earl. Missed a few good bits after that. I learned to drive, hot-wired a car and robbed a store."

"You what?" Panic slammed into my chest. "What did you do with Earl?" He had been the reason I followed her. My fear of her doing something to him. She was a Demon, after all.

"We got married in a chapel on the way, then I sold his soul to Lu and killed him." She pointed at herself, "Proud widow here."

I stared at her and she burst into laughter.

"Death and damnation, you are so easy to fool. Would you truly believe I –" Her eyes met mine. "Ah. Of course, you would. No, Earl is fine. He was getting weird about the hospital thing, so I had him drop us off in the next city and decided we would make our own way." She grabbed at something on the passenger seat and threw it my way. "You should try and get dressed. I won't let Dax grow up with a complex just cause you're angelically well endowed."

I looked at the pants now in my hands and felt a blush creep up the back of my neck. Pushing the facts of the last, God knew how many, hours to the side would be best. For now, at least. I wasn't ready to deal with what I had done, and to be honest, a Demon seeing me naked was one of the smaller problems I had right now. Still, her cheeky wink when she'd said the part about my... endowment had my breath short, and that stupid blush flooding my cheeks.

To flee the discomfort – or whatever it was – I stuffed my good leg into the pants, then stopped. My ruined calf had been bandaged, perfectly. Slowly this time, I placed that leg into the pants as well and tried to wriggle it up my legs and over my ass. It took a lot longer than I thought it would, and my back often hit the padded leather seat, robbing me of breath each time. When I finally zipped up the fly, sweat ran down my face and back, burning in the wounds like fire. Exhausted and out of breath, I tucked what was left of my wings around me. I wished I could retract them, but they were so badly damaged that I didn't dare to.

"Who is Dax?" I asked instead.

"You'll meet him soon enough."

"Where are we going? Does your kind have a refuge up top we don't know about?"

"First off, if we had, I'd never tell you. Secondly, you'll see when we get there. I told you we'd go where I wanted. And you are in no condition to decide. Once you are well again, you are free to leave to wherever. Provided the cat will be safe with you."

Said cat had woken and was busy stretching, making its needle-pin claws appear, then yawned to show off tiny, poisonous fangs. It traipsed over and pawed at my thigh, its curious red eyes firmly holding mine.

I stared down, not knowing how to react to it, but just like before, its red eyes drew me in. I was too exhausted to marvel at the feeling of connection I felt and sighed. "Do you know why it chose me?" I asked.

The Demon shrugged. "*She* must have somehow gotten out of the Hellcat pens in the Incubi ring. Then she found you."

"Yes, but Hellcats only ever chose Incubi or Succubi, I have never seen another Demon ride one into battle."

"True. But that is because those are the only Demons they are presented with." Fane grimaced, glaring at the road ahead. "Fucking Lustdemons and their prized monopoly on these magnificent beasts. Truly, Hellcats simply bond with the strongest warrior they find. In this case, it was you."

I frowned at the kitten, who broke our staring contest, hopped onto my lap and started purring while rolling itself into a ball once more. "Great."

"Hey! She saved our lives. In Hell more than once and yours even on the surface. I would have left your ass in that desert, no two fucking ways about it. The reason I didn't was that I knew she'd die by the hands of your brethren once they found her with your corpse." A crease appeared between her brows. "You have been bestowed with an incredible honor. You should be thankful."

"Honor? Thankful? I blessed two of the Hellspawn. And now I am on the road to who knows where, with those very same children of Lucifer."

She rolled her eyes. "Ugh, forgot who I was talking to. I got you out. You'd be dead by now. And you agreed to bless me before I freed you, so you knew exactly what you were getting into."

The truth ringing in her words wasn't comforting. I had no idea how Heaven would react to what I had done. Maybe if they never found out... I nearly scoffed at my own thoughts. What would I even tell them about how I got out of Hell? And lying to the Lord? *Impossible*. It was not a true intention anyway, just a thought. Because I was nervous. Nervous about what blessing a damned one would mean for me. There wasn't a lot of precedents on the topic.

It wasn't done. And yet, I had done it.

Tentatively, I placed a palm on the furry ball in my lap. It was soft, the leathery wings warm and smooth. I spread one wing up and studied the form and mechanics. Much like a bat's wing, it was essentially an extra arm and paw. The bones were just a little different and a lot longer. Curious. As fragile as the soft wing felt in my fingers, the cat didn't object to my perusal. Instead, it purred and rubbed its little cheek against my upper leg. Almost of its own accord, my hand let go of the wing and wandered up to scratch behind the cat's minute ears. I could hardly believe that this little piece of fluff would one day grow as big as a horse.

I looked up and caught Fane smirking gleefully at me and the cat. I cleared my throat, feeling that blush come on again. This time because I felt caught. The cat was Hellspawn, I shouldn't be petting it.

"You said you learned how to drive and hot-wire a car while I was unconscious," I said, desperate for a change of atmosphere. "How long was I out?"

"Two days."

"Two… days? Seriously?"

"Yup. That wound on your back has taken everything your body could give. It was caused by a ball of Hellfire. And the tear in your calf is more of a burned gash – a fire-clawed Ifrit being the one who gave it to you – so that is taking its sweet time to heal. I guess you'll be out of commission for at least a few more days."

"Hellfire? That would explain it." I grimaced as a subtle shift of my legs made searing agony race across my back. For a few seconds, I was busy catching my breath.

She was right, I would have to wait for a few more days until my back healed. Hellfire wounds did not heal as normal ones did. It also explained why I had been unconscious for such a long time. My body had needed everything to keep me alive despite of my wounds.

"So, who taught you to drive, not to mention hot-wire a car?"

"I did," she said, pushing forward her lower lip in a small pout. "I have seen enough movies about blond-locked pretty-boys and bemuscled bald men to figure out the driving. Although, they grossly exaggerate the amount of gear changing in those movies, let me tell you."

I had no idea what she was talking about, but she rambled on.

"The hot-wiring was exponentially easier. I only had to take a look at the wires behind the keyhole, the magnetic pull of electricity told me which to fuse together for the car to make a go-go."

"Go-go?" I whispered. This woman was speaking in riddles. What was more, I had never heard of a movie-watching Demon. Where? There was no such thing as technology or electricity in Hell, and in this, Heaven was similar. Our kinds inherently stuck to the ways of old, mostly because most of us were of those olden days ourselves. Some of the made, or re-born, Angels – those who had died and ascended more recently – did Surface Saturdays sometimes. They snuck off to indulge in stuff such as movie nights and bar-crawls. A waste of time to most of us older ones. Movies didn't seem all that interesting, and we couldn't get drunk easily.

Personally, I could not find any appeal in either. But Demons? They came to the surface to tempt and corrupt those Humans susceptible to such things. Humans might not be able to see them, but their energy was enough to push certain buttons. And a group of Demons, like the one Rapha and I had encountered, could do serious damage, even to the purest of souls.

The humming from when I woke picked up again and I noticed it was Fane. She softly hummed along to the music from the radio. Terribly false, and she obviously had never heard the song before, but that did not deter her. She grabbed something from the seat next to her and offered it to me. A crinkling bag.

"Chili chips?" I read the label.

"Yuppers. Love 'em. Try one, they are delish!"

"Why? We both don't need to eat."

"Well, I also don't *need* to fuck, I still like doing it." She shook the bag. "Besides, as I said, they are delish."

Ignoring her lewd words, I hesitantly stuck my hand into the bag and fished a chip out. Fane watched me in the rearview mirror as I stuck it into my mouth and gave it a taste. It burned on my tongue, the flavor rich and spicy.

"Huh? Great, right?" She pulled the bag back, making it crinkle loudly as she dove a hand into it and stuffed a fistful into her mouth.

I had not decided on whether or not I liked them, which probably meant I didn't, so I withheld my answer.

"Almosht shere," she said around her mouthful, pointing at a sign reading 'Emerald Falls 20 Miles.'

I had never heard of this place and curiosity brimmed the surface of my mind. Knowing that I should be more excited, more worried, more… everything, I tried to plan my next steps and think up scenarios. What if she took me to a surface den of Demons? How would I fare? Try as I might, I found it hard to rustle up anything but nonchalance. I couldn't bring myself to care more. My body was tired and heavy, despite the lapse in consciousness, I needed sleep. Badly.

I ended up fighting my lids, which were set on closing. The sound of the car, mixed with Fane's humming and the decidedly different tune from the radio, and the cat vibrating on my lap, all of it was lulling me deeper into a relaxed state.

If she wanted to harm me, she could have just left me, or killed me while I had been incapacitated. Strange Demon. Bandaging an Angel. Taking him on a journey to… wherever.

"Sulfur and onions!"

I snapped my eyes open fully at the cry from the front seat. "Wah – ?"

"Would you look at that?" Fane asked and pointed out the window to the right.

We had entered a wooden area, the forest getting ever thicker around us, now the thick canopy of leaves had parted and we drove along a mountain, a valley sprawling to our right. A huge lake, fed by a waterfall crashing from the mountain further ahead, glittered in the sunlight. Houses lined the lake, covering much of the valley below. It was a quaint sight. One that could bring feelings of peace and home.

"I had no idea this was what it looked like."

I straightened and sucked in a sharp breath. My back was killing me. "Y-you have never been here? Then how did you know how to find it?"

"Of course, I've been here, silly. But it was always night, and I never left the house."

I grabbed hold of the seat before me, the smooth, red leather creaking beneath my grip. "What does that –" I swallowed, "You have been summoned here." It was the only thing that made sense.

Her guilty glimpse in the mirror told me I was right. "Are you insane? You are going to see Humans? To what? Kill those that enslaved you?" I tried to lean forward, but the skin on my back was taut as a wire, a bit more and the edges would tear open.

"Calm your tits, Veronica," Fane said. "I have never been enslaved by the people I am looking for, and I am not planning on killing anyone." Her amber eyes found me, burning with intensity. "Unless you decide to be anything less than a gentleman, then it might be your time."

I blinked, not knowing what to do with that. "Then why look for them? If not to exact revenge for a summoning? As I understand it, you must obey those who call on you."

She gripped the steering wheel tightly and maneuvered the car down, following the twisting and turning road. "Never you mind. You will see soon enough. It's not like you'd believe the truth if I told you."

Too tired to argue, I decided to conserve what little strength I had left, in case I had to save the Humans from her.

Once we drove past the first houses of Emerald Falls, Fane stopped. She fiddled around with what I assumed had something to do with the brakes and stepped outside. I fiddled with the button on my armrest until the window whirred down. Wind carried the scent of pine and water my way, as I stuck my face outside to see what the Demon was up to. A loud 'meow' from my lap told me that the cat was curious as well and I lifted it up. Now we both ogled the Demon, who crouched on the pavement, both palms on the floor. She hopped in a circle, dragging her palms with her, her eyes closed. The small crease between her brows made an appearance as she looked to be completely concentrating. Her luscious lips moved as she whispered beneath her breath. Then a smile grew on them and the crease vanished. Fane patted the pavement like one would a pet, making a passer-by shake his head and speed up his steps.

"Car sick," I told him when he looked at me questioningly.

He grumbled something and walked away as fast as he could.

Fane sprang up, slid into the car, and on we went. We drove around for a few minutes, every other block, Fane got out and did her pavement patting routine.

Until we stood before a small house close to the lake. It was built of whitewashed wood, with accents of dark blue around the windows. Small as it was, it had two stories and looked much too welcoming to house an evil sect of devil worshipers or shady people who would need to summon a Demon. This, like the village, was quaint. The yard was graced with a gnarly, old oak, from which a swing hung, lazily moving in the wind.

The Demon dashed from the car and sprinted into the yard, clearing the picket fence with a vault, before running up to the front door.

"Cam! Dax! I'm here!" she cried and slammed her fists against the door.

The door was ripped open, and I let out a gasp when a woman nearly took Fane off her feet in a tackle-like hug. Following her was a boy of maybe eleven and the three of them sank down in a laughter-filled hug.

What. The. Hell.

Chapter Eight
Fane
The Surface,
Emerald Falls

I made it. I truly made it. The thought kept repeating over and over in my head as I sat on the wooden porch, arm in arm with Cam and Dax, breathing in their beloved scent and hearing their voices rife with wonder and tears.

"How did you…" Cam pulled free to palm my face with both hands. "After the last time we thought you might never come again. What about your Maester? How are you here?"

"Did someone else summon you?" Dax asked, a hint of jealousy in his voice.

I laughed, the reality of what I had accomplished now settling in fully. I had escaped Hell and broken my bond to Ragon completely. I was free. My own person. For the first time since I could remember.

"I…" I chuckled some more, gripping Cam's hand with one of my own and cradling Dax closer with the other. "It's a really long story and I'll tell you all about it, but I didn't come alone, and I need to ask you guys to help me." Turning to the car, I saw Mihr staring at us, his face incredulous, if extremely pale. He needed rest and I had to check on his back.

"Wh – There was no one there a second ago," Cam said. "Now there is a guy in your backseat and… Wow. Fane, who is he?"

"He got me out of Hell, but he has been injured doing so and he needs a place to rest and heal. I hate to ask, but I couldn't leave him behind. Can he stay with us? Just until he is better, then he will be off." Of this, I was sure. No matter what he had done in regards to get out, he would want to go back to Heaven.

"Of course. You know you are welcome for as long as you want. And anyone who is responsible for your freedom is welcome too," Cam said.

"Come on, guys." I stood and took each of their hands in mine as we began to walk across the yard and toward the car. "I'll introduce you."

Mihr's eyes got wider when he saw us coming at him, specifically as it became apparent that both Cam and Dax could see him. It looked like he had been trying to hide himself from them, but either me telling that there was someone, or his waning powers had somehow broken his glamour.

His breathing was short, and he was even paler than I had thought from further away.

"This is Mihr," I said. "Mihr, these are Camille and Daxter, my favorite Humans in the whole world."

The Angel stared, obviously not used to talking to Humans, much less being seen by them.

"Hello Mihr," Dax offered. "Fane says you helped her escape Hell and her Maester, Lord Ragon. He sounds like a really mean guy. What type of Demon are you?"

Mihr snorted in answer, obviously offended by Dax thinking he was a Demon. "I am no Demon, child. I am," his mouth clapped shut, "something else."

"He isn't really allowed to tell you guys what he is, but I don't mind. Mihr is an Angel."

"Fane!" Mihr thundered. "You can't just…"

Cam gasped. "An Angel? Are you serious?"

"Of course, mom. Don't you see his wings?" Dax pointed and Mihr awkwardly shifted to tuck his ruined wings closer.

"Wow." Daxter leaned closer. "Those look so pretty. I have a million questions."

"I'm sure you do, champ," Cam said, tucking him into her side. "But do me a favor and run inside and place one of the blankets from the hall-cupboard on the couch, will you?"

"Sure thing, mom," Dax smiled and sped off.

Once he was gone, Cam pegged me with an uncertain look. "I know I said anyone who helped you is welcome, but…"

"I would never harm you or your child, Camille. My kind, unlike hers," he jerked his chin at me, "would never put your kind in jeopardy. You are the pride and joy of our Lord. His most proud creation."

"Yeah? Well, your *Lord* can take a turn on it," Cam said, her pale green eyes sparking with rage.

"Cam," I said. "He would truly never hurt either of you. In fact, he would die before harm came to you if he was close enough to do something about it." I raised a brow at Mihr. "That is the one thing I can tell you with absolute certainty, and something I could never vouch for if he were a Demon."

"Fine, you can rest in my house until you are better," Cam said. "Let's get you inside."

Mihr's face relaxed a fraction, but whether it was because he was so tired and didn't know where else to go, or if he was glad to keep an eye on me while I was with Humans, I didn't know. I knew that was why he got into Earl's car with me in the first place. And while I wanted to be offended by that, I could understand the sentiment. My kind didn't normally befriend Humans. Besides, had I not met Cam and Dax, I wasn't sure I would have left

Earl intact. Interacting with a Human and not corrupting them was unheard of. Every chance had to be taken, that was the motto drilled into my kind. But I did have the advantage of not being as brainwashed as my peers who went out to specifically do harm to this world and its inhabitants.

I put the thought to the side for later and opened the door. A hissing sound greeted us, and the kitten swiped at me when I reached for Mihr.

"Really, madam? I thought we've been over this." I lined my face up with her. "You know I'm trying to help him, right?"

The kitten stopped hissing and mewled.

"Kitty?" Cam tried hard not to squeal. "I like you better already," she told Mihr.

I snagged the kitten and draped it around Mihr's neck, then I went about pulling him from the car, diving under his arm once more.

"I should get a medal for carrying your heavy ass around all the time," I said.

"You didn't get hit by a ball of Hellfire," he griped.

"True. But you haven't had to schlepp around a judgy Angel."

Cam took his other arm and together we braved the way to the house.

Mihr was feverishly warm, and I knew it took much for him to not lean his entire weight on us, he was almost out of juice. I worried that he'd pass out any second again.

Dax opened the door just as we stumbled up the porch. "Couch is all set up," he said and led the way into the living room, which was to the right of the small hallway. As always, my perception was hit by the wooden floorboards. It felt like walking on nothingness. Only my continuous exposure to it every Saturday kept me from missing a step and taking the three of us to the exquisitely smelling floor. Wood was awesome, and scary.

Eventually, we maneuvered Mihr next to the couch and helped him sit down. His face was a mask of agony by now, his jaw clenched so hard that his muscles were ticking like mad.

"Lie down on your stomach and I'll take a look at your back and leg," I said and turned around. "Do you have a —" Dax presented me with a first aid kit. "Nevermind," I said and smiled at him. "Thanks, love. Can I get a bowl of hot water and some towels?"

"Of course," Cam said, and she left the room with Dax.

Mihr lowered himself to his stomach and groaned when he finally lay sprawled in front of me, his feet sticking out over the couch by quite a bit.

The kitten hopped from her position and took up vigil next to him. She sat like a sphinx, watching every move I made.

"Judgy Angel, judgy cat," I said.

"Kitty!" Dax exclaimed, nearly spilling the water he carried in a big bowl.

"Careful, sport. Set the water down on the coffee table." I winked at him when he did.

Dax did, his eyes not leaving the kitten. "Can I pet it?"

"Not sure," I told him truthfully. "She's a Hellcat, and her teeth are poisonous. Right now, Mihr is the only person she likes, but you can try sitting next to her, and let her do the first move, though. And be very gentle, her poison is potent, even though she is small."

Cam strolled into the room, towels in her arms. "A Hellcat? What is that?"

"They are the steeds of Incubi and Succubi," Mihr rumbled. "But this one has taken a liking to me. She'll grow as big as a horse and will be able to carry a grown man to battle."

"She has wings!" Dax marveled when he sat down and the kitten flapped her wings a few times, then tucked them back.

"She sure does," I said. "You okay with Mihr and the kitten for five minutes? I'd like to speak to your mother quickly."

Dax nodded, his eyes rounding when the kitten slowly traipsed closer.

I pulled Cam with me, over to the hallway and out of earshot. Making sure she still had an unobstructed view to her son I whispered, "Are you okay? I wouldn't have thought learning he is an Angel would be a problem. If you want, I can take him and leave, whatever makes you feel comfortable."

She had her arms crossed and shook her head, making her black curls bounce around her shoulders. "No. You stay. If you say Dax is safe with him here, I believe you. I just…" She bit her lower lip. "His kind is your enemy. What makes you think that *you* are safe around him? What if he attacks you once he is strong enough? He doesn't seem to like you very much."

I grinned. "That is probably an understatement. He thinks I'm a vile creature. But no matter, he will not harm me in your presence." I watched him lying very still, concentrating on the kitten, who slowly snuck closer to Dax. "I doubt he'll hurt me even if he is better."

"But you aren't sure, are you?"

"Not one hundred, but I'm not planning on leaving the safety of your company with him, so I won't have to find out. Besides, he thinks that I am a danger to you."

Cam clicked her tongue. "Ridiculous."

"Yeah, he doesn't know that though." I reached out and squeezed her shoulder. "You really okay with this?"

Cam held my gaze. "I am."

I nodded once and walked back to kneel next to the couch, Mihr had taken up all the space, except for where the kitten balanced closely to the backrest, closing in on Dax. The boy sat stock-still on the far armrest and looked like he tried not to breathe too much. His mother stepped up behind him and drew a palm through his tightly curled hair.

I plunged a small towel into the bowl of water and wrung it out. "Ready, Mihr? Gotta clean your wound."

"Ready." His voice was strained, and the kitten immediately stopped what she was doing and eyed me.

Tentatively, I cleaned out the edges of the circular burn. It was smaller than it had been in the beginning, but the Angel needed serious rest to speed up his healing process. The cross-country road trip had been less than ideal for his body.

Lint and dirt had collected in the edges of his wound and cleaning it out was grueling work.

To his credit, he didn't move and he made no sound, but the muscles in his back bunched up and spasmed uncontrollably. Sweat soon covered him and I couldn't help but feel respect creep up inside my guts. I knew Demons who would have been sobbing messes given the agony he was exposed to.

And I decided I had been wrong about him. His suffering wasn't as sweet as people had described it to me. It wasn't an involved process, or a giving-into-it kind of thing. It was like iron. He was. Unyielding, hard, and strong.

It nearly had me wincing when his fists clenched around the blanket Dax had laid out beneath him. The first sign he let show, other than the involuntary reactions of his body.

"Almost done, Angel," I murmured, rinsing the towel once more.

"I can do this all day," he rumbled.

"Sure you can."

"It looks so bad," Dax said. "Are you gonna be okay?"

"I will be fine, Daxter. Fane has kept me alive," he sucked in his breath when I dabbed his wound, "this far. She won't let me die now."

"No, she won't," I said. I refrained from adding that it wasn't for his benefit, but for the kitten's. She was the only other free Hellspawn, apart from me, and I would be un-damned if she came to harm because Mihr died. And yet, a small part of me wondered if I would have truly let him die in that desert, had she not been there. *Of course, I would have,* I told myself. *He would have killed me if he saw me out in the open, not knowing me.* It's what our kinds did. The question was, would he still do so, after all we had been through together?

Seeing as I had nearly finished with the wound, Cam rounded the couch and knelt next to me. She opened the first aid kit and pulled out some iodine.

"Thank you," I said and placed the towel on the table before taking the iodine. "Mihr? This will hurt. Do you need to be held down?"

He turned his face into the blanket. "No. Do what you must," he said, his voice muffled.

This time, his whole body bunched up like a fist. The muscles in his back and arms vibrated with how hard he was clenching them, still no sound came from him and this time, I definitely felt a pang of something painful in my chest. *It is respect*, I told myself. My kind revered strength, seeing his probably spoke to a hidden part of my inner wiring. I hoped this was the case, as the alternative was unthinkable. Because the alternative meant that I cared for his pain, and by extension him.

Thankfully, that train of thought was snuffed when I was done and gave Cam the iodine. I quickly changed the bandages on his leg, but that wound was healing fine and would be gone long before his back was healed.

Without thinking, I brushed strands of his dark-blond hair from his face. "All done, Angel."

"I think he might be more comfortable in the cellar," Cam mused. "We have a bed down there for guests."

I raised a brow at her. "Guests?"

She gave me smirk. "Dax and I thought that if you ever got out, you needed a place to stay. So, we made you a room in secret."

"You did?" I stared at her. "B-but you knew I could never get out."

"We always hoped, Fay," Dax said.

I felt tears brimming close to my eyes. "I don't deserve you guys."

Cam raised a brow, looking at the Angel. "Looks like your room will have another inhabitant for the time being. Think you can make it to the cellar, Mihr?"

He groaned and fought himself into a sitting position. "If we go now," he said. "Might pass out soon."

"Let's go then. I need to see this room," I said and heaved him to his feet with Cam's help.

"Will you get the door, champ?" Cam asked Dax, who sprang up and led the way into the kitchen and through a door I had never seen. He clicked on a light and walked down a narrow flight of stairs. It took a while for the three of us to follow and looking back I saw the kitten hopping down one stair at a time in pursuit.

Finally, we made it and my breath caught in my chest. "You guys!"

The room was exquisite. It had a stone floor made of slate tiles and both a normal bed and a cot made of sandstone. It was a huge slab of red stone and it must have been a bitch to get down here.

"We weren't sure if you slept on stone or not," Cam explained.

"I normally do, but I have always wanted to try a real, human, bed. This is epic! I love it!"

Had I not been weighed down by Mihr, I would have pirouetted through the room and checked out every nook and cranny, that was for sure. Speaking of which, we got him to the bed and Cam drew back the covers before we set him down. He breathed hard and almost immediately sank to the side. We helped him settle on his stomach and I drew up the blanket to the small of his back.

A loud meow to my feet made me laugh and I snagged the kitten up and placed her on the bed as well. She climbed up Mihr's legs and rolled into a ball. Looked like she wasn't going to be moving for a while.

"Come on, Fane," Dax said. He dragged me to the far-right corner of the room, were an arch opened into a small bathroom.

"You even have your own bathroom," Dax said, beaming. "We also weren't sure if you used them, since you never did during the summonings, but we thought…" he shrugged, "just in case."

I bent over and drew him into a long hug. "Thank you. Thank you a million times." I let go and kissed his forehead, then I pulled Cam in for a hug. "You have no idea what this means to me."

They truly didn't. I had spent my life building houses, rooms, thrones, and vanity projects for others, having someone make – build – something for me… It was beyond comprehension. I felt ugly tears coming on and freed myself from Cam's embrace.

"I uh… Imma try the bathroom if that is okay."

Cam gave me a warm, knowing, smile and a nod. "Dax and I'll be upstairs and make some dinner. The sun is almost down, and I think – if you want – we can have a nice outside dinner. On the back terrace?"

All I managed was a tear-stricken noise, then I watched them leave and finally let my eyes spill over. I took deep breaths as I walked across the room, running my hands over the concrete walls, feeling them. They did this for me, words could not express how beautifully close to pain my chest burned. I loved these two more than I could ever express.

With a deep sigh, I eyed the bathroom and decided to try it out. I had always wanted to try a shower.

Chapter Nine
Fane
The Surface,
Emerald Falls

"Now what?" I scrutinized the dials in front of me. "Red means hot, I think. Hot is good." I turned the dial and squealed when water shot from the showerhead, ice-cold. Jumping back a little I kicked my clothes further away, lest they get drenched. When I looked back, steam rose from the spray and I stuck my hand under it.

A deep sigh escaped me as heat flowed over my fingers and I shuffled into the curtain of water. This was great. Where I came from, the way to go about cleanliness was – if even a thing – to bathe in the caves close to the third ring. I knew a secret cave with a seldomly frequented pool of heated water I used, but it had always been an anxious affair for me. The pools were frequented by many and I didn't like the company. Especially that of Demon men.

The bummer was that I needed the pools almost daily, to recharge my powers and undo the stiffness and knotted muscles my job brought on.

This shower was of the same soothing nature. Granted, my body had largely recovered from how I had pushed it during our escape, but I had been on edge the entire time traveling.

Reading the magnetic field of the earth, the movement beneath my feet, the stone, and plotting a course accordingly was one thing. Having an unconscious Angel with me while figuring out the Surface and learning as I went, had been quite another matter. Learning to drive had not been as easy as I had made it out to be, though I had enjoyed it once I picked up on how it worked.

Now, I felt the anxiety, bunching up the muscles in my upper back and shoulders, slowly leaving. It washed down and curled into the drain along with the dirt and golden blood on my hands.

I fingered the small bottles in a metal nest hung next to the dials and examined several. Opening one that said 'shampoo,' I sniffed. "Uhhh! This is amazing."

As I worked the gooey contents into my hair and over my body, bubbles and suds grew and I giggled like an idiot, while making shapes before washing off. I knew in that moment that I loved showers and most of all soap.

Smelling like a fairy fart, I turned off the shower and stepped from the stall. I couldn't remember ever feeling this refreshed, or hopeful. What lay ahead was exciting, now that I was the master of my own fate. I knew that sooner or later I would be stumped as to what to do next, but right now, I had no desire to ponder it. I was in the house of my favorite people. I was safe. For the first time since Lev died, I felt giddy. Happy. For a second, I wondered if I had rediscovered my true self. The one that piped up and held onto happiness with everything it was worth. Because I had survived all I had due to my gift of clinging to hope and looking on the bright side, no matter what. Only what happened to Lev had broken me. But now… Maybe now I could finally move past it. Cam and Dax had helped me through my grief, being free could help me find myself again.

"Aha. I see you have eventually left his side," I said when I nearly tripped over the kitten, who sat next to a basket reading 'dirty clothes go here.'

I picked up my ruined shorts and the top I had stolen, when getting a few items for myself and Mihr to wear, and threw them into the basket.

The kitten watched, her red eyes laden with intelligence. She gave me a commanding 'meow' and trotted from the room, in the door she turned once more and mewled the same command once more.

"Want me to follow, madam?"

She flapped her wings and was off. I shrugged, draped a towel around me and followed. She led me – as if it could be any other way – to the Angel and clawed her way up the bed on a piece of blanket hovering close to the floor.

"You need something, Angel?" I asked and gingerly sat down next to him.

His tired eyes found mine. "How did you…?"

"Your cat told me to come." I held out a hand to her and, for the first time, she leaned her head into my palm. A smiled broke from my lips and I marveled at the softness of her fur, it was hard to imagine that she'd grow up to be one of the deadliest creatures known in Hell.

"I tried to get up when I heard you scream," Mihr said, making me refocus on him. "She probably thought I needed your help. What happened?"

"The water was cold."

"Seriously?"

I glowered at his frown. "Hey! I haven't taken a shower before. Stop judging, you… judgy piece of… heaven trash."

"Wow. Even I know that was lame." For the first time since knowing him I saw the corners of his mouth lift slightly. The change it brought to his face was extreme, the stoic mask slipped, revealing something close to roguish mirth. I bet a full smile would blow me away. To save face and regain my composure, I did the one thing I knew would get to him. I got up, dropped the towel and walked my naked ass to the dresser, maybe there were – "Bingpot!" I exclaimed, pulling out some yoga pants and a shirt. The gasp from behind me was expected, I still had a hard time suppressing a giggle.

Taking my sweet time, I dressed with my back to him before returning to his side.

His silver-gray eyes held me as I sat down. "You find satisfaction in testing me, don't you, Demon?"

"Well, your prude reaction to me is certainly entertaining, and I am supposed to be evil, remember? Don't they teach you in Heaven that bodies are all the same? It's the thoughts and emotions that should be private." I leaned closer, "They are important. They are what make us individual. Bodies are just flesh, made to enjoy, to fight, to live in."

That small, almost-smile, was back. "It is an interesting take on things, but your disregard for my comfort only shows how devious you are. Still." His expression grew solemn, his dark brows drawing together. "I wanted to… thank you. For not leaving me behind. And for taking care of my wound."

I was taken aback a little. "Didn't really do it for you, but you're wel –"

"Just so you know," he interrupted. "We shouldn't be here, and I will not let you harm anyone as long as I am close."

Shaking my head, I huffed out a dry laugh. "And he goes and ruins it. I would never, ever, harm Dax or Cam."

His storm-colored eyes narrowed. "You seem to like them, but your kind always has an angle, a goal, some scheme. I will find out what it is. Besides, you should not have told them what I am. You know I'm not allowed to directly interact with Humans."

I got up, done with his judgmental bullshit. "Listen, Cam and Dax are the closest thing to family I can imagine. I have no angle, I left Hell, broke out. You know as well as I do that I will likely be killed if any Demon ever finds me." I walked to the stairs and stopped with my foot on the first one. "Concerning you, you have already committed the most unholy act and blessed a damned one – two if you count the madam on your legs – so, I don't see a problem in breaking a few more rules."

"You have exposed them to our world, Fane. It will cost you. Think about what happens if anyone – Demon or Angel – finds you here. What will they do to Camille and Daxter?"

I snorted, leaving him and his accusations behind as I trampled up the stairs, firmly shutting out what he'd said. I wasn't going to let his poor opinion of me ruin the high of feeling safe and free. Not even that last little nugget he left me with.

"Fane, there you are," Cam said when I entered the kitchen. "Oh, you smell amazing. Not charred as usual."

I grinned at her. "I love showers."

"Great. You needed one." She winked and pointed at the oven dinging to my right. "Would you mind getting out the gratin? Dax has set the table out back, you can bring it to him." She presented me with mittens and I laughed, opening the oven door and grabbing the baking dish, making my veins light up from the heat.

"Hah, forgot about that neat trick of yours." Cam bumped my hip as she passed me to get to the fridge.

The dumb smile I carried through the house – along with the gratin – did not seem to want to leave. Even being as different to them as I was, she viewed me as the same. Not a Demon. It was a strange sensation knowing that to Cam I was just a normal person.

I passed through the open door leading to the backyard and gasped. Beneath the canopy between two huge trees was a table, set for three. The sun was about to hit the lake and sink into its waters, making the rippling waves appear gold and red, like a sea of fire.

Dax was busy arranging cutlery around the plates and waved me over when he noticed me. I breathed in the scents in the air deeply, set on committing this view and moment to everlasting memory.

****

For the first time, we didn't have to watch the clock, the atmosphere was light, and we laughed, chatted, and joked through dinner. My first real dinner. The heavens got dark and soon stars twinkled in the inky blackness, while a cool wind lazily grazed my skin, carrying with it the scents of grass, water, and flowers.

Try as I might, the last thing Mihr had said hovered close to the surface of my mind and I spent the whole evening suppressing it.

After the hour turned late, and Dax had said his goodbyes, hugging me tightly, Cam and I sat under the trees, a bottle of wine shared between us. Finally, I couldn't help it and voiced my concern.

"The Angel said something that made me think," I said. "I am what you might call an outlaw. I tricked my way out of a place that should have been impossible for me to leave. I'm pretty sure they will be looking for me, specifically my Maester." I turned the glass in my hand and took a sip. "Me being here could spell danger for you, which is the last thing I want for you or Dax."

"How would they know?" Cam asked.

"Maeve might tell them I have Human friends. I can't rule that out. But she knows you by Cam and Dax, no more."

"No one besides you knows where we live, right?"

"No. I was very careful to never even mention a continent to Maeve."

"Then you might be worrying for nothing." Her smile was meant to be warm, but there was a slight tremble in her lower lip.

"Yet I am, and so are you, babe. I can't have Dax or you being at risk because of me." I leaned back in my chair and placed the wine on the table. "And the truth of the matter is, I am too weak to protect you, should they find us. Maybe it's for the best —"

Cam laughed and tugged her mane of black locks back with a palm. "You? Weak? After what you did to Jake?"

"Jake is a Human, and I was pissed off, royally. He was trying to hurt you," I growled, reliving the emotions of that particular night. The night Dax had summoned me because Cam's ex had gotten into the house and was threatening her.

"You picked him up and threw him out, literally. I have never seen anything like it. The knife he had didn't even nick your skin." Her eyes glinted with unshed tears. "You saved our lives that night."

"And I would fight anyone who wanted to harm you. But imagine someone ten times as strong as me wreaking havoc, and you've got an idea what a Raider would do if he found me. And that would be just one, they normally travel in groups." I downed the rest of my wine. "No, I think the safest thing — and I can't believe I'm saying this — would be to leave once the Angel is better."

"That is bullshit," Cam said. "Where would you even go?"

"No idea. And it's not like I'd want to leave. I came to be with you guys." I swiped my eyes with my fingers. "I'll have to think on it, maybe… maybe there is something else I can do."

"If you can think of something other than leaving, we'll try it," Cam said. She filled up my glass and we toasted silently, then just sat together for a few moments. The song of the night creatures was thick around us. Somewhere an owl hooted, and crickets chirped from all around us. The rustling of leaves to my right told of something small sprinting through the foliage and I gave myself over to the unfamiliar sounds, enjoying them as something nonthreatening. It was a blessing.

"So, will you tell me about the Angel?" Cam asked.

"What do you want to know?"

"How come I didn't see him at first? And when I did, his wings were hidden? And how come you drove around for days without anyone noticing your… redness?"

"The short answer? Glamour. Angels can hide completely from Humans, as they aren't allowed to interact with them directly. If they make themselves visible, they can still hide their true nature. Only Humans who believe and know what is before them will see the truth. When it comes to me, I appear as Human to everyone apart from you and Dax. It's fascinating, really. I have no idea what I look like, I would love to know."

Cam worried her lower lip. "You know, you have never told me much about your world, apart from what you do and who you are. My best friend is a Demon, yet I don't even truly know what that means."

"I didn't want to… sully you with what I am. Hell is a vast void of sin, gruesome acts, and power moves. You either thrive being an asshole, or you suffer under one. There is nothing else." I breathed against the memories long locked away. Before my contract, before Lev. "Here, I can be who I am, not who I am supposed to be. But if you want to know things, you can always ask, and I will answer truthfully."

Cam was quiet for a while and the longer the silence stretched on, the more antsy I grew.

"Where is Hell?"

"Hah. That is a tricky one. Hell and Heaven both exist on a plane right next to this one. You can enter both through death or portals. The portals have rules. The ones for Heaven are in the sky, and only Angels know where they are and what to look for. The ones leading to Hell are like holes in the earth, and they only let a specific number of Demons through per day. Unless you are not of Hell, or blessed. That's why Mihr, the kitten and I popped up from the Ascent like a zit without anyone following us."

"Another plane? Seriously?"

"Absolutely. What? You thought you could just dig and end up in Hell? If that were the case, the chase for oil would have already yielded swarms of Demons escaping from drill holes." I sniggered at the idea of a group of pissed off Ifrits lighting up an oil rig because they had been disturbed in their slumber.

"Are there more planes than Heaven and Hell?" Cam's eyes were trained on me and the glass in her hand was tilted precariously.

"Possibly, but I personally know of none. Then again, I am of the lowliest Demons. Which means I am pretty uneducated when it comes to such things.

109

Knowledge is kept from most of us, as the most important thing is the war, and we should all concentrate on it."

Cam pulled her glass upright without spilling and took a sip. "Ah. And you decided to 'make love, not war'?" Her grin was as dirty as one of her laughs.

"Love? Hah. Not likely. I just didn't let the Angel die."

"But you have to agree, he is magnificent. Sure there isn't a little... some something going on?" she wiggled her brows.

"Camille! I am appalled." I slapped a hand to my chest feigning outrage. "He is my mortal enemy, this isn't Romeo and Juliet. Besides, he is a judgmental, overly righteous ass and doesn't think much of me. I kinda disgust him, I think."

Cam giggled at that. "Yeah, yeah. You guys have banter, even when he is nearly unconscious. That, my friend, is rare. And no one would ever think of you as disgusting. In another life, I would have made you my wife."

I whooped, "Ooof! That was a rhyme lads and ladies!"

Cam raised her hand and opened her fist, "Mic drop, bitch." She picked up the wine bottle and turned it over. "Empty. Figures. Gotta get more tomorrow."

We decided to call it a night and I stumbled down the stairs after hugging my friend. My head was light and my spirits high, my footing just wasn't up to par. It took me a minute to light my hand to find my way, as I didn't want to disturb Mihr.

"Shhhh," I made when the cat glowered at me from the bed. I rounded the bed and sat down on the slab of sandstone. Patting it fondly, I formed it a bit for more comfort. The stone was as malleable as thick clay beneath my fingers, and I lay down a minute later, very happy with the world and my current place in it.

My gaze wandered to the Angel, his grey wings hanging off the bed in drapes of silken feathers. They looked better already. In the back of my head, I wondered what he would look and be like at the height of his power. Would I still find him pretty if he wasn't bruised, plucked, and singed? As my lids slid shut, I smelled his scent of clean air and spring and decided it wasn't the worst scent to fall asleep to.

Chapter Ten
Mihr
The Surface,
Emerald Falls

Time and reality swam together around me like inkblots dropped into water. There was no telling how long I lay on my stomach, agony raging on my back, or which of the people around me were truly real.

I was pretty sure I had an animated conversation with Michael wearing a melon-helmet at one point, and that had to have been a dream. Michael would neither wear a melon-helmet, nor had I really had a conversation with him in… some time. I also hoped that the Demon bringing me into a human household and telling them what I was had been a dream, as well. At times, I felt sand beneath my fingers and smelled dirt and dust, so there was a possibility I was still back in the desert and the Demon had left me there. But as more and more glimpses of memories and a room I didn't know came through, I decided that my wishes of being left behind had to be just that. Wishes.

The only constant throughout my ordeal and the coming and going swirls of lucidity and weird hallucinations, was the cat. I felt her weight on top of my upper legs, where she lay curled into a fluffy ball. Sometimes, she slunk up to stub my face with a silken paw – mostly when my fever-dreams got heavy – only to lick over my nose and resume her position on my legs once more.

Her presence was comforting in a strange way. It grounded me in the fact that I had truly left Hell, even when flashes of my torture in the cells of the Deep breached the corners of my mind with the gentleness of a sledgehammer.

Other than her being a constant, I heard the voice of my Demon talking to me. I also saw and felt her at my side from time to time. Her red skin was like a glowing sign in my murky world, and sometimes I got very close to breaking through the curtain my fever had drawn. She cleaned my wounds, which was excruciating, and talked to me in that velvety, raspy voice. A voice that left thoughts of unfulfilled desires in my mind. She had a voice like sin.

The more she appeared, the clearer it got. I was, in fact, not in the desert. She had taken me on a road trip to her human friends. Those memories had been real. Which meant the Humans were in danger.

"Shouldn't have come here," I mumbled, seeing her red skin as she reached out a palm to feel my forehead.

"Yeah, yeah. You have told me already," she said. This time, her voice carried farther and pierced through. I blinked as she grew sharp in front of my eyes.

"You back?" she asked, bending over and bringing her face closer to mine. "Mihr?"

I blinked once more and finally pierced the veil surrounding me. Like waking from a very animated dream, I emerged, gasping for air.

"Fane?"

She smiled, showing off her subtly pointed incisors. "There you are. The pain in my ass I have been waiting for."

"Where am I?" I tried to push my torso up, but she pressed a palm to my shoulder.

"Easy, tiger. If you move too fast, you'll get dizzy."

I slumped back down and raised a brow at her. "Where are we, Fane?" I repeated.

"Where we have been for the last three days. With my friends Cam and Dax. Do you remember them?"

"Little boy, likes the cat. His mother does too, she doesn't like Angels though. Right?"

"Right on the money, Regina." Fane patted my shoulder.

"You shouldn't have told them what I am. And you definitely shouldn't have brought me here. Or come here. You are a danger to these people."

"Yes, thank you. You have said as much for the past few days. By now, I know how you think on the topic."

"I'm serious, Fane," I glowered at her.

"I. Know. Now stop being a prick and let's see if we can get you up." She shooed the cat from my legs, resulting in a rattling growl, but the kitten did move away and jumped to the floor.

The skin on my back pulled tight uncomfortably and throbbed when I turned on my side and Fane helped me sit up. It felt like being sliced across the back by blades on fire.

"You know, your pain tolerance is pretty high," my Demon said. "It must hurt like a bitch, yet your stoic face never changes." She pouted and frowned, seemingly trying to mock-mimic me.

"Very funny," I heaved out.

"I know, thank you." She winked, her amber eyes aglow with glee. "Now, let's see if you can retract the wings. You'll move more freely if you do." She stood and pulled me up by my wrists, until I towered over her.

Wobbly like a reed in the wind, I tried to balance and get my head to stop swimming.

"Whoa." She steadied me and after a few seconds the world stopped spinning. She let go of my wrists slowly. "You okay?"

"Yup. Seems like I am." I took a tentative step and, though unsure, I didn't keel over immediately. Counting that as a win, I turned my head and tried to spread my wings out a tad.

"Retract, remember? Not widen and flap around," Fane said. "They're healed. Give it a try."

Looking at my left, I surmised that she was right. Both my left wings looked healthy and strong as ever, but still felt heavy and sluggish. I breathed in and pulled them closed, then back. It took a few times before I was able to retract all four of my wings fully and hide them from view. Instantaneously, I felt the skin around the wound on my back slacken. Relief flooded me as the pain lessened. I sighed and gently rolled my shoulders, then my head.

Once I looked down, Fane was smiling at me. "I think your wound will heal a lot faster, now that the weight of your wings isn't pulling at it anymore. You up for joining us for lunch? Dax has just come home from school and we tried making spaghetti before Cam gets home. I think we could use your input on the sauce."

Everything she said sounded… so normal. Like she had lived here – like we had lived here – for years. As though we were friends. "We don't eat, Fane."

"Well, I think I have told you already what I think of that sentiment." A cheeky smirk played around the corners of her lips.

"You have. It involved a crude statement on intercourse if I remember correctly."

"True. But human food is so good. You should totally try it."

"It leads to using the toilet. I do not desire to do so."

She stuck out her tongue. "You, sir, are the biggest stick in the mud since Michael. And from what I have heard, that guy is bad."

"Michael wa-is my best friend," I said, nearly speaking in past tense. I hadn't spent time with him in a while, but I was not going to let Fane sully his person. "He is the epitome of virtue and righteousness. A model —"

"Yeah. A stick in the mud. I heard he once burned out his eyes because they strayed to a Human woman." She grimaced. "I mean, they grew back, but eesh. Talk about over-fucking-compensating."

"Desire for a Human is a sin, he did the right thing by repenting."

"Oh, for the love of granite, you don't truly believe that."

"What if I do?"

She drew the nail of her index finger up my naked stomach, over my torso, and flicked my nose. "Then I'd say, you'd have to gauge out your eyes as well. Twice, by now, if I remember correctly."

"Right," I scoffed. "Seeing you in your unholy nakedness is one thing, I would have to desire you for it to be a sin."

"Poor Angel. I might not be strong, or highly regarded in Demon hierarchy, but I know I am fucking magnificent. And I know of your desire." She breached the distance between us, pressing her chest to my torso. "You have asked me often enough why I test your conviction."

Her being this close, the heat of her skin, only separated by her shirt from mine, it did spark desire. As did the depth of her amber eyes, holding me captive as if she were holding onto me physically. She was like fire herself, hypnotizing, blinding, dangerous.

I placed both palms on her shoulders and pushed her back, gently but firmly. "You might be magnificent, but don't look for desire where there is none. I prefer a woman who is pure, not a sinful daughter of Lilith."

"You keep telling yourself that," she whispered, her gaze still as intense as ever. "I bet you don't even know the depth of your own deprived longing, or what you truly want."

"Fay?" Small feet drummed down the steps, preceding the boy, Daxter.

The Demon turned from me, breaking the spell engulfing us. "What's up, Dax?"

The boy stopped dead and stared at me. "You are up. And your wings are gone."

"He sure is, and he can retract his wings," Fane explained. "All Angels can."

"Are you going to join us for lunch? Fane and I made spaghetti." The boy beamed at me, so welcoming and hopeful that I had no other choice but to acquiesce.

"I will try your pasta dish," I said.

Daxter's smile widened even more and he puffed up his little chest with pride. A long-lost feeling stole itself into my heart, a lightness I hadn't felt in years. It took me a minute to understand it as the delight coming with making another happy. Not in the way I was used to – making my peers proud or doing God's work – but bringing true joy to an innocent.

"Huh. Did I just see an almost-smile?" Fane teased when Dax had sprinted up the steps and we followed suit.

I only braved the steps slowly, letting my palm glide over the drywall at my side for balance. To my left, the kitten hopped up every step alongside me. "Could very well be. Humans are pure beings at this age, most of them, anyway. They do spark happiness, you know."

"Oh, *I* know. I wasn't sure you remembered what that was."

Her statement irritated me, and I glowered at her, "What would you know about me, or what I would remember?"

"Did some research. Dax once accidentally summoned me to this house using an old tome containing not only my name – he was fortunate he did pick mine, mind you – but those of countless Demons and Angels."

That stopped me short. "The boy summoned you?"

Fane dragged me on. "Yeah. He was lucky it was me, because he had such a shock when it worked that he broke a line of the pentagram with his foot as he stumbled back."

"Unbelievable. You know that summoning you means –"

"He can possibly use basic spells? Perhaps even more? Yes," she nodded. "Which is why I have forbidden him from trying out any more of the rituals in his book," Fane said, leading the way into a kitchen I hadn't seen yet. "Isn't that right, squirt?"

"That's right, Fay." Daxter was busy stirring the contents of a pot on a gas stove situated next to the refrigerator on the far side of the room. On the other side was a sink, followed by a long, gray countertop, overlooked by a window that allowed a beautiful view into the yard. I made out the lake in the distance, glittering in the midday sun.

I looked around the kitchen some more, trying to orient myself in this alien place. The cupboards and cabinets were a dirty, rustic white. Painted to look used. It gave the room charm in a way.

"I would like to take a look at that tome later, if I may," I said, wanting to add more but deciding against it for now. If the child could summon Demons, and possibly use other spells… he himself could be a danger.

Daxter nodded, while pouring the pot into a ceramic bowl Fane held for him. "Course," he said.

"You think you're up to taking these to the table? Through the arch in the living room is the dining table," Fane nodded at a pile of four plates with cutlery on the countertop.

I rounded the kitten, who had taken to sitting beside me, watching our conversation unfold. After a double-take I stopped. "Wasn't the cat smaller?"

Fane smirked at the black feline. "She was. Her kind grows very fast. In a week she will be the size of a grown house cat."

"You really should give her a name," Daxter said, scaling a stool to get out glasses from an overhead cabinet.

I supposed, I should. She had stayed with me the entire time and I was sure Fane had told the truth, she wasn't leaving me. As always, when I met the cat's gaze, I felt a strange sense of grounding. Of belonging. It was a feeling that was as soothing as it was unwelcome. There was no way I would be able to go to Heaven with her. My brethren would surely kill her. That was if I even *could* go back.

I slowly made my way to the countertop, grabbed the plates and turned for the living room. Two arches on either side of the couch led into another room, the dining room. The table was sturdy, but old. It looked like it had been passed down from an older family member. It had been the same with the leather couch, the one I had lain on when Fane had first brought me here. The leather was thick, the seams sturdy, done over in places.

One at a time, I set down the plates around the table as Daxter strolled in, clad in oven-mittens, carrying the pasta. The boy gave me a shy smile, then placed the pasta on the table. He tugged off the mittens and bent down toward the cat. Stretching out his palm, he waited.

Knowing that the Hellcat was poisonous, I was close to intervene, but she elongated her body, sniffing the boy's fingers before she took a step forward. A soft purr floated through the room when the cat let Daxter stroke her head. She had truly grown in the past few days, her size now close to an adolescent house cat.

Fane strutted through the arch and her face lit up in a warm smile when she saw the interaction between Daxter and the cat. Her expression was one I hadn't seen before and it was still confusing to grasp what I saw. It was plain as day that she adored the boy. Something that shouldn't be. Where was the malice of her kind? The angle? The plan to twist him and his mother to evil? If it was there, I couldn't make it out. Nothing in any interactions between Fane and her Humans had spelled danger.

I watched as she rounded the table and put down the sauce she had brought along. "Salad," she said and jogged from the room once more. My Demon was an enigma. She should have killed me the moment she had the chance. She should have killed that old man, Earl. She should not feel for these people what she obviously did. Love. Her kind wasn't supposed to even know what love was.

I nearly scoffed. Just like my kind shouldn't know what it was to hate. Yet, I did. And I knew enough of my brethren who did, too. I knew those whose hate had grown until it bordered on fanatical rage, like Michael. Something unbefitting of our kind. So, who was I to say that a Demon couldn't love?

"She is so soft," Daxter said, breaking me from my thoughts.

"Pardon?"

"Your cat. She is amazing, and soft." The boy was sitting down, stroking the cat over her back, gently patting her wings as he went. "We could name her together," he suggested. "If you have no ideas, I got a few."

"That would be very helpful, thank you. I suppose it is time she gets a name."

The boy beamed again, his back straight as a rod. That feeling from before was back again, as I witnessed my words being the cause of his pride. It was something so simple, but I had never known it to be this meaningful.

"Since she's from Hell, how about Lilith?"

I nearly laughed out loud but was able to turn it into a cough. "Uhm… not really an option," I told him.

"Shiva?"

"That is a Hindu God. Also, a male."

"Hm." Daxter frowned and stroked the cat, his scrutinizing gaze as intense as if he could learn her name by looking at her. "Kasha?" The cat meowed, then purred even louder. Daxter grinned, "I think she likes that name."

I grunted as my back spasmed while I sank down next to the two of them. Immediately, the cat rubbed her sleek body against my knees. "Kasha it is," I said.

The moment I said her name, her red eyes zeroed in on me. As if an invisible thread connected us, she pulled me in, and I sank ever deeper into her mystical stare. The connection grew until it felt as though I was stretching out to touch her, even while she sat in front of me, and my hands rested at my sides.

A feeling of coming home, of belonging, of utter acceptance seared through my entire being. I had no idea why, but I knew that I could trust this being with my life, and strangely, I felt an overwhelming sense of protectiveness rise inside of me. It filled me up, overflowing everything else. Until all that was left was Kasha, and the irrevocable knowledge that I would walk into danger, and even death, for her.

She blinked, her regal face satisfied, and I sucked in a breath and shook my head. "What was that?" I choked out.

"Ah, you named her, didn't you?" Fane asked, carrying a glass bowl filled with salad.

Chapter Eleven
Fane
The Surface,
Emerald Falls

It was good that he was up. The sooner he healed fully, the sooner he'd be gone. As I took the salad I whipped together to the dining room, I saw Mihr and the cat caught in a staring contest, a mad energy radiating from both of them. It could only mean one thing.

"Ah, you named her, didn't you?" I asked, just as Mihr shook his head and mumbled something.

"Yup," Dax said, a proud expression on his face. "Her name is Kasha."

"Good name," I told them and set the bowl down. So, the bonding was completed, he would not be able to leave her behind and he would be unable to let anything hurt her. My conscience regarding her was now clear. He could leave.

I watched as the Angel stood shakily, his wound still worryingly big. He was up and walking though, and that meant it wasn't long now.

The sound of a car pulling up to the house broke my trail of thought. "Sit, guys. Cam is home."

Sure enough, as soon as we had taken up our seats, Mihr lowering himself down gingerly, the front door opened, and Cam stomped inside. She plopped down her keys and bag and headed through the arch. "What is this?" she asked, drawing a palm through Dax's curly hair before she kissed his forehead.

"Fay and I made spaghetti for everyone," Dax announced.

Cam blew us both a kiss.

"Well, Dax made most of it, I was allowed to cook the water," I said.

"We still have to see if it's any good," Dax said, his expression serious.

"Then let's begin, before it gets cold," Cam said, taking a seat next to her son, who started filling their plates at once.

I couldn't wait for Mihr's reaction and slyly peeked at him taking his first bite. His eyes popped as he chewed, then closed. I heard a very soft sigh come from him and was completely floored by his face. Usually hard, and looking perpetually unimpressed, Mihr's expression was one of sensual abandon and satisfaction. *Damn, if that was his face during sex...* I found myself debating whether it would be worth it to see it in person. But I knew the answer, given the chance, I would go to town on him. Angel or not.

I inwardly shook my head. Had to be the long abstinence, and the fact that there was no other man around, or the fact that he looked like a statue cut from marble. Or the fact that I hadn't felt any type of threat come from him yet. Maybe it was just my Demon nature relishing hedonism. Had to be. Ever since Lev, I hadn't trusted another Demon man with my body, for a good reason. But it also meant the long dry spell was eating at me. It had to fuel my naughty thoughts regarding the Angel.

Twisting my pasta into a nest, I took a bite and groaned unabashedly. "Dax, this is divine." I pointed the fork to my plate. "The sauce is amazing."

"And someone *did* cook the pasta-water just right," he said with a chuckle.

I mock-glared, "Smartass."

"Fane is right," Cam said. "Does this mean you cook from now on?"

Dax drew in a big breath. "Maybe," he huffed out with grandeur. "If you pay me. In books, and movies, and games."

"Huh. I think cooking myself will be less expensive," Cam said.

"But less tasty." I wiggled my brows, earning a scowl from Cam. Then the three of us broke out into laughter.

Mihr looked from one to the next silently, but I saw a small twinge in the right corner of his mouth.

****

After lunch, I found myself in the backyard. Dax and Cam had left for work and school respectively. Dax had decided to try out band practice a few weeks back and today was the day he got to go. To my ears he was a whiz with the Cello, but I also only ever heard *him* play. Nevertheless, I was sure they would take him.

Digging my fingers into the sandy ground, I reveled in the utter vastness of what I felt. The roots of the trees on either side of me spiderwebbed through the soil, drawing on minerals and water. In the distance to my left, the lake made the sand feel cool and runny. It was an unusual feeling, runny sand. Not something I would have ever felt in Hell. As well as the sheer abundance of life. Bugs, worms, and critters swarmed the ground underneath me, their shells clacking against the sand. Their little hearts beating fast, sending the tiniest of vibrations to my fingers.

I did not fight the smile washing over me. This was living. This was freedom. Hard to think that a few days ago everything had seemed hopeless. Now, I was here and I could stay for as long as I wanted. Or rather, as long as I dared.

Very soft footfalls traipsed up behind me and I reached out one hand to my side. My palm was hit by a fluffy head, the action eliciting a purr. I let my hand glide over her back, skimming her leathery wings. "You wouldn't happen to be alone, would you, Kasha?"

She meowed, looking past me, back at the house. In that moment, I felt him step from the porch onto the sand. His steps were unsure and slow, but he didn't waver until he shuffled past me, reached the metal table and leaned his butt against it.

"What is it with you and the ground?" he asked.

"Stone is my element. I can feel through it, manipulate it, and shape it into anything I want." I glanced at him. "Who do you think builds everything down there?"

"That seems like a great talent, how come I haven't heard of your kind before?"

I pulled my remaining fingers free from the sand and scratched Kasha with both hands. She plopped to the side and gave me her belly. "I am extremely talented among my kind. Not many Embers can do what I can. Besides, there is a slew of Demonkind that never leaves Hell, so I bet there are more you don't know about. But I won't tell you." I gave him a sweet smile. "You'd use it against them in some way."

"Yes, obviously. But you know first-hand how bad it is down there."

I raised a brow. "So what? I should help you and *your* kind win the war? No fucking chance."

His brows drew together, and he crossed his arms. "But you left…"

"That doesn't mean I think *you* guys should win."

A tinge of outrage colored his features for a second, then it was gone. "Why did you leave? Breaking me out was a huge risk, you must have been desperate."

I tickled Kasha's paw beans and she mewled, revealing the tips of her claws. "That is my business. Suffice to say that there was the possibility of never seeing Cam and Dax again. I wasn't down with that."

Mihr's hands fell to his side in surprise. "You broke out an Angel, you fled Hell, and fought your own kind... for Humans?"

"Seems like it." For a second, guilt slid into my belly at the thought of Maeve. I really hoped she hadn't taken the fall for helping me. But I firmly covered the guilt with the thought that she would have surely thought of something. She was quick on her feet, and a bona fide badass.

"But..." He blinked in confusion. "That would not make sense, unless you..." His eyes found mine. "Are you and Camille in love?"

I chuckled. "Close, but no. They are like family to me. Dax summoned me during a difficult period in my life. I had given up on myself, close to giving in to the system of Hell I had fought for so long. They both brought light into my life. Being with them means happiness for me. I was not about to have that taken away from me again. Besides..."

"What?"

"Never mind." I decided against telling him that I watched out for them, that, at one point, they had needed me to.

"That sounds like your reasons are selfish."

"Excuse me?"

Mihr placed his huge palms on the table on either side of him. "You are here because they make you happy.

But as long as you are here, they are in danger, you *must* know that."

"No one knows where *here* is. No one will find them, or me."

"Are you sure about that?"

I stood, glaring at him. "I am. You think I haven't thought about it? You think I would deliberately put them in danger?"

"I do. Your kind —"

"Oh, fuck off with that. *Your kind this, your kind that, you evil, I good.* Blah, blah, blah. I am done with your holier-than-though shit. You are no better than us. You have killed us just as we have killed you. What makes your side any more valid?"

His eyes darkened. "We don't steal and corrupt souls of the innocent."

"Hah! But you use the most innocent of souls to fight for you, don't you? Turned Angels fight in the war, just like turned Demons do. Tell me, how different is one from the other really? You eradicate — no, obliterate — souls by making Angels. When they die? They are gone from this life and the next, utterly lost. Forever. Just. Like. Made. Demons."

"You can't possibly think that is the same."

"Why the fuck not? Why is it different? What is the difference, Mihr? Tell me."

A muscle in his jaw jumped. "We give them a choice. The souls that come to us can either live out eternity with those they love, they can go back, or they can fight alongside us. Those that choose to fight are highly honored. The souls of the damned? They are fodder of Satan's war machine."

"Right. You have to know that the math on that does not add up."

"What do you mean?"

"If every damned soul is turned into a Raider or something similar, and you guys *supposedly* give the innocent a choice, how come Hell hasn't won by now? The sheer numbers would overwhelm you."

He barked out a sharp laugh, "Angels are more powerful, and no Demon knows how to enter Heaven, so they can't attack directly. That you would even think we would… No, that is your evil nature speaking."

"Evil nature? Really?" I threw my hands up, noticing that my veins had begun glowing with the ire racing through them. "I took care of you. I took you to the most important people I have, not knowing how you would react. I could have let you die."

"You should have. Now, all we have are problems."

"You are alive because of me, not to mention free, a little gratitude would be appreciated. But you know what? If you think you have problems, you are free to fucking leave, anytime." I smelled smoke on my breath by now, knowing that I was a hair's breadth away from being on fire completely. I had worked on my temper in the past, and truthfully, the last time I had been unwillingly burning all over was the night Dax summoned me to protect them. Which meant that this Angel was getting under my skin – literally – in a way only very few had ever managed.

His stubborn face was back to looking like it was cut from stone. Pretty and unmoving. *Bleh.*

"I thanked you before already, you know of my gratitude."

"You have a very funny way of showing it."

"Doesn't matter. I can't in good conscience leave you here, endangering these two innocents," he said. "If you are too weak to fight in the war, you are also too weak to protect them from those that will come for you. That

131

is, if you are being truthful in wanting no harm to come to them."

Yup, definitely getting under my skin. I clenched my fists to keep myself from tackling him across the table. "Be very careful what you say next, Angel," I growled. "I might be a weakling compared to you, but you are still in bad shape. I'm pretty sure I could give you the thrashing of a lifetime right now."

"All you are doing by threatening me is proving my point," he said. "You are aggressive, prone to violence, and deluded when it comes to your own nature." This time, his expression was very clear. Disdain. "You can leave behind the cursed depths, be friends with Humans, even call them family, but you can't change what you are."

Sparks flew from my skin, which looked like glowing coals, and I smelled my clothes catch fire. They burned to a crisp in seconds. "You have no fucking idea who, or what I am." I shook off the charred remains of my clothes and stalked across the yard until I stood nose to chest with Mihr. He didn't move, his storm-colored eyes steady, his arms crossed. He didn't even take a fighting stance. That fact ticked me off even more as he seemed to not deem me a threat, at all.

"I do," he said, calmly. "You are riled by a few choice words, ready to set anything and everyone on fire." He leaned closer and I felt his breath fan over my scalding cheeks. "Humans are not safe around someone as combustible as you. You have no self-control."

Wrangling my inner fire into submission I glowered at him. "I have control. You are just being an ass to prove a point. I know I could bend you over my knee and spank you in your current state."

His brows shot up.

"I won't, though. Because I know you are weaker than me right now and I understand weakness. You knowing how to set me off doesn't make you right. Yes, this is very visible anger," I held up a burning palm. "But just because I have easier tells than most, doesn't make me act on them."

It was hard, but knowing he had riled me up on purpose helped, and I blew out a smoky breath to calm my fire. He thought he could make me attack him and prove his point? He had another thing coming. I turned from him slowly, letting my skin dim.

"Fane," his voice was soft, the sound close to… sadness? It made me stop. "You might think you have control and I wish you were right, I truly do, but creatures like us are not meant to live in this world. No matter how good our intentions, we are too different, too dangerous, and eventually things will turn out bad. You know I'm right. I implore you to leave. As I will."

The sadness creeping through his voice doused my fury like sand poured on a campfire. My skin dimmed to its normal red and my shoulders sagged. "I know I am a danger to Cam and Dax," I said. "But not because I would hurt them, I know I'd never. You can think what you want regarding that. I told Cam already that I'd likely leave once you were better, unless we found another option. Because if I were found by one of our kind, I could never protect them."

"You are planning on leaving? Why didn't you say so in the first place?"

I turned. "Because you were being a dick, and I don't owe you an explanation."

"Fair enough." His glance flitted around, looked like he was coming to grips with what his riling me up had done to my clothes. "Where… uhm, where are you going to go?"

I shrugged, "I haven't really thought on it. I'd like being surrounded by wood, or water." I gave him a very fake grin and crossed my arms. "I'll find something. It's not like I can go to either of our realms. What about you?"

His head sank down, and he looked at his feet. "I'll probably find some of my kind and return, so judgement can be passed on what I did. Then I'll either be welcomed back or die."

My arms fell to my sides in shock. "Excuse me? You'll let yourself be judged and the only two outcomes are death or returning? And you are okay with that?"

"What else is there? It is my duty to serve. I need to tell them everything I know about Hell, maybe that information can help in the war, help save lives. But if I am deemed unworthy of forgiveness, nonetheless, so be it."

"Satan's ass, you have serious priority issues. Mihr, that can't be your only option. You can't let yourself be punished for something that was outside of your control."

At this, his face shot up once more. "I had control. I should have said no to your offer of freeing me. I didn't. If I have to pay for that decision, I will."

"Wow. Just... wow. That is fucked up. You had no choice at all. It was either letting Lucifer get the information that could have given him an advantage, or blessing me and live to fight another day."

"I don't expect you to understand my convictions, as –"

"Before you put your foot in your mouth, I do understand. I have known countless men and women with the same mindset. Duty above all. The war is everything. Because it means the eradication of one of our kinds. We kill to not be killed, right? We are a part of something bigger. We seduce – in your case protect – the innocent just so we can fuck them in the ass when they die." I spread my arms in welcome. "Hey, you won! You get to fight for the side you chose, and probably die for it. Yay!"

His lips thinned with anger.

"I also know how to rile people up, you know. And you can't tell me that both of our sides aren't using Humans to our respective ends. The war you are fighting for, the one you find so much honor and duty in? It's bullshit."

Now *he* was glowering. "How can you say that?"

"It is my truth. I have lived in Hell for three hundred and forty-two years, and I have suffered under the war as much as anyone who fought it. I have lost people, I have been worked to the quick, I have been owned by Demon princes who lusted after me, and I am sick of it all. This has never been about good versus evil, it has always been about the two petty idiots who can't stand to see each other alive and thriving. All of us suffer for it. I am done with suffering. I'm done. I can't believe you'd return to all of it willingly. And you really shouldn't. You have a chance at a new life. One of your own choosing."

His face had turned a peculiar shade of red during my speech. "Stop your blaspheming at once."

"I am a Demon, it's what I do. Apparently," with that, I left him fuming and walked back into the house to raid Cam's closet. Maybe I'd use her bathtub before I got dressed. As true as my words had been, and as many shitty memories as they brought, seeing the Angel's stoic face change color because of it had been… gratifying. I was nothing if not a tit-for-tat kind of girl. Or a petty bitch. Both were good with me.

Chapter Twelve
Mihr
The Surface,
Emerald Falls

The pain in my back lessened during the day and I knew it would be nearly gone in the morning. Now, the only problem was that I couldn't fly to the heavens, I had to find my kin here on Earth. Luckily – mostly courtesy of Rapha's incessant rambling – I knew of many places young Angels would sneak off to in the night. And thanks to Dax and his internet, I had found a city nearby they always hit on their tours.

Thinking of Rapha brought a twinge of sadness, a bit of guilt, and a whole lot of rage. Most of that rage was aimed at the Demons, specifically the Incubi, we fought, but some of it was because of the reckless young Angel himself. He should have listened to me. Then he would still be alive, and I wouldn't have half the problems I had now.

One of my problems lay across Dax's bed, her almond-shaped, red eyes on me, while she purred lazily. If Fane was right and Kasha would follow me everywhere – considering the connection I felt to her, I found it more than probable – she'd be in trouble if I met my brethren. They would not accept her. I pondered if I was able to let them kill her. I wanted to believe I could. She was Hellspawn, connection or not, I should have no qualms with her dying. She was the enemy, just like Fane.

My hand reached for Kasha almost on its own, and I stroked her silky head, feeling a sense of deep peace as I did. She was like a small warming fire at my side. A pulsing connection of warmth and companionship radiated from her. There was no way I could let her be harmed, she would have to stay behind. I'd go to meet my kind alone first and see what the verdict was. If my life was forfeit because of what I did and they killed me, Kasha should be free of me. I hoped. I could ask Fane about it, and how the connection worked in case of a death. But I didn't feel like talking to my Demon.

Fane, who had many… opinions. Her views were blasphemous for sure, yet I found myself thinking about what she said. Not that I believed any of it, but it made me wonder. Still, it wasn't my place or my job to concern myself with such things.

The clicking of the keyboard and a small 'aha' uttered by Dax broke me from my thoughts. The boy sat in front of his computer, madly hammering onto his keys and clicking around with what he called a mouse.

"Found it?" I asked.

"Hmm. A bus leaves for Portsmythe tomorrow afternoon at four. It should take two hours till you're there." He swiveled around so he faced me. "You'll need money." He got up and unzipped a backpack that was tucked away at the side of his desk. Dax counted out a few bills he pulled from it and offered them to me.

I slowly took them. "Thank you. I'll pay you back. Once I can." *If I can*, my mind added.

Dax waved me off. "You don't have to. Fane keeps us afloat with as many precious stones as mom will let her give us. But… you sure you want to go?"

He looked partly worried and partly sad, as if the short time we had spent together had meant something to him. Maybe it was because I was an Angel, and one didn't see those every day as a Human, but he didn't seem to care about that so much, there had been no questions regarding me being one. So, I couldn't place the origins of his worry or sadness.

"I'm sure," I said. "Would you do me a favor, though?"

His face lit up with sudden joy and pride. "Of course."

"I will be going alone. I think the guys I'm meeting won't like Kasha so much. Would you watch over her while I'm gone?"

He smiled, looking at her, "Absolutely. You'll come back for her though, won't you?"

"If I can," I said.

The boy's lips thinned as his smile faded to nothing, making my chest tighten somewhat.

"How was your… thing?" I asked, nodding at the huge black case he had left with earlier, to change the subject.

Daxter looked at the case and shrugged, "Band practice? It was okay. I like playing with people, but I'd rather play my own music."

"You write your own music?"

"I'm not good, but I like the process of composing a song." He twiddled his thumbs in his lap. "It helps me escape, when…" He trailed off, then looked up, a very carefully placed smile on his lips. "You wanna hear something?"

"Sure."

Daxter shot from his chair, opened his case and sat back down with his Cello in hand.

"This one I wrote about Fay," he announced, before breathing out and placing the bow on one of the strings.

At the first deep vibrating sound, Kasha straightened and fixated Daxter, her ears snapping in his direction. I watched on, as the boy closed his eyes and his

139

hands moved with grace, calling forth a dark and beautiful melody. There was an underlying danger to it, a sound like flames flickering, moving back and forth, fleeting. Cheeky. Beckoning. Sultry. Then it morphed to a deep and full sound, mournful and sweet at once. Lonely.

I stared, captivated by the richness of the melody. Of course, Daxter knew the Demon longer, not to mention better, but I discovered her in the lush song, catching glimpses of her I had only seen hints of, until now.

I turned my head as I caught movement from the direction of the door and there she was. Fane leaned against the frame, her head tilted, her cheek resting on the wood. Her expression though… The smallest smile tugged at the corners of her lips as she gazed at Daxter, tears glinting on her face. The look in her eyes was one of absolute love. Something I had never seen in a Demon. I nearly huffed. This look of unconditional love was seldom, even in Heaven.

****

That night I lay awake for a long time. Flipping through Daxter's book of spells – the one he had used to summon Fane – I gathered that it was the grimoire of a long dead sorcerer, or devil worshiper. From his writing, he was both. When I read the incantation that the boy had used, I snorted. It was a summoning spell for Gazeroth the Deviant, but one of the runes in the pentagram was smudged, altering the whole incantation. It was pure luck that Daxter had misinterpreted the rune, otherwise he would have had one of the five Demon princes ruling the eighth ring standing in his room. And both he and Camille would be dead now.

140

If a Demon was summoned in his true form and there was even a kink in the chalk of the pentagram? He could get out and wreak havoc as long as the summoning lasted, including killing his summoner. And everyone else he so happened across. If what Fane had said was true, and Dax had opened the pentagram by stumbling back... He and Cam had truly been lucky that it had been Fane, not Gazeroth. The real question bothering me was quite a different one, though. There were loads of spells in this grimoire, some harmless and some downright grueling. If the boy tried out any of them, would they work? The fact was, the grimoire was filled with dark magic. The kind which came with unpredictable costs. Then again, he had been summoning Fane for the past year and was the sweetest child I had ever seen.

"You shouldn't go," Fane said, from her stone bed, ripping me from my thoughts. She had her back turned to me since she had walked into the cellar an hour ago without a word and gotten on her slab of stone.

"She's talking to me again," I observed.

"Ditto."

"I had nothing to say."

"Likewise."

"Good."

"Fine."

I groaned. "You're being childish."

She turned around, her amber eyes glaring across the room angrily. "Excuse me? Who is ready to throw his life away for some stupid reason? You or me?"

"It's not stupid. It's the right thing to do. Not that you'd know anything about that."

"I know plenty about right and wrong, and this is wrong. I just hope you aren't planning on telling your ilk about Cam and Dax."

I frowned. "Why would I?"

141

"Because they know about you, and I am with them."

"You're leaving though, right?"

"Right. So?"

"So, what?"

"Will you tell your brethren that two Humans have seen you in your true form?"

"I don't know, I might have to."

Fane sat up. "Mihr, don't. Please. You committed no sin, I told them what you are. Leave them be. No good will come of you telling them."

"I can't promise anything."

"Damn you, stubborn Angel."

"I won't lie for your mistakes, Fane."

"You *should* lie to protect innocents, isn't that what you guys are all about?"

"I don't lie."

She glared at me, then folded her hands and let her head sink. "Please try not to tell them. I beg you." My Demon looked up once more, a silent plea accompanying her words.

"I promise I'll try. But if I'm asked directly, I don't believe I'll have a choice but to tell the truth."

"Guess that is as much as I can expect from you," she rumbled and lay back. "What about Kasha?"

"She'll stay here. I might not know how I will be received by my kin, but I know she won't be met with tolerance. And I have a feeling that I might side with her if it comes down to it." Knowing my last sentence to be true was disconcerting, but it didn't change a thing. "Will she… will she be free of me when I die?"

Fane snorted and gave me her back once more. "How should I know? Hellcats and their masters normally die together. One will always protect the other."

"That doesn't answer anything," I said.

"Tough shit, Raquelle, I'm not your walking Hellicon."

"Hellicon?"

"Hell-Lexicon. I'm not it. Now, quit bothering me." She shimmied a bit, bunched up her shoulders, and curled in on herself. Her body language could not be clearer, and I refocused back on the grimoire, done with her childishness.

****

The bus ride was something to behold. Not used to human transport, I sat wide-eyed and alert, swaying with the loud smelly beast carrying me to Portsmythe. A long time had passed since I had really gone out into the human world without searching for Demons. As I watched the people around me – a boy playing cards with his father on the bench in the space between them, an old lady animatedly telling the man at her side about a memory from long ago, her gnarly hands flitting around like little birds – I realized how far removed I was from all of them. They were oblivious to the war raging around them, on their behalf.

I did get strange looks from many, making me uncomfortable. The reason for the stares was clear, I was large in statue, filling a good part of my bench. Humans weren't used to men of my size and built. And I wasn't used to them gawking at me. Normally, I would have preferred to be invisible to them. But a glamour would have taken too much energy, energy I still needed to heal, if I wanted to fly by the end of the night.

Letting my head sink and my shoulders slouch, I tried to make myself smaller and less intimidating.

"Where you headin'?" a voice to my right said and I looked up. A young woman stood next to me

143

smiling down, while a couple of rows behind us, a few girls her age giggled. She had long brown hair, styled into lavish curls, her green eyes sparkled with sass, and her full lips were pulled into a sexy pout.

"Portsmythe," I said.

"What a coincidence, us too," she pointed over her shoulders at her giggling friends. "I'm Cloe, need someone to show you the best watering holes?" She leaned forward, lining up her cleavage with my face. "Or anything else?" she whispered close to my ear.

"No. Why?"

She ignored my answer and continued to whisper, "We could have some real fun, handsome."

I jerked back, realizing what she was talking about. Frowning, I asked, "How old are you?"

She winked, "Old enough. Definitely."

I shook my head. "I seriously doubt that, Cloe."

"Oh, come on, gorgeous." She cocked her hip and bit her lower lip. I sighed and got up, towering over her. She shrank back a bit and I squeezed past her and walked to the doors.

As I reached them, a gong ran through the bus and a creaky, robotic voice coughed out "Portsmythe." The doors squeaked open and I ducked outside, speeding up my steps and telling myself that I was *not* fleeing the tittering of Cloe and her adolescent girlfriends that click-clacked off the bus behind me.

A few blocks down, I saw the ocean. The smell was fresh, as was the wind, and I was briefly taken back to the night Rapha died. I sped up my steps once more, this time fleeing the thoughts and the mixture of feelings conjured by the memory of the young Angel. It might well be that I would meet none of my peers, but Rapha's incessant rambling of the gins in stock, not to mention the burgers and fish, gave me hope that I would find some of his companions at 'Pints by the Shore.'

I fished the folded map Dax had printed out for me from my pocket and surmised that I was only two streets away. A few minutes later, I saw the neon sign glow through the night. Two glasses clinking, each carrying a drunken lobster that leaned back – their claws grabbing the edges of the glass – like the crustaceans were taking a bath in beer. I snorted and headed up the two steps to the automatic glass door that swished open, allowing me to enter.

Music, delicious scents, and laughter, fanned my way and I quickly took in the place. A terrace opening to my right had many tables, looking out over the water, while a long bar to my left was the site of many small groups lounging around standing tables and the bar itself. Off to one side, a pool table and some dartboards were frequented by groups of people, giving the whole scene something cozy, while the restaurant part looked elevated and almost rustically chic.

I walked to the bar and took an empty stool on the far side to wait. The bartender, a black-haired man with a heavy golden chain, smiled at me winningly and asked for my order. Deciding to honor Rapha's ramblings, I asked for a gin and tonic, which resulted in the guy asking which gin and which tonic I would like.

I blinked, confused. "Surprise me, "I said, and he was off.

Shortly after, I was handed a long glass. I paid with some of the money Dax had so graciously given me, and took a sip. I nodded at the bartender, who had waited for my reaction and he smiled, continuing on with the other customers.

The drink was really good. It had been a while since I'd drunk alcohol, and for the most part, I hadn't liked it to begin with. But this was good.

I could almost hear Fane say, "Yeah, we don't need it, but isn't it fucking delicious?"

A small chuckle surprised me, and I wondered what she would do now. When she left Cam and Dax behind like she planned. What would a truly free Demon do in this realm? I should be concerned, yet I found nothing but curiosity and a strange heaviness pulling at my gut when I thought about it.

Shaking the thought, I turned on my stool so I could see the entrance better, and readied myself for a long wait.

****

A few hours in, I saw them, five young Angels came walking through the doors. Four large men and a woman, easily recognized by the glow coming off their backs where the wings were retracted and hidden. The glow was only visible to me, but they would have turned heads no matter where they were. Tall and beautiful, starkly different from the Humans around them. I knew none of them by name or face, though.

They entered the bar area like they owned the place. And the locals reacted like they did, greeting them with handshakes and high fives all around.

They shouldn't be interacting with Humans like this. Nothing more than was necessary was allowed. They seemed to know some of these people by name. Three headed for the bar and ordered drinks, while the other two joined the small group playing pool.

I nearly choked on my drink when one of the Angels picked up a Human woman and kissed her deeply as she wrapped her whole body around him.

Putting down my current glass, I stood and walked up to the pair. I cleared my throat and after a few seconds, their mouths parted, and I met the annoyed gaze of the young male. He let go of the Human immediately when he recognized me and she stumbled back, bewildered.

"Mihr," the Angel gasped, bowing curtly. As I was fairly known in Heaven, it wasn't a surprise that he knew who I was. "I-I wasn't expecting –"

"Clearly," I interrupted him. "Call upon Michael, immediately."

He straightened and looked confused. "They are saying that you fell. We found Rapha's remains, but you were gone. What happened?"

I narrowed my eyes. "Michael. Now."

"O-of course." He stumbled back and sprinted from the building as though on fire.

It took but half a minute and I was swarmed by the remaining four Angels, the Humans around them all but forgotten.

"What happened?"

"How did Rapha die?"

"Where were you?"

Question upon question bombarded me and I nodded at the door to our left, reading 'exit.' They took the hint and we collectively left through the back exit, which led to a sandy back, filled with dumpsters, cars, and wooden boxes.

"So, will you tell us now?" the woman asked. "What happened to you and Rapha?"

"Sumu-Incubi," I said. "And a group of Raiders and Wanderers. We fought them off, but Rapha got

147

caught by an Incubus. They killed him and took me to Hell."

Silence and bug-eyes followed.

"You were in Hell?" a deep voice asked behind me.

I spun around, seeing Michael and the young Angel I sent for him glide down from above.

"If that is true, how come you are standing here?" the female asked.

Chapter Thirteen
Fane
The Surface, Portsmythe,
behind Pints by the Shore

"I can't *believe* I let you come along," I grumbled, ducking behind a few wooden crates close to the back exit of the bar Mihr had gone into. Kasha mewled, having clawed her way atop a crate at my side and I snorted. "You're just too persuasive, that's all."

In truth, I had only discovered her following me once I was almost on the bus. To hide from the Angel, I had stuffed her into a duffel bag I had borrowed from Cam. The Angel might think things would turn out fine, but I suspected differently and was there to make sure he didn't out Cam and Dax for harboring me.

For all I cared, the idiot could go on and get himself killed, but I would be damned if I let harm come to my friends because he was being an upstanding simpleton. The small voice in the back of my head that whispered 'you know you're lying,' I consequently ignored.

Kasha sat down and flapped her wings once, then meowed in an annoyed tone. "Oh, yeah? Got a better plan? We can't well cozy up to the guy at the bar and wait with him, can we?" I flipped over a crate and sat down myself. "They won't want to be seen talking, and since Mihr can't fly yet, this back exit is our best bet. I wonder what Angels are doing at a bar though... Thought it was forbidden."

Kasha licked over a paw and scrubbed behind one of her ears in answer. I shouldn't have taken her with me. But it'd been either that, or risk losing my tail on Mihr, so there really had been no choice.

We waited for what seemed like forever, and more than once, I was tempted to crash the bar as the sounds of people having a blast and the music sang to my hedonistic soul.

Trying to keep my impatience in check, I thought on my next steps. Mihr had asked where I would go once I left, and I still had no answer to his question. With the possibility my freedom provided, this realm had opened up to me. It was overwhelming, to be honest. I wanted to go everywhere and nowhere. I didn't want to leave Dax and Cam, feeling as though I hadn't spent enough time with them yet.

A huff left me, and Kasha paused her cleaning, her pink tongue sticking out for a second. It wasn't like I'd ever spend enough time with them. The Angel was right though, I had to leave. Chances were that Ragon would pull some strings to get me back, not that I thought he valued me enough, but the slight of me running from him and severing the bond of slavery would be something he wouldn't likely ignore. If I was lucky, he'd just shrug it off and go about his business. The thing was, I wasn't a particularly lucky person, and the way he had always looked at me… More alarming than him though, I had cost Lucifer a born Angel. And if the Prince of Darkness was after me, I should be as far away from Cam and Dax as possible.

"Should have thought of that," I murmured, picking at a rusty nail poking from a crate stacked up next to me.

The urge to run and be free had been the main focus on my mind. Now that I had somehow managed the impossible, the consequences of my actions would probably come a-calling soon. Which lead me back to my initial thought, *Where would I go?*

Just like I had told the Angel, I'd love to hide away and wander a dense forest, or an island surrounded by water. As far away from the wasteland of rock and lava I was so used to. A place where the sun either shone mercilessly or filtered through a thick canopy of leaves. Oh, I could picture it so clearly.

My bare feet in hot sand, the taste of the ocean on my lips. Bark beneath my fingers, as I learned how to traverse a space made by roots and leaves.

I had to be clever about it too, I still needed to be able to use my powers in case of danger.

Wiggling one of my nails beneath the rusty nail on the crate, I crooked my finger and loosened the metal. Bit by bit, I pulled it out.

Danger. Who was I kidding? If I was found, I would be taken, there were no ifs, buts, or maybes about it. Powers or not, I would surely lose any fight coming my way if I wasn't clever about it. For a minute, I wished that I had been instructed in the art of fighting, but that wish quickly evaporated into nothingness. I would have been thrown into the war, not a price I was willing to pay just so I would know how to protect myself.

Wrenching the nail free, I turned it over between the pads of my fingers, flaking my hands with rust.

No, the only chance I had was to run and hide. Forever. A grimace took hold of my features. Before I could mope any further on my new life as an eternal fugitive, the backdoor to the bar opened, making a wave of noise wash over Kasha and me.

I ducked lower and held a finger to my lips to shush Kasha. The cat sat upright, nearly invisible in the dark, spying through a gap in front of her.

Within a few seconds, I had my skin turn to an oily black and crouched next to Kasha, pressing my eyes to a crack between the crates to see what was happening.

It was Mihr and four other Angels – if their shining backs were any indication. They conversed in hushed voices and I placed a palm on the ground, adding the vibration of their voices, travelling down their bodies to my senses. Drenching my senses in their conversation, I listened, now able to understand what they were saying.

Mihr was telling them something about an Angel named Rapha, then a louder voice – this one without added vibrations – asked, "You were in Hell?"

I looked up and two Angels came floating down from above, their wings masked, but I was able to see them as echoes, like the flickering of heat in the air. One of them was an ordinary Angel, a made one, as his two wings indicated, but the other one… I pressed my free palm to my lips to stifle a gasp. He had three pairs of wings, one more than Mihr. An Archangel.

"If that is true, how come you are standing here?" a female Angel asked.

The Archangel and his made companion reached the ground, their feet making the softest sound on the sand.

Mihr ignored her question, his gaze focused on the Archangel. "Michael, it's so good to see you."

"Michael," I whispered. The notorious killer of my kind. He truly was a sight to behold, even in his diminished, human form. His blond hair shone like dark gold in the night, and he was taller than even Mihr, his face a mask of pristine beauty. Flawless.

I twisted my lips. He had nothing on Mihr, in my opinion. Too pretty. Yet, there was no denying he looked fearsome. Like he would be able to ram my little self into the ground head-first, without breaking a sweat. I was absolutely positive he could.

Michael walked up to Mihr and they clasped arms in a warrior's handshake. I rolled my eyes at the pretentiousness of their antics.

"It is good to see you too, my brother," Michael said. He released Mihr's arm and stepped back. "But I would like to hear your answer to Pheydra's question. How did you escape Hell?"

Mihr nodded once. "A Demon broke me out of my cell, and we fled through the second and first ring together, then she showed me how to get out and…" Mihr pursed his lips, "and we did."

"A Demon helped you?" Michael asked, his brows raised. "Why?"

"She wanted to be free of Hell and her Maester." Mihr shrugged, "Something about being a slave all her life."

The other Angels spoke over each other and it was hard to make out what was being said.

Michael held up a hand they all fell silent at once. "Where is her body now?"

When Mihr didn't answer I cursed under my breath.

"You did kill her once you got free, right?" Michael asked, his tone hard.

"I was…"

"Yes, tell them yes, you idiot," I whispered.

"I was in no condition," Mihr said instead, and I grunted in disappointment. Stupid, honest, pissant. He was well on his way to get himself killed.

"A ball of Hellfire hit me when we ascended, and I was close to death." Mihr looked at his feet for a second. He swallowed, straightened, and fixated Michael. "The

Demon looked after my wounds and took care of me until I was better and able to find you."

Once again, the voices overlapped, but now so loud I didn't need to touch the sand to hear them.

"Why?"

"Seriously?"

"Impossible!"

"Again, I will ask, where is her body? Tell me you killed her once you were able, Mihr," Michael said.

Mihr didn't cower under the Archangel's stare. "I did not. She saved my life, without asking for anything in return. Killing her would not have been right."

"She is Hellspwan! What more reason do you need?" Pheydra fumed.

"Where is she now?" Michael asked, his face calm. He had trouble keeping his voice level, though. I felt its tremor in my fingertips.

Mihr slowly unclenched his fists and shifted ever so slightly. I would have missed it, but I felt his feet scoot further apart as he took a stance. "Why?"

Michael looked taken aback. "So, we can right your mistake and eradicate her, of course."

"No."

"No?"

I pressed my eyes closed in both relief and anger for a second. When I opened them, I saw Mihr staring down Michael. "It's what I said, isn't it? No. I will not tell you where she is. She was never part of the war, as she is a lowly kind of Demon. She does not harm Humans. All she wants is to be free. I will not let you kill her."

"Mihr… Listen to what you are saying. You'd choose to give your life for a… a Demon? She is filth, like all of her kind are."

"If she is, then why did she save my life? Why not leave me to die?"

"I don't know!" Michael thundered. "It's certainly not because she felt compassion. That isn't something Demons are able to do."

"They are. At least this one is. I saw…" Mihr shook his head slowly, "I saw love in her face, Michael."

"Love? For whom? You?" Michael laughed and the others joined in. It wasn't joyful, but strained. Uncomfortable.

"Not for me, no. But I know that she is able to feel love, something we've always been told Demons cannot do. And If she is capable of that, she is capable of good. I can't let you kill her."

The laughter stopped abruptly, and Michael huffed out a breath. "Are you sure about this? You know the consequences."

"I do. I came to tell you what I have seen and experienced in Hell, so that our kind gains an advantage in the war. I broke my holy oath to our Lord by blessing the Demon so she would be free. It was either that or let Lucifer get to me." He smiled bitterly. "And we all know what that would have meant. If I am to die for what I have done, even if that means at your hand, I will accept it."

"You did *what* to escape?" Michael snarled.

"How else would she be out and about? She freed me with the condition that I bless her, which I did, to get away. It wasn't really a choice, between breaking the rules and divulging everything I knew to Lucifer."

Gasps and whispers followed Mihr's words.

"Death is too good for you," Pheydra said. The other Angels nodded along.

"You disappoint me, brother," Michael said. "You should have died fighting the Incubi."

"Don't you think I know that?"

"Now you have done the unthinkable and refuse to tell us where your mistake is hidden." The Archangel shook his head. "We'll take you home, to the Seers. They will give us the answers we need, including where the Demon is hidden."

Mihr blanched at his words. "You can't mean that."

"You have failed to protect your charge, you let yourself be taken captive, and you helped a Demon escape Hell. Now you have the means to give us a living Demon with no attachments to Hell, who could be a well of information, and you refuse to do so. Once the Seers have emptied you, we will know all." Michael shrugged, "The fact that you will be nothing but an empty shell is something you should have thought about before getting captured."

"Screw me sideways," I whispered. I could not let this happen, if they would know everything Mihr knew, they'd know about Cam and Dax. Digging both hands into the sand I concentrated and started pulling. Absentmindedly, I kicked my shoes off, I'd need my feet to connect to the earth if I wanted to pull this off.

"Come quietly, Mihr," Michael said, reaching for him.

As sweat ran down my face from the strain of the pull, I saw my Angel falter. His beautiful face was contorted with the battle waging inside of him. Duty against his conscience. But no matter who won, I needed to get him out of there.

Kasha stood, her housecat-sized-body ready to spring into action.

"No, Kasha," I whispered. "You stay here."

But I could well have been talking to the crate next to me, as the Hellcat had sensed her warrior in danger, and she was about to do something about it. With a rattling growl, she jumped over the crates and landed at the feet of the Angels. He leathery wings spread, she hissed and snarled at them, her back arched to make herself bigger.

"Kasha?" I heard Mihr's surprised voice, but I reached further down and pulled. Finally, slowly, pieces of iron and other metals melted together beneath us. Like sucking ice through a straw, I pulled it up. Up, up, up, until it was just a foot under the Angels, lying in wait. I grunted as I strained to get more.

"What is this, Mihr?" Michael asked, looking at Kasha.

One of the younger Angels laughed and lunged at her. She jumped back, her ears flat while she uttered a low growl. Tiny as she was, the growl didn't impress the Angel, and he pursued her. With an incredibly fast move, he grabbed the back of her neck and snatched her up. Kasha's body went limp as she hung from his arm like a sack of flour.

"Let her down," Mihr said. His voice was calm, but dangerously cold.

"Why? What is it?" the Angel asked, swinging Kasha from side to side. A feeble mewl was all Kasha managed.

I balled my fists, drawing more metal to the surface, and I knew this was as much as I could muster on such a short notice. It would have to be enough. Snatching Cam's duffle bag and throwing it over my shoulder, I stood.

Strutting from the crates, I let my skin turn to red once more. With each step, the veins in my feet and calves glowed a bit more as I connected to the metal.

"She is a Hellcat," I said.

All the Angels whirled around to face me, gaping stupidly, while Mihr groaned.

"Sure, she is a baby, but wait till she's grown, then she'll swallow you whole, pissbrain," I told the young Angel holding her.

"Fane," Mihr croaked. "What are you —"

"This is your Demon?" Michael asked, a smile growing on his pretty mug.

"Dunno about being his, but I surely am a Demon," I told the Archangel. My heart beat fast as fear spread through me like wildfire, lighting me up with something close to panic. Being eye to eye with an Archangel wasn't something I'd ever thought would be on the agenda.

It was silent for a few heartbeats as the Angels sized me up. Then several things happened at once. Kasha squealed because the Angel holding her pulled on her wings, Mihr let out a roar and plowed straight into the young idiot, who let go of Kasha. The other Angels got ready to jump me and I crouched down and dug my toes and hands into the sand. Then I pulled. Yelling with the effort, I aimed the metal outward. It shot from the ground, spraying sand everywhere, snatching the feet and ankles of the Angels coming at me. Four of them fell over, but Michael broke free and accelerated into a sprint, his blue eyes trained on me. He'd be outside of the metal's range in seconds.

Behind him, Mihr sat on the chest of the young Angel and pummeled him into the ground. Kasha dashed after Michael, a blur of black fur, and slammed her small claws into his calf. The Archangel stumbled for a moment, but it was all I needed.

Once more, I pulled and aimed. Hot, liquid metal snaked over his feet and up his legs. Kasha hissed and let go as the metal rose higher, well past his knees.

I was drenched in sweat, my muscles pulsing with agony as I pulled up more. Encasing the Angels in metal up to their hips, I didn't stop, instead, fusing stone and sand into my efforts.

Michael screamed at me, trying to wrench himself free. He tugged his sword from his back and began hacking at the mounds covering him, but there was too much. I smiled stupidly while my body gave out and I slumped to the side.

Footsteps came my way, and I was picked up gingerly. Mihr drew my arm around his neck and helped me stand.

"What the Hell, Fane?" my Angel asked. "You could have been killed."

"Still possible," I mumbled. "Let's go."

Michael and the other Angels strained and grunted in their restraints, but they were strong, and surely would be able to free themselves soon. Especially now that I had no control over anything anymore.

"Kasha," Mihr called, and the cat bounded up his leg and settled on my arm, around his neck.

"This is vaguely familiar," I said.

"Hold on, crazy Demon," Mihr said.

"If you leave now, there will be no place in this realm you can hide from me," Michael shouted. "We will hunt you till the ends of the Earth, Mihr."

"Eat shit and die, blondie," I murmured.

"Mihr!" Michael hollered. "It's not too late."

My Angel turned to his peers and drew both of his broad arms around me. "It was too late the moment you denied me an honest death to pay for my missteps," with that, he bent his knees and flung us into the air.

<h1 align="center">Chapter Fourteen
Mihr</h1>

The Surface,
between Emerald Falls and Portsmythe

My back hurt like hell, but we needed to get away fast. Still, every wingbeat felt like being stabbed in the spine.

I had no idea how Fane had been able to ensnare the young Angels – not to mention Michael – like that, but it seemed to have taken a huge toll on her. Her skin was clammy with sweat and her arms were draped around me rather than clutching me like the last time. Also, she wasn't screaming.

A soft moan drifted to me and when I looked down, I saw her smile softly with closed eyes, her long lashes starkly contrasting the red of her skin. She sighed and burrowed her nose into my chest. "Safe," she muttered, making a strange pressure build up in my chest. I drew my arms tighter around her and sped up my wingbeats. Painful or not, we needed to get as far away as fast as possible.

I followed the street leading out of the town and soon, woods and hills swished past us below. I kept my eyes open until they blurred from the sting of wind, fighting hard to not let the mix of feelings galloping through my chest take charge and overwhelm me. Luckily for me, the searing in my back felt like Hellfire running up and down my skin, so my mind was occupied with staving it off as best I could. But dread, anger, and a bout

161

of full-on terror trampled through me with growing urgency.

I have betrayed my kind, I thought. *Betrayed Michael*. The words in my head made as little sense as my actions just now did.

I dipped lower to hide us against the dark trees, on the chance the others had gotten free and were searching for us from above.

In my heart, I knew I'd made the right choice, but my head was not on-board with it. *She is Hellspawn*, I thought. *A child of darkness and evil*. Why hadn't I been able to do what my upbringing dictated? If Michael saw her as a chance to get an upper hand in the war, I should have put my conscience aside and jumped at the opportunity.

Yet, as Fane's hands slid over the nape of my neck and she drew her legs around my hips, locking her feet behind my back, a warm shiver danced over my entire body. For a moment, the pain between my wings and the chaos inside me subsided to background noise. My body reacted on its own as if it was the most natural thing, and I hiked her closer, digging one palm into her fluttering hair, while I spread the fingers of my other over her lower back, almost spanning the entire breadth.

For a few precious seconds everything quieted down, and I was able to breathe deep lungfuls of night air. Then I shook my head. This needed to stop. Not outing her to my peers was one thing. She didn't deserve to be caught right after getting her freedom, and she *did* save me without asking for anything in return.

"Did the right thing," I whispered into the wind.

But whether I had or not, lusting after her was definitely wrong. I was an Angel, she a Demon. Our kinds killed each other, we did not want, or desire, the other. Not voluntarily, at least. Incubi and Succubi could seduce us – as I had recently been reminded – but their pull over others was not genuine.

This… attraction I felt was genuine. I frowned and leaned to one side, following our path around a mountain. It could also be because she was just too close. She was a beautiful woman and she'd fused herself to my entire body, it was only natural for me to react this way.

Regardless, I had bigger problems right now. As I pushed at the thoughts and the feel of her, everything else came crashing back down on me with a vengeance.

I sighed with relief at seeing the twinkling lights of Emerald Falls in the distance. I'd sort it out once the pain in my back subsided and once Fane wasn't so… close anymore.

Sure that I could think more clearly once those two problems were solved, I circled the small town a few times, watching the skies for my kin, before I swooped down and landed in Cam's backyard. The back draught of my wings to slow us was excruciating, and I clenched my teeth to stop an agonized groan. My feet connected hard with the ground and I stumbled a few steps.

I retracted my wings and relief washed over me instantly. Kasha jumped from my shoulders and wound around my legs, purring, nearly making me fall over her as I ascended the steps to the porch. Slowly, I let Fane slide down my body until her feet hit the wooden boards.

"Can you stand?" I asked.

Her arms didn't let go of me. "Hmm?"

"We're safe, Fane. Can you stand?"

"We-what? Oh, yes," she stammered and let go. Swaying back, she swung her arms to regain balance and I quickly grabbed both of her hands to steady her.

"Sorry. I must have zoned out." She gave me sheepish grin. "I'm good." The Demon pulled her hands free and held them up. "Just used too much power, that's all. A good night's sleep will take care of it."

"We should head inside," I said, checking the sky with a quick glance.

"Right on, Florence," Fane said and wobbled into the house.

I shooed Kasha after her and took one last look around before I followed.

Cam met us in the living room, she had been sitting on the couch and sprang up as soon as she saw Fane. "You okay, sweetie? You look like hell. What happened?"

Fane threw an arm around her friend. "Fine. Superfine. Mihr is in trouble, though. He was veeery naughty."

"Never mind me," I said, crossing my arms while Kasha continued her journey around my legs. "Why in the name of all that is holy did you follow me there? And on that note, *what* did you do?"

"Pfft" Fane waved me off. "I was there to make sure you wouldn't tell them about Cam and Dax, and to get a head start in case you did, to get them to safety."

"I told you I wouldn't tell on them."

"You also said you wouldn't lie if asked directly, so excuse me, but that wasn't a risk I could take."

I scrutinized her for a moment. Her amber eyes glinted with anger, and her chest heaved as she leaned on Cam for support more and more.

"Fair enough," I conceded. "What did you do to the Angels?"

"I drew up metal from the earth and wrapped their feet and legs in it. Then I added some rock and dirt for good measure. It won't hold them long, though. And since you pissed off an Archangel, chances are they are free already. The six-winged guy was hacking at the dirt with his sword like a madman. Took everything I had to encase them like that." Fane swayed a bit, and her friend adjusted her arm around the Demon.

"Can someone *please* tell me what is going on?" Cam demanded. The Human woman looked even more pissed off than Fane, and I told her in a few words what had transpired.

"So, you are what? A rogue Angel?" Cam asked.

"Oh, he is much more than that." Fane grinned, her lids drooping a bit. "He is, as of now, the undesirable number one in Heaven. They will send a whole squadron to capture him. Angels don't like betrayal very much."

"Which effectively means I will have to leave as soon as possible," I said. I nodded at Cam. "I will not put you and your son in danger. If you'll allow it, I will rest for the night and take my leave in the morning."

The Human blinked at me. "Of course. But since Fane has told me that she is about to leave herself…" she trailed off and bit her lower lip nervously. "They are looking for her now as well, the Angels?"

"Yes."

Cam continued worrying her lip. "Will you take her with you?"

"What?" I asked, perplexed.

Fane just burst into tired chuckles. "What are you saying, love? I should run away with an Angel?"

"He could keep you safe," Cam said. "You could both watch out for each other."

"Yeah, and Hell could freeze over," Fane slurred.

Cam took hold of Fane's shoulders and plopped her onto the couch. She turned so she was looking at the both of us. "The way I see it, you guys potentially have the same people coming after you. Your chances would be a lot better if you stuck together."

Her reasoning was met with silence. She looked from me to Fane and back at me. "Please. I would feel so much better if I knew you had Fane's back."

"Hey," Fane said, straightening a bit. "I am more than fine on my own."

I knew differently. If she was found by either side, alone, her life would be forfeit.

Cam wrung her hands in a pleading gesture. "You denied telling on her, resulting in being outcast yourself, Mihr. What use would that sacrifice be if you split now and got picked off one by one?"

"I'll think about it," I said and walked over to the couch. "You need to sleep, now." I offered a palm to Fane and she looked at it for a second, seemingly contemplating if she wanted to accept my help.

The Demon placed her hand in mine and I pulled her up. "This does not mean that I agree," Fane said.

"I know," I said.

"I'm good on my own."

I led her to the basement stairs. "I know."

"I'm very good at being stealthy and hiding."

Throwing a look over my shoulder, I caught Cam smiling softly before she waved at me. "I know that too, Demon."

"Well, stop knowing everything, you show-off."

****

There was no sleep for me. Other than Fane, who had fallen asleep the moment her body had hit the slate of stone next to the bed, I was kept awake by my roiling innards.

I paced the room for a few minutes, then noticed that my shirt was sticky with new blood from my back, not to mention ripped to tatters by my wings. Kasha

166

followed me into the bathroom, jumped onto the toilet seat and watched my movements closely with her calm, red eyes.

My hands shook as I grabbed hold of the sink and stared at myself. Curious, no one would know of the havoc inside of my chest by looking at me. I was paler than usual and my lips were a thin line, but other than that, I looked like I always did. I shouldn't. I was a traitor, a deserter, an apostate. "For a Demon?" I asked myself.

Lifting my shaking hands, I rubbed my bloody knuckles, thinking of how I had fought one of my kind because he'd hurt Kasha. A snort left me. Even now, dark anger rose at the memory.

I let my hands sink and reached for Kasha. Stroking her behind one black ear, I had to smile despite everything. "You tried to protect me, didn't you? Tiny thing that you are."

She leaned into my touch, her daunting eyes not leaving mine. It was like an answer, as if she was saying 'and I'd do it again.'

"Yeah, me too, Kasha. Me too." I straightened and peeled the bloodied, ripped shirt from my torso. "That right there is my problem. I shouldn't feel this way. It should be simple, always has been. You are evil, and my kind fights yours. Black and white." I threw the shirt to my feet and stepped from my shoes. "Now everything is a murky gray, and I have no idea what I am doing, or going to do. No clue."

To her, I could voice my worries. Her steady, warm presence was a comforting anchor as panic mixed with wrath overtook me.

"They weren't even listening, were they? I would have happily given an account of all I had seen and then died for my sins, but Michael wanted to take me to them…" Bitterness boiled up my stomach. "The Seers pierce the mind and split it open. A practice reserved for Demons and Hellspawn, and Michael wanted to subjugate me to them?" I trudged to the shower and turned the dials.

"It's a horrible fate, and he wanted..." Bit by bit, the true meaning of my friend's words filtered through my fear. He had decided to do the unthinkable to get what he was after, information on Fane. All of it without consulting Him. And he would surely have done it behind His back. Because subjugating an Angel to the Seers wasn't allowed.

"Something is up with him, you know? Michael. Why would he...?" I bit my teeth together, knowing I had seen my friend change over the last years. There had been many instances where his views had shifted from driven to almost fanatic. His brutality had risen steadily, so much so, that I had pulled back from him. Truth be told, I had been a recluse from my brethren – especially Michael – for some time now. And obviously, he had gotten even worse.

"Unheard of," I stuck my hand under the spray and adjusted the temperature before I looked back at Kasha. She had rolled up into a ball and was happily snoring by now.

No Angel could be sentenced to the Seers, and yet none of the younger Angels had found Michael's decision strange.

None of it mattered now, though. I was a wanted man. Michael would make sure of that. There was no way for me explain myself and my actions to anyone, least of all Him. I would be dead before I even reached Him. And even if I did, He wasn't known to be merciful when it came to his soldiers. Besides, He Himself only knew what Michael was telling him right now, justifying a manhunt. I had no doubt it would come to exactly that. Which was why I had to leave these lovely Humans, sooner rather than later.

I slipped off my pants and got in the shower. Squeezing my lids shut and clenching my fists, I turned. Even expecting it, I had to stifle a yell when the water ran over my back, burning like my skin was melting off. A shaky breath left me, and I opened my eyes to watch a stream of golden blood curl into the drain. It took a while, but I got used to the feeling and when the water was clear, I began washing myself.

Rifling through the soaps in the basket fastened to the shower wall, I sniffed at a few of them. I recoiled when I smelled the one Fane had obviously used, as the image of her clinging to me came back instantly. Her hair had smelled of this. Sweet and smoky.

Camille's request ran through my mind. Her worry for Fane was obvious, and her wish for me to keep her safe valid. My Demon was no match for the forces being unleashed on us. I wondered though… She had incapacitated five Angels at once, an incredible feat. Her kind clearly had no idea how her powers could be used if one was creative, or Embers would have been used in the war.

Fane may well be physically weaker than most of her kin, but her powers were incredible the way she used them. I doubted that her kind knew just how ingenious she was.

Bottom line, she could be of help to me. And being together would mean we could alternate watch and sleep times if needed. A huge plus when one was on the run. Alone, I would have to be vigilant the entire time.

I chose a bottle reading, 'for men,' and lathered up my skin.

The question was, would we be able to trust each other enough to work together? There was always a chance of her betraying me if it meant getting out of a tight spot safely for her.

I rinsed and shut the shower off. Stepping from the stall, I dried off, careful not to let the towel rub over my back.

If I was honest with myself, and if Fane wasn't a Demon, I would have said she is not that kind of person. But she was a Demon, and I didn't know her all that well. The link was Kasha.

I smiled as I slid on a pair of comfy pants Cam had, no doubt, laid out for me.

As long as the Hellcat and I were bonded, Fane wouldn't harm me willingly. I didn't know why she cared so much for the cat, but she had been the reason why Fane hadn't let me die in the first place. It was something I could use. And we'd need weapons, preferably swords. Angels and Demons both didn't care much about being shot. Our rapid healing and strong skin meant that bullets didn't make much damage. The swords did need a special combination of metals though. I wondered if Dax's computer would find a place where we could get what we were looking for.

I picked up Kasha as I walked from the room and switched off the light. On her slab of stone, Fane glowed subtly, radiating enough light for me to find the way to my bed. Her veins pulsed with fiery light and I wondered if it would burn my skin if I touched her.

I stopped short. Seemed like I had made my decision. I'd take her along. Now, all that was left to be done was convincing my Demon that being on the run together was safer.

Chapter Fifteen
Fane
The Surface, Emerald Falls,
Camille's House

"I have decided it would be good if we traveled together, Fane."

"You decided?" I stared at the Angel, seated across from me at the breakfast table.

"Yes," he said.

The piece of scrambled egg I had just scooped up flopped from my fork and rolled over my plate uneaten. "You have to be joking."

"I am not."

"Why, by Satan's hairy hooves, should I agree to that? What if you change your mind, being the upstanding tool that you are, and give me over to your feathered friends? You might have denied telling them where I was, but I'm pretty sure you did that because of Cam and Dax." I waved my empty fork from my friend to her son and back again. "I don't trust your holy ass."

Daxter, who wasn't a morning person, leaned his elbow on the table and watched the both of us, mildly interested. I was sure he had no idea what was going on. Cam pursed her lips repeatedly, probably to keep from saying something, then hid her mouth behind a cup of coffee.

"This is your fault, you know," I accused her. "I distinctly remember you filling his head with this very idea last night."

Cam nearly spat out her mouthful of coffee and glared at me, but before she could say anything, the Angel had started counting off reasons on his fingers.

"First off, what good would it do me to hand you over now, after I am wanted by Heaven myself? Secondly, we could look out for each other, and if we were found, we would stand a better chance together than alone. Thirdly, Kasha will come with me and you are the only one I know who can help me take care of her."

I let my gaze flit to the black cat, who obviously had a growth spurt overnight, as she sat on a chair of her own and was able to look over the edge of the table. He had me there. She was kin. The only one from my world who was as free as I was.

"Whatever," I snapped and frowned at Mihr. "You can't just decide things like that. I'm my own person, you know."

"I haven't —"

"You said you decided we are travelling together from now on. Or did my hearing fail me?"

"Yes, but —"

"What gives you the right to think you can speak for me?" I sprang up and stomped from the room, heading for the back porch, seething with anger. Several things bugged me about what had just happened and none of them really had anything to do with him wanting us to travel together. Hell, it was the sensible thing to do.

I huffed and trampled down the wooden steps until I stood in the yard. Kicking my shoes off, I stuck my toes into the sand and crouched down, doing the same with my fingers. Maybe it would help calm me, or take my mind off… Him.

Trying hard to listen to the tiny vibrations of the critters around me, I closed my eyes and bit my lips. But it didn't help.

"Fane?" Cam said beside me. She sat down on the ground next to me and stroked a palm over my back. "What is going on?"

"Sorry I yelled at you," I murmured. "It's not your fault."

"You clearly thought it was." I heard the smile in her voice and knew she wasn't angry at me. I didn't deserve a friend like her.

"No. Your idea was good." I opened my eyes and pulled my hands from the sand. "It's just… the way he said 'decided,' it rubbed me the wrong way. I didn't get my freedom to be bossed around again. Never again. And I fear if we travel together, the bossiness will only grow, and I won't deal well with that."

"Sweetie, please don't take this the wrong way, but I really don't get the problem. I'm sure Mihr didn't mean it as a decision he took on your behalf, but rather one he made for himself."

I snorted. "Yeah, probably. But what if not?"

"Then you leave his ass behind."

We were quiet for a while, but I could tell Cam was mulling something over. "Ask," I said.

"What?"

A deep sigh escaped my chest and the anger I had felt dissipated into a pounding ache. Sadness deeply nestled inside of me. One that would never leave. "You want to know why this bothers me so much."

"Well, I assume it's because you never had a choice before and now you do. The prospect of someone deciding for you pisses you off," she paused. "But it's more than that, isn't it?"

I picked up a handful of sand and let it run through my fingers. "It is. I don't mind assholes thinking they have a say over me, they usually assume they do, and in Ragon's case, the asshole was right. What bothers me is that Mihr is no ass. And I once knew a guy with the potential of being good, who fell into a pattern of ordering me around because I belonged to him."

"You mean Leviathan?" Cam asked softly. "He wasn't a good man, love."

"Maybe not entirely," I said. "But he was the first man in my life who gave a shit about me." A small smile flashed over my lips thinking of him then, a Demon prince who had fallen for a lowly Ember. He had saved me, cared for me, and loved me.

"The bad parts of him got worse because he could control and govern me. Being able to control the one you love is never good, and in the end…" Sadness engulfed me and pulled me down. "In the end, it killed him."

"Oh, sweetie," Cam said. "I know. But It's not your —"

"It *is* my fault, Cam." I blew out a breath. "But it's done. Past and gone." I swiped at my misty eyes. "He's been gone for a while now."

"But it still hurts." She squeezed my shoulder softly and I reached up to lace my fingers with hers.

The ache in my chest pounded as if in answer. "It does."

"Will you go with Mihr, though? I-I feel awful thinking of you running alone."

I chuckled, a sound thick with tears. "You are a pain in my ass, you know that?"

She smiled and leaned against me.

"Yes, I will go with him. But I have no idea where, or how. I mean, since his peers know the vicinity we are in, we'd probably have to change continents."

"I thought so too. Come on, love." Cam gave my hand another squeeze and got up, pulling me with her. "Let's plan it out."

I quickly wrangled my shoes back on my feet and followed Cam inside.

Mihr and Dax still sat at the table, their conversation animated and filled with laughter. It looked like Dax had finally woken up.

The Angel glanced at me as I entered, and I stopped short. His storm-colored eyes seared into mine and a shiver danced over my lower back. In that moment, I knew exactly why I had reacted so strongly just now. I remembered last night clearly.

I had felt safe in his arms, trusting him fully to carry me back here. Trusting him to protect me.

The feel of his arms tightening around me, then of his hand digging into my hair, it had me weak in the knees. True, I had always seen him as a beautiful man, but last night, he had become something more. A man I had trusted with my life. For me, trusting someone – other than Cam and Dax – had never resulted in a happy ending. It should be enough of a reason for me to run the other way.

Instead, I said, "I will come with you. But don't you ever think you get to just decide over my head."

"It was never intended that way, Demon," he rumbled with a nod. "I worded it wrong, and I am sorry. It was insensitive of me."

He apologized. To mask my surprise, I rolled my eyes. "Ugh. Stop being a mushy Angel. We got planning to do."

****

"Sooo… Fake passports are a no go," Cam said, looking at the camera in her hand.

"What, why? Lemme see!" I grabbed the thing and stared at the picture she'd just taken. My likeness was

175

so blurred, not to mention black as shadow, that one couldn't make out anything.

"What the hell?"

Mihr stood in the doorway, his arms crossed, making the muscles of his lower arms bulge. "I told you it wouldn't work. Neither your nor my kind can be photographed."

"Sucks," I said. "I would have liked to know what I look like as a Human." I lifted a red hand and turned it in front of my eyes. "And passports would be handy to have. How else are we supposed to get out of this country?"

"Well, I plotted a course that will take care of that," Dax said, perched before a computer, clicking around wildly. "You'll fly over the border into Canada, then head further north-west into Alaska." He scrolled and leaned closer to the screen, his crinkled nose blue with the shine of the monitor. "There is a place called Wales, you could fly from there to these islands here… the Diomedes Isles, then rest and fly to Russia. It's around 53 miles in total, 28,5 to the island. Could you make that?" he turned to Mihr.

The Angel smirked. "Easily. But that won't be the problem we'll face."

"Russia? Bering Strait?" I ogled Dax. "Are you serious?"

"It's the easiest way to switch continents," Dax grinned.

"There is 'getting out of the country' and then there's 'making a world tour'," I mused. "I don't know if we need to go so far. Up north there are so many reclusive places – Canada is filled with uninhabited islands – can't we just go there?"

"Fane is right," Cam said.

Dax frowned, then his brows shot up. "I just remembered something. There is this spell in my book —"

"We need none of this," Mihr said. "Heaven has many portals that lead to different places in this plane. All we need to do is fly up, find a portal and exit at another one and we're on the other side of the world." His face froze for a second. "I know a place where we would be safe. At least for a while."

"Where?" I asked.

"There is a hut in the German woods. I go there when I need time for myself. It belongs to an old couple, but they don't use it anymore. It's secluded and uninhabited, as far as I know."

I placed my fists on my hips. "And why — pray tell — didn't you tell us about all of that in the first place?"

His stormy eyes found mine. "Because it means entering Heaven with a Demon and a Hellcat. It is forbidden, not to mention secret. I don't know whether I can trust you with the location of a portal."

"Seriously?" I glared at him.

"Oh, come on, it's not like you trust *me*," he waved me off. "Besides, there is no telling if we're able to slip through unseen. If we are, and they know which portal we exit from, they can pinpoint our location." The Angel leaned his head against the wall behind him. "And I haven't been to the hut in some time, I have no idea if it is still safe."

"German woods sound good, but why not just rent a hut?" Dax asked. "That would be the simplest solution. Mom could pay with her credit card and you would be able to move in at short notice."

All of us stared at the boy and the nape of his neck reddened slightly. "It's just an idea," he mumbled.

"That is —"

"Perfect," Cam interrupted me. "Knowing where you are will help me sleep at night, and it sounds better than you getting captured by Russians because you crossed a border you shouldn't have."

"We would still cross a border we shouldn't," I said, subtle fear spreading in my gut. "Sneaking through Heaven does not sound like child's play."

"It won't be," Mihr said. "But I know my way around and we would save time. So, it's either traveling for days, or weeks on end, with the probability of getting caught, or a short yet dangerous trip."

"Won't the portals have sentinels?" Dax asked.

"Most of them, yes." Mihr stared into the distance, looking deep in thought for a second. "But there are portals that have been all but forgotten over the years. We would still have to travel to one of those."

I eyed Mihr suspiciously. "And how do you know about these 'long-forgotten' portals?"

"My father was one of the library keepers in Cyrisas – the holy city of God – and when I joined the warriors, he made me read every book on portals he could find." A twitch ran over his full lips. "He was adamant that I knew all the escape routes I could, in case I needed to get out of a hairy situation here on Earth."

For a short moment, no one said anything as Mihr stared into the distance, a forlorn expression on his features.

Cam cleared her throat softly, "Where is the nearest portal?"

Mihr blinked and focused on her, "Nova Scotia."

I scrunched up my nose, trying to jog my memory of the world-map. "That's pretty close, right?"

"One state over," Cam said. "Maine, then across the border and through New Brunswick."

"That should be doable," I said. "Right?"

"We'll need weapons before we leave," Mihr said. "Or, rather, I do. If we choose to enter Heaven, I will need a sword and – why are you smiling like a demented goblin?" he narrowed his eyes at me, irritated.

I cracked my knuckles, excitement building in my gut, chasing the hint of fear away. "In Hell, I built houses because my talent is exceptional and not many Embers can shape the amounts of stone that I can, not to mention, at the same speed and quality. Instead, the majority of my kind fashion weapons for the war. All Embers learn how to do it. I haven't made a weapon in ages." The grin wouldn't lessen, no matter how much I tried. "But I used to love it more than anything. Oh, and I know the exact mix of metals to fashion blades that will do maximum damage to Angels *and* Demons."

"I don't know whether to be glad or unsettled by that," Mihr stated.

"You'd be safe feeling both," Dax said sagely.

****

"A little bit further," Dax shouted, waving a hand back at himself. I inched the car backward and punched the brakes when he threw his palm up. My fingers found the handbrake and I pulled it, then put it in park and shut it off, so it wouldn't roll from this steep location.

I sprang from the vehicle I had stolen and trudged up to meet Dax, who popped the trunk and heaved out four bars of carbon steel. He turned and lumped them onto the ground.

"You sure we won't be seen here?" I asked, glancing into the forest surrounding us as I walked up to the ledge of a small plateau, overlooking the lake.

"Pretty sure, this is mom's thinking spot, and she has apparently never met anyone up here."

We had decided that me making weapons with my bare hands in Cam's backyard would have been a tad too conspicuous, so we came up here. Away from prying eyes.

Dax raised a brow when he scrutinized the anvil still sitting in the trunk. I smiled and picked it up without effort, then placed it next to the steel ingots.

"You know, it's hard to believe you are weak when you do stuff like that," Dax mused.

"You better believe it, sport." I bent over and stacked the steel onto the anvil. Placing my palm flat on the ingots, then the anvil, I closed my eyes and nodded.

"Can you really make weapons with nothing but your hands?" Dax asked. He had been excited as a puppy since I said what I was about to do.

"Yes, and it is epic!" I patted his back and we both watched as Kasha lunged from the backseat, sailed through the window and landed on the dirt road gracefully. She lifted her head and meowed in a demanding way.

"He should be here soon, madam," I told her.

As if on cue, Cam and Mihr arrived in Cam's car. My friend didn't bother to back up her pickup, but just parked it in front of my car.

"Did you get it?" I asked.

Mihr, his face dark, nodded once and held up a lump of rusty-brown stone. "I'm not okay with this."

"Yeah, you told us. More than once," Cam said as she got out and slammed the door shut. She rolled her eyes and shook her head. "He bitched the whole way."

"Excuse me for not being completely on board with stealing from a mineral museum," the Angel griped.

"'Not completely on board'?" Cam asked. "The way you were going on, one would think we had stolen the Pope's huge white hat."

"Stealing is stealing. And it's not right."

"Hand it over, goody-two-shoes," I said and reached out a palm.

With a soft growl and a resting bitchface, Mihr placed the piece of a meteor into my hand.

I weighed it and turned it over several times. "This alloy will work nicely."

"Why a meteorite?" Mihr asked.

"The kamacite. Your kind doesn't like it," I answered and turned from him. I sat down next to the anvil and balanced the lump of space rock on the rest of the metal at my side.

"Did you bring the hilts I asked for?" I asked Cam.

My friend nodded and rummaged around her huge handbag, unearthing a bag that clattered softly with wooden hilts. I was excited to use wood. In Hell, we learned how to make hilts from bones and horns, but I liked neither the smell nor the feel of them.

I took a deep breath, then palmed the ingots, the anvil, and the meteorite, arranging them as I needed. As before, the grin would not budge from my lips. This was what I was born to do.

Chapter Sixteen
Fane
The Surface,
above Emerald Lake

My hands warmed on the metal, my veins crackling with energy and my inherent fire. An itch, starting in the very tips of my fingers, raced along my skin, up my hands, my wrists and arms, until it met the heat in my very chest. The seat of my unholy fire. As they met, my skin burned bright red, my fingers turned red-hot, and I took up one of the steel ingots.

It was good material, very malleable and soft, once heated to just the right temperature. I pulled the ingot until it resembled a piece of red dough, then I folded it and pulled it again. I repeated it over and over, at a steady, yet fast, rhythm.

"Would you be a dear and get me some water, Mihr?" I casually asked the Angel ogling me with an open mouth. "There's a bucket in the trunk."

Dax quickly fetched it and elbowed the Angel in the side, then held out the bucket to him. Mihr absentmindedly took it and strode to the cliff overlooking the lake. He looked back once more before manifesting his huge, gray wings and diving over the edge and down.

It was my turn to stare this time. I had known he had to be magnificent in his full angelic glory, but I had never really seen him sprouting his wings fully. Most of the time he had, I had been clinging to him for dear life.

The color of his wings was a bit darker than his eyes, and he looked absolutely glorious as he dove down, his huge body arching with surprising grace.

"It's really something," Cam said. She too was staring after him.

"Don't tell him that, though," I said. "He'll get bigheaded."

My friend chuckled and sat down on the edge of the trunk. She threw an arm around her son and both of them watched in wonder as I continued to stretch and fold the steel in my hands.

Kasha meowed and peeked over the cliff, flapping her wings anxiously. She didn't have to wait long for Mihr to shoot up again, the filled bucket in his hand.

Wind blew stray hair strands from my face as he landed and retracted his wings. He put the bucket down at my side and stepped back, crossing his arms. Kasha wound around his legs, happily purring. In a smooth movement, Mihr crouched down and drew his fingers through the Hellcat's fur. She plopped onto the floor and gave him her belly, which he scratched while raptly focusing on the metal I formed.

I dumped the elongated ingot into the water where it sizzled and hissed, then took the meteorite and infused it with heat. Twisting off half of it, I put the rest back on the anvil, then stretched and folded the metal.

Once the consistency was to my satisfaction, I placed the long piece of meteorite between the soles of my naked feet to keep it heated.

I plucked the steel from the bucket and reheated it, then twisted it into the meteorite. Using the pads of my fingers, I pulled, pushed, and formed, until the meteorite was spanning the outside of the blade. Then I stretched the whole thing and got up. I walked to Mihr and measured the blade to him.

"Do you have a preference when it comes to form?"

He blinked at me. "I-I used to have a Wingspine, I guess the closest to it would be a Claymore, in human terms."

"Pfft," I waved him off. "I know what a Wingspine is. Who do you think you're talking to? But I wonder…" I pulled the blade some more and directed the metal into the right areas to make it both durable and strong, yet flexible enough so it wouldn't easily break. After everything was where it belonged, I straightened the sword using the anvil and formed the cutting edges on either side. Now the real work began.

I sat back down, balanced the sword on my knees and closed my eyes while letting my hands wander. Every crack, every bubble of air, every imperfection manifested at the pads of my fingers, and I drew them out, smoothing them, and eradicating each one. From time to time, I flicked the metal with a nail and listened to it sing, determining how many imperfections were left and where my next focal point was.

It took a long time, but the total focus felt good. I loved the in-the-zone feeling I got when concentrating this hard, and it was one of the things about my power I truly loved. I could get lost in it completely.

With my nails, I carved out small decorations and spells. Things that would give this sword an upper hand in a fight. I had never been allowed to truly make weapons, since my talent was discovered so early, leading to me building houses and fashioning rooms, furniture and the like. Shame on my first Maester, because this would be the finest weapon ever forged in all three realms. And had he not forced me to build for his profit, who knew what the war would look like now.

My last spell incorporated Kasha – a tiny etching of the grown Hellcat, carrying an Angel – and once they rode into battle together, it was bound to manifest. A sly smile spread across my lips, I was so looking forward to seeing the Angel's face when his sword suddenly erupted into a fiery blade. Having Kasha be part of the spell meant that it would be flaming with Hellfire, cutting anyone and anything down in their path.

"Epicneeess," I sing-songed and opened my eyes. Hours must have passed, because the sunlight had changed from morning softness, to midday harshness and my skin prickled pleasantly in its shine. Earth was dope that way.

I looked around and found that Cam and Dax had taken refuge beneath a few trees and were busy eating some sandwiches Cam had brought.

Mihr stood where he had hours ago, his gaze trained on my fingers with rapt attention.

"Hand me the bag with the hilts, please," I said to him.

He dashed over and a second later, the bag dropped down at my side. I gave him a thankful wink, which he ignored, judging by the way he was still staring at my hands.

I grimaced when none of the hilts were long enough to hold the sword of this size. On the spot, I decided to improvise and broke a piece from the anvil. I formed it, then added it to the grip and fanned it out at the guard, adding a little more detail to it.

"Your belt," I demanded, stretching out a palm to Mihr.

The Angel raised his brow but undid it and handed it over.

I sliced off a part with my nail and rubbed it between heated fingers until I was able to dilate and thin it. Once I was content with the size and malleability, I wrapped it around the guard. With both hands, I cupped the leather to the metal, warming it from the outside and within. Smoke rose from the guard as I fused the two materials to one another.

I stood, my joints cracking and popping from being in the same position for so long. Turning and twisting the blade in my hand, I inspected it one last time, before handing it over to the Angel. "Here you go."

He slowly took the offered sword, his eyes big as saucers. "This… the way you… absolutely amazing." Mihr weighed the blade, tried its perfect balance and swung it about a few times, getting used to the grip and feel of it.

Packing the rest of the metal, the anvil, and the hilts into the trunk of my stolen car was the work of a moment, then I strolled to Cam and Dax, joining them in the shadows of the trees.

"Want one?" Dax asked, offering me a sandwich.

I gladly accepted and sighed with delight at the taste of ham and cheese. "We should leave now," I said between bites.

"Yeah, we know." Cam reached out and squeezed my upper arm with a worried look on her face.

"I got you this," Cam said and held out a phone.

I gasped and took it from her, then looked up. "This is amazing! Thank you so much."

"It has a pre-paid card right now. You'll probably have to change it in Europe once the credit is empty. Please text me your new number as soon as you're there."

I scooted over and hugged her with one arm. "How will I ever thank you for everything you've done for me?"

When I pulled back, Cam smiled at me with misty eyes. "You saved our lives that night, sleaze, we'd do anything for you. Besides you know we love you, don't you?"

"I love you guys, too." I wound my other arm around Dax, and we sat like that for a moment. Finally, we pulled apart and I went back to eating my delicious sandwich, but the atmosphere remained a bit heavy.

"I'll – we'll be alright," I said, watching Mihr swing his new blade, a look of concentration and drive coloring his features. Kasha lay on her side, basking in the sun, while her red eyes never left her Angel.

"If not, you can always come back to us," Dax said. "Right, mom?" He looked at Cam.

"Of course." Cam ruffled his curly hair, but I saw the worry still etched into her expression, even through her smile.

"Nothing's gonna happen." I took another bite, chewed and swallowed. "Mihr is probably overstating the danger, and who would ever come looking for us in the Black Forest?"

Cam and Dax both gave me unbelieving looks and I knew my sunny disposition didn't fool them.

"You stay safe, you hear?" Cam said. Her palm found mine and she laced our fingers for a second. "I wish you could stay."

"Me too. But I would never forgive myself if something happened to you because of me."

****

I hated parting from Cam and Dax, had already hated it every Saturday, but this was worse. Knowing that I probably wouldn't see them for a long time, I'd held them all the tighter.

188

The road wound ahead of us as I drove down the hill we had hid on and into town, through it, and out the other side. Absentmindedly, I reached for the piece of paper Dax had given me, containing the address of our rented hut in Germany. My chest was tight, and a tear escaped my eyes that I angrily wiped away.

"You'll see them again," Mihr rumbled from the passenger seat.

"How do you know?" I whispered, expressing the fear clawing at me. I swallowed, hoping he hadn't heard that vulnerable slip-up.

He turned his head, and I knew my hope was in vain. "I promise you will, that is how I know." His deep voice sounded so sure, so filled with truth, that I had to hold back even more tears. Was it a bad thing that I wanted to believe him? That I wanted to scoot closer to him and his steadfast conviction? That I wanted to trust in the promise of an Angel?

Yes. The answer was clear and simple. It was bad. People promised all sorts of things and barely any of them ever followed through. Lev had promised me things, again and again, and believed he'd be able to keep them. Yet, Mihr couldn't be more different from him. The Angel was stoic, strong, upstanding, and frustratingly righteous. Lev... Lev had been a Hellion – obviously – a proud prince who decided with his gut, was as fickle as Hellfire, and as unpredictable as a volcano. He had always acted with the authority befitting his station, knowing that his commands would be followed, with no regard to anyone else.

Mihr cared. Deeply. I knew that much. And he did the right thing, no matter if that meant being hunted by his kind for being a traitor. I doubted Lev would have made the same choice – the repercussions were too severe. So maybe Mihr's promises were different from Lev's.

"I'll hold you to it," I said.

The sun drifted closer to the horizon and the next few hours we spent in silence, each one alone with their thoughts. It was a comfortable kind of silence, and very unusual for me. There weren't many people I could be silent with.

Kasha lounged on the backseat, mewling occasionally, and sharpening her claws on the leather. Whenever he heard the sound, Mihr would cast a glance over his shoulder, and she would stop immediately. But she was a cat, so sure enough, after a while she'd do it again, resulting in the same stern, silent look from Mihr each time.

The Angel stroked over his new sword, which he had placed in his lap – against my warning – and not in the trunk. His long fingers drummed down the blade and felt over the etchings, but his face darkened the more time passed. The silence grew from comfortable to heavy and dense, and I wondered what was going on in that pretty head of his.

We spoke at the same time.

"You think they are looking for us right now?"

"What are these etchings in the blade?"

He uttered a small huff, something close to a laugh and I giggled softly.

"The etchings strengthen the sword, and they are infused with my magic."

"Really?" his brows shot up. "In what way?"

"Well, there is a word you can say to make this blade heat and/or melt the weapons it clashes with. Another will harden it so you can sever even an Archdemon's head, but you shouldn't use that if the strike

190

would hit any kind of metal or rock, as it could burst if that part of it is activated."

Mihr sat, his stormy gray eyes fixed on mine, his lips opened slightly. He had beautiful lips, I noticed. The bottom one was a bit fuller than the top and both their curves looked absolutely kissable.

"Oh," I shook myself inwardly to stop gawking, "and there is the one etching that will only manifest if you ride Kasha into battle." I squinted over my shoulder at the cat. "Once she is fully grown, of course. If you call on that magic, the blade will flame up with Hellfire."

The Angel's mouth was still open. After a few seconds, he cleared his throat and lifted his sword to look at it more closely. "I-I have heard of magical blades, some of the Archangels use them, but never of one who can manifest different kinds of spells."

"That is because none of them were made by me."

"If you can do this, why didn't you fashion weapons for the war?"

I grabbed the steering wheel tighter. "My talent developed so early and in such a huge way, that my Maester at the time decided I was best suited to fashion his new home. I did it in record time. From that point onwards, everyone and their grandmother wanted me to decorate, remodel, or build them things. I was never told to make weapons – a grand misjudgment if you ask me – instead, I became the most known shaper throughout all nine rings." I jerked my head over to the sword in his lap. "That is the first weapon I have ever made, and you will find no better blade in any of the three realms."

"Your first weapon?" he asked. "How do you know it will work the way you said?"

I snarled. "Don't insult me, Angel. Of course, it will work. But I'm debating whether I even want to tell you the magic words to unlock the spells."

"I meant no offense, Demon. It was only a question."

His gaze met mine and for a moment no one backed down. "Your turn," I said and turned my head to look at the road. "Do you think your peers are looking for us right now? That is what you have been thinking about, right? Turning all gloomy on me like you did."

"They are. Most likely they have called a squadron to comb Portsmythe and all surrounding areas and towns. Eventually, they will reach Emerald Falls, I estimate in one or two days."

"Do they have any way to tell that we were there?"

Mihr drummed his nails on his blade. "I don't think so. I mean…" he trailed off and breathed in deeply. "Demons normally leave a lingering scent, especially Raiders, and we will sniff them out, so to speak. But in your case… I don't know. They won't catch it. You don't smell of Demon. More like sandalwood."

That last part slipping from him made him visibly uncomfortable. He twisted his torso to face the window and fell silent, but the nape of his neck reddened.

For a second, I felt like calling him out on it, but the itch faded as fast as it had come. Curious. "Looks like they have no way of tracking me then. What about you?"

"Blood," Mihr said. "That's why I burned all the bandages and shirts I bled on. We find each other's bodies because our blood sends out a pulse if we are close enough. A call, if you will, one that every Angel knows and can follow."

"Rad. You sure you burned it all?" I scratched the back of my hand, sudden unease gripping me.

"Now you insult *me*, Demon. I burned every last bit of it. Cleaning up messes made by Angels and Demons alike is part of my job. Or it was." That moody look was back on his face.

"You really thought they would take you back," I surmised.

The hand gripping the hilt of his sword cracked, his knuckles turning white. "I thought they'd at least grant me an honorable death. But Michael… I never thought he would dishonor me so. I have spent hundreds of years fighting at his side, fighting for our cause, and now he would have my mind shredded for evidence I would have gladly provided."

"To be fair, you didn't want to give him what he was really after, me. Why is that? Was it because it would lead them to Cam and Dax?"

A muscle in his jaw jumped. "Partly. But what I told Michael is true, I believe you mean no harm to the people in this realm. And you did save my life. Where would my conscience be if I repaid that debt with betrayal?"

"I would have told on you if it would have saved my ass," I said.

He faced me and for the first time a full-on smile – directed at me – spanned his lips. It was every bit as panty-melting as I had expected. His face was a beacon, radiating with that smile. Warm, inviting, and with a hint of devilish cheek, completely catching me off guard. "I don't believe you, Demon."

Chapter Seventeen
Mihr
The Surface,
on the road

Our talk had taken some of the bite from my thoughts. But once Fane fell silent after me telling her I didn't believe she would have betrayed me, they slithered back into my head.

I did not regret my decision, something had been clearly off with Michael, but the consequences settled with me fully, as we sped up the coast of Maine, passing Portland and headed for Bangor.

True, I'd enter my birthrealm tomorrow, but it was bound to be different. I'd never again walk the valleys, or fly over the mountains freely, and with a sense of home. I'd never enter the Heavenly city again. Cyrisas, with its marble streets and shimmering walls, the high towers and white trees, was lost to me now. Forever.

My friends, all the people I knew, they'd learn of my actions and think me a traitor. *He,* would know me as a failure. Yes, I was both and I should be furious because of it. I should feel... something besides of what I did. Hopeless. And it was her fault.

My eyes wandered to Fane, who slurped milkshake from a polystyrene cup we had picked up, along with some food, at a drive-through. Yet, I felt no anger when I looked at her. I understood her motives. What I didn't get was how I could have been so wrong about her. My Demon was no hellish monster, she had no interest in corrupting Humans, she didn't care about her side winning the war, she even thought it to be 'bullshit.' All of it wasn't what got to me though, it was the fact that she cared. More than most Angels I knew. I had found the one Demon in Hell who had compassion – or rather, she had found me – and it was a shock to my system. How many like her were in Hell? How many hated the war just as much as she did? On that note, how many Angels felt the same way?

I had believed the war to be righteous, a true cause. But what if Fane was right? I didn't want to think it possible. It would render so many things meaningless.

This constant conflict had taken everything from me. My parents died for it, many of my friends and countless brothers and sisters in arms, as well. It had made me harden to the point of a peculiar numbness. I had eventually started hiding away from remaining friends and any encounters that would shake me awake, that would risk me getting invested in anything, or anyone. It had been stupid on my part, or I would have noticed Michael changing sooner. Perhaps, I would have even done something about it. I huffed. Maybe I would have changed as well, like he did, so it could have been a blessing.

Either way, the past few days had rattled me. And my front of cool disregard didn't hold up to my inner scrutiny anymore. I had attacked my kin because of the cat in the backseat, and I would do so again without a second thought. Just the thought of her jumping out, miniscule against the five Angels, but determined to have my back, had me furious.

I shifted in my seat and the leather creaked.

"We can stop two towns over, Dax has booked us a motel there," Fane said.

Once more, my gaze wandered over. Her red skin was stark against the beige seat, her long brown hair curled softly around her shoulders, and her amber eyes held a gentle, pulsing glow, like the gleaming of coals. For a small second, I felt a chuckle bubble up my chest. She thought her nakedness shocked and provoked me, and while she was right, the way she had made my sword… it had been the single most magnificent thing I'd ever seen.

I had found myself wondering how her talented fingers would feel on my skin, as they danced over my sword like artists. Fane had used her entire body to shape my blade and she had spellbound me the entire time.

Slowly, my eyes dipped to her lips, those beautiful lips that smiled so easily – despite the life she had lived – but spewed crude words and sharp thoughts. *What would they taste like?* The memory of her head nestled to my chest while she mumbled 'safe,' flashed through my head and I nearly groaned.

I shrank back from my thoughts, they were improper. Still, I couldn't help but steal glances at her. Fane had never needed to shock me to test my conviction, she tempted me plenty just by sitting next to me.

"Mihr? You okay with that?"

"What?" I asked, ripping myself loose from my indecent musings.

"I said we can stop two towns over. It's still an hour till we get there, do you want to call it a night, or keep going?" She squinted at the lights of an oncoming car, her upper lip peeling back in a small snarl, revealing her subtle fangs. She had to be exhausted from today. Not only had she used a big amount of her power to make me a weapon, but she had driven the rest of the day. I shouldn't care, and I definitely shouldn't think about her in improper ways. I glared out of the window on my side. *Stupid.*

"We can stop. You should rest."

"I'm fine, Angel."

"That may be, Demon, but I'm not fine with ending up wrapped around a tree because you are pushing yourself too hard."

She snorted. "Is this your pathetic way of telling me you care about me being tired?"

"No. This is me telling you I care about staying in one piece."

"Ass."

"What else is new?"

"Jeez, what plucked your feathers, Angel? I was beginning to think you weren't all bad but –"

"Just drive, will you?" I snapped.

"Right." She fell silent for a few breaths, then turned to me, "You know what? No. Fuck that. I will not be snapped at without any reason whatsoever. You were the one who wanted to travel together, you were the one who 'decided' it would be best."

I groaned, "This again? I worded it wrong, and I told you I was sorry about it."

"That is not the fucking point!"

"Then what is?"

"That you suddenly have a stick so far up your ass you are coughing splinters. What is with the snapping? And with the glaring, and growling? What did I do?"

"Nothing," I grumbled, knowing full well that I was being an idiot, but anger at myself and her coursed through me. Red, hot anger.

"Excuse me? Did you just 'nothing' me?"

I took a deep breath. "You did nothing, is what I meant."

"Then what is wrong?"

I paused, "I don't want to talk about it."

"Well, I can deal with that. Just stop snapping at me, okay?"

Perplexed, I looked over. "What do you mean?"

"What I just said. If you are cranky because of some personal reason you don't want to talk to me about, I understand, but I won't have you biting my head off about something I didn't do."

Still angry, and feeling like a moron, I sat next to her in silence until we reached the motel Dax had booked for us. Fane headed inside while I retrieved the suitcase Cam had lent us and picked Kasha up from the backseat.

Fane strutted from the reception, a card in hand, and waved at me to follow her. "Dax booked us *one* room. Apparently, he thinks since we shared the basement..." The Demon slid the card into the lock of the room number 4. It clicked and she opened the door, leading the way inside.

"Oh, Dax," Fane mumbled when she switched on the light, revealing one big bed.

"Scared to sleep in the same bed as me?" I asked. Maybe this time, I would catch *her* off guard for a change.

"Nope, I know you want to." She winked at me. "It's just... never mind."

I placed Kasha down, closed the door and threw the suitcase on the foot of the bed. All the while watching Fane stroke over the duvet softy, visibly chewing on her inner cheek. She didn't look at me, and there was no shyness. As much as I would have liked her to be a little... well, *affected* due to the prospect of sleeping together in one bed, this was something else entirely. She didn't seem to be worried about me, but the bed itself. Curious.

It frustrated me, as well as the fact that she had stumped my pissiness in the car. Why did she always make me feel like I was either not understanding, or overreacting? And why couldn't I shake the flutter in my lower belly when looking at the bed?

I opened the suitcase and gulped. Cam had packed it for us, I'd had no idea what was inside. One side was filled with jeans, shirts, socks, and boxer shorts. The other contained smaller clothes and the occasional dress. When I picked up one of my shirts, I saw Cam had opened it twice at the back – for my wings. I turned it in my hands, gratitude heavy in my chest at her thoughtfulness, before I placed it back in the suitcase. I had no idea how I'd ever repay Cam for… for everything, really.

After rummaging through my side, I snagged underwear and a black toiletry bag.

"Going for a shower," I said as I passed Fane.

The Demon gingerly sat down on the bed, looking deep in thought, not acknowledging me. A small 'hmm' was all the answer I got, and I chided myself for feeling like rolling my eyes.

****

Fane

The floor was wooden, as was the bed. I tested my weight on it, bobbing up and down carefully. It was like I imagined Humans felt on the high seas. My head grew light, and I tried hard to stay steady and not panic. There was nothing to ground or anchor me to the earth. One of my senses – the one I relied on to keep me safe – was essentially gone. How would I ever get sleep without feeling safe? I had wanted to try a human bed, but I'd always thought I'd do so at Cam and Dax's, where I felt safe to begin with.

A shaky breath left me, and I tried concentrating on the sound of Mihr's shower. At the thought of him, my lips lifted a fraction. The inner image of his glorious naked body being all wet and sudsy…

My head swam even more, now for a different reason. Back in the car, being cramped in that small space with him, and feeling his eyes flit my way, roaming, it had gotten me all hot and bothered. I still felt him looking, his gaze as intense as a touch.

The question was, why had he snapped at me? Was it because things with his people hadn't worked out, and he was having a hard time coming to terms with it? But then why steal looks with those heated stormy eyes of his?

He was hard to read, and I hadn't had the need for it so far, as the Angel had always told me what was on his mind. Annoyingly. Now he was moody and didn't want to talk about it. Strange.

I slowly stood and spread my arms out to help my balance. "It's just like Cam's living-room," I told myself. "You've done this a hundred times."

Why was this suddenly so hard? I jumped when Kasha wound her body around one of my legs. She glanced up and mewled softly.

"Damnation, Kasha," I gasped. "I nearly tripped over you."

I got another meow in answer, then she rubbed her head against my leg and purred.

"Yeah, I know. I am being silly. You are here to protect me, right?"

Her purr got louder, and I stepped over her, heading for the foot of the bed to rummage through the suitcase. My breath grew short and my throat tightened when I smelled Cam's fabric softener and saw what she had packed for me. I already missed them with an intensity that astounded me. It actually hurt.

My back pocket vibrated, and I slid out the phone I had stashed there. As though she knew I thought of them, the screen revealed a text from Cam.

Hey, sleaze. Everything good?

I fiddled around until I had formulated an answer, my fingers not used to the sensitive touch interface. *Yup. Just arrived at the motel. Dax reserved a room with one bed.*

Lol. Should be interesting ;)

I chuckled. *You bet.*

Well, don't do anything I would do.

I'd never.

Right. Gotta go make dinner. Just checking in to see how you doin. But if a shared bed is your only problem... You'll be fine.

Thanks, Cam. Tell Dax I love him.

*I will. *hugs you into oblivion**

hugs back

And don't be scared out there without us, you got this.

Tears ran down my cheeks and I sniffled to get a hold of myself. I wiped the tears away texted a short, non-convincing answer, and placed the phone on one of the bedside tables. She was right. No matter how exciting being free and in this amazing plane was, I was scared. Without the safety-net that was Cam and Dax, I had no idea how to navigate the unknown.

Much like I had no idea how to navigate this night, without stone touching me. It angered me. The Surface was synonymous with safety and warmth for me because I had found my footing here, I had healed here. I had become accustomed to being loved without conditions, had grown fat and safe on it. Now, my future was as shrouded and unsure as it had ever been.

"You're a grown ass, Demon, act like it," I chastised myself. "Fucking pathetic."

"Fane? You okay?" Mihr said from my side.

I hadn't heard the door opening, so deeply in thought and I looked up. Satan's fancy hoofhair, the guy was… mouthwatering. He stood in the door, only clad in boxer shorts that left little to nothing to the imagination. Drops of water blinked from his shoulders and his towel-dried hair was marvelously disheveled. Steam from his shower billowed around him, making him look like the ethereal being he was. I wanted to lick every inch of him. And decided that I'd be fine. Scary or not, I was on the run with an Angel who had the ability to melt my insides with a look. With exactly the one I got from him now.

His storm-colored eyes rested on mine, intense and almost branding. "I'm fine," I said, my voice disturbingly thin.

"You look… flushed."

I chuckled and grabbed a few things from the suitcase. Then I sauntered up to him and placed a palm on his naked pecs. "I am face to face with a practically naked, sinfully hot Angel, and I haven't fucked in a while, so yeah, I am flushed."

He gulped in a lungful of air and I gently nudged him out of the way as I passed him. I closed the door with a hearty laugh, his derailed face vanishing behind wood and white lacquer.

I was busy nestling with my pants when the door flew open. Surprised, I squealed and turned to face Mihr.

"You," he swallowed, a muscle in his jaw ticking. "You shouldn't say things like that."

"Mihr," I gasped mockingly, clasping imaginary pearls. "How dare you enter the bathroom when a lady is getting ready for the night?"

For a second, he looked taken aback, then his face hardened. "You are no lady, and if you don't want me pinning you to the next wall, you will stop goading me. Stop making fun of me," his voice was raspy, deep and sensual, making me shake inwardly. "I may be more proper than you, but I have limits."

"Don't tell me that the upstanding Angel lusts for this filthy Demon," I purred.

He stalked closer, until my butt hit the sink and he bent over me, crowding me without touching. "You know I do, so there is no need to pretend differently anymore," he rumbled, his gray eyes scorching me. I wanted to get lost in those eyes, wanted to ride that storm. A devilish smile spread across his heated features, making my knees weak. "But I know that you do too, despite all the teasing."

I swallowed. "Who said I was teasing?"

He huffed and placed his mouth next to my ear. Goosebumps covered me with lightning speed when I felt his breath caress my neck. He breathed in deeply, inhaling the scent of my skin. "No one. And now I know I was wrong. You meant every crude word just now, didn't you? Hmm?" He turned his head, nearly brushing his lips down my neck and over my shoulder, and I trembled beneath the almost-touch.

"You smell different now. Like *burning* sandalwood." Mihr let his face almost graze mine, then looked at me. "And your eyes are aglow. Tells, I will remember."

I stood stock-still, waiting for him to surge forward and kiss me. But instead, he straightened and backed away. "Two can play the teasing game, Demon." He walked from the room and closed the door.

I blinked at the door, my breath ragged and my heart hammering away in my chest. *What the Hell had just happened? Had the virtuous Angel flustered me? On purpose?*

I blew out a breath and turned to the mirror, leaning on the sink with both hands. My eyes shimmered and pulsed with fire, and small veins creeping along my face glowed to the same rhythm. I was of half a mind to barge from the bathroom and mount that cheeky Angel, but as he'd said, two could play the teasing game. I bit my lower lip and smiled. I wondered how long it would take him to lose control, all that pent up desire… it was going to be glorious.

Stripping down, I got into the shower and turned on the cold spray. I just had to keep myself from being the first to give in. "Game on, Angel," I said into the spray.

Chapter Eighteen
Fane
*The Surface,
a motel between Bangor and Saint John*

When I walked back into the room, clad in a tank-top and very cute pink panties, Mihr lay in bed with his back turned to me. Kasha was purring from somewhere beyond, sounded like she was tucked against his chest or belly. *Lucky cat.*

I was done teasing for the night, or I might have undressed and snuggled up against his back naked, to see what reaction it would elicit. But as I traipsed to the bed on unsure footing and got in – my stomach clenching with a bout of unease – I knew I wasn't up for games. Concentrating on my breathing, I braved the unfamiliar softness and absolute lack of safety around me. With shaking fingers, I reached for the light switch and plunged the room into darkness. The flimsy curtains on either side of the door let in slivers of light from the neon sign buzzing on the side of the house. From time to time, the sign flickered and I tried to predict the rhythm of the pulsing light. Anything to keep my body from shaking, and my fear from taking over.

I am safe, I told myself. *No one knows we're here, so no one will come looking. I don't need to feel stone. I am safe.* But no matter how often I repeated that top-notch reasoning in my head, the flutter of panic in my chest didn't let up. It didn't help that my stomach was almost queasy from being this close to Mihr. If I had been in my right mind, I would have laughed, then scooted

207

closer to get a little sumthin sumthin. The last time I had a giddy stomach around someone had been when I met Lev, which did not bode well for me. If it meant that I actually felt something other than lust, I had to figure out a way to stomp it out as fast and as effectively as I could.

Pulling the blanket up to my chin, I blew out a breath and closed my eyes. My body hummed with warring sensations and I hoped that my exhaustion would make short work of them. I needed sleep if I was to bust into Heaven tomorrow.

Ugh, stupid, I chastised myself. *Why did you go and think of that? On top of everything else?* It made my gut twist and bunch up like a fist. I squeezed my lids shut and clawed at the blanket. My kind had never breached the portals of Heaven, we weren't meant to. And truth be told, I had no desire to see it for myself.

As I warred with my innards, my thoughts and fears, a small body suddenly landed on my chest and I nearly jumped out of my skin. My hands flew up to find fur and leather, my wide eyes met red, glowing ones and I sighed in relief, stroking Kasha's soft fur. The Hellcat purred and kneaded my one arm with her front paws, then turned a few times and rolled up on my chest. Her purr vibrated through my torso, soothing my haywire nerves while I pulled my fingers through the black sleekness on Kasha's back.

"Thank you," I whispered.

Kasha raised her head and uttered a small, demanding meow and to my utter surprise, Mihr turned to face me at the sound.

"What's wrong?" he asked.

"N-nothing," I stuttered, wishing to sink into the mattress and disappear. Him seeing me weak and afraid was not something I wanted.

Mihr slid a hand under the pillow and rested his face on his bulging bicep. "You're lying, Demon. Kasha would never have left my side otherwise, and your eyes are pulsing like crazy. Also, you have been shaking since getting into this bed." He drew his brows down a bit. "Is it because of me? Should I sleep on the floor?"

I nearly laughed, but my throat was too tight. "No," I choked out. "I… uh… I have never slept in a bed before," I admitted. "Normally, I sleep on stone."

He frowned, obviously not understanding.

I licked my dry lips nervously. "Stone is my element, Angel. It is my strength. The only defense I have ever had. Sleeping on stone not only grounds me, it tells me if someone is coming for me. It protects me, anchors me, and I can hide inside it if I need to."

"You're afraid," he deduced.

"No shit, Sherlock. I can't feel *anything*. The floorboards are wood, this bed is wood, I am far away from actual ground, and it's freaking me out. I don't imagine you could understand. You never had to sleep with one of your senses awake, in case someone came to… to hurt you."

"No, I suppose not. It pains me that you do."

I had no time to voice my surprise at his words, as he pulled his arm from under his face and reached for me. "Turn your back to me," he said.

"Why?" I asked, fear ratcheting up a notch.

"Trust me," he rumbled.

I swallowed, staring at him for a few heavy seconds, but there was nothing I feared in his eyes. Only understanding shone back at me.

Slowly, I turned, sliding Kasha down, so I hugged her to my belly. Mihr slid one arm under my neck and wound his other around me from above, then he pulled me flush against him.

I stared into the semi-darkness when my body molded to his.

"No one will hurt you, as long as I am here, Demon," Mihr rasped from behind me. "You are safe."

My heart hammered for minutes, but the Angel was as still as a statue, yet warm as a hearth of coals. I shimmied closer and very slowly, my breathing calmed. As time passed, my bunched-up muscles uncoiled, and relaxation flooded me.

A tingle in my lower belly and on my skin, where the Angel touched me, was all that was left after a while.

I felt his steady heartbeat against my back, while his warm breath tickled the nape of my neck. It was a steady rhythm, lulling me in and my lids grew heavy.

Safe. I laced the fingers of one hand with his and pulled his arm tighter around me. As my exhausted body finally got the rest it so badly needed, my last thought flickered like a warning sign.

Never, in all my three hundred and forty-two years had I felt safe in a man's arms. Lev's touch had burned like Hellfire, filled me with desire and heat, but even he had never made me feel safe.

****

I woke rested and calm, unusually so. The warm body fused to my back moved slightly and a huge leg twined with mine. A very awake crotch pressed into my bum and my eyes snapped open. I wiggled my butt a bit and was rewarded with a twitching hardness. I smiled like an idiot and did it again.

"Careful, Demon," the Angel rasped against my shoulder. "Keep it up and I won't care how uncomfortable this bed makes you."

"As much as I'd like to find out if your bulge has as much potential as its feel promises, we have a long way to travel today." I scooted away and we untangled our limbs from one another. Kasha plopped from the bed in the process and hissed indignantly, before starting to clean herself, throwing me scathing looks every now and then. I stretched out my arms and arched my back off the mattress.

Mihr watched me with a cocked brow and sat up. I yawned. "What?"

He shook his head and slipped from the bed. The Angel tried to hide his raging morning wood, but neither his hands, nor his boxer shorts were able to shield it from my bemused gaze.

"*Big* potential," I whispered as he vanished in the bathroom. I sat up and rolled my shoulders. There was no stiffness, no pain, and no lasting lethargy. I had slept like a baby, snug and safe.

"Huh," I mumbled and got up. "Who'd have thunk?" The floor seemed a lot less scary today than it had last night, and I skipped to the suitcase and threw it on the bed. Picking out jeans, a bra and a new tank top, I got dressed. I gathered what we had strewn across the room and packed it up, done in a few minutes.

Once Mihr emerged from the bathroom, I did a quick morning routine – very human-like – and shortly after, we exited the room. All the while, our gazes met every few moments, as his eyes followed me and mine him. It was strange, a chasing of looks, without uttering a sound. I even blushed from the intensity. My stomach fluttered like it was swarming with bugs. Something had shifted during the night, something big. It added to the pull I felt toward him. I wasn't sure if it meant I'd follow my original plan of teasing my angelic volcano until he erupted or not. I was of half a mind to leave well enough alone. He had made me feel safe. *Yes*, a small voice in my mind purred, *and just imagine what else he can make you feel.*

I hushed that thought as we pulled from the parking lot after having paid with some of the cash Cam had given me.

The next few hours remained heavy with glances and silence, and I repeatedly shifted in my seat as the fluttering in my belly didn't let up for a second. His smell, proximity, those stormy eyes of his… It was enough to have my breath short the entire time.

But I wasn't the only one affected, clearly. Mihr's huge hands clasped the hilt of his sword repeatedly until his knuckles turned white. He too, shifted a lot in his seat.

After two hours, I couldn't take it anymore. "You should name her," I suggested to keep myself from pulling over and jumping his bones.

"What?" Mihr asked.

"The blade." I nodded at the weapon in his lap. "Every good one has a name. And she is one of the greatest, if I do say so myself."

"I have never named a sword," he said, his brows bunching together until a crease appeared between them.

"Well, you should. She deserves a name."

A loud meow from the back seat interrupted our conversation. Mihr glanced back and reached for Kasha, to pet her.

"Hey!" He pulled his hand back and stared at his index finger, "She just bit me."

"Did she break the skin?" I asked.

Mihr turned over his finger, looking at it from every side. "Nope. It's just… surprising."

I glanced into the mirror at Kasha, who paced the back, a low growl tumbling from her muzzle. "She is bound to be hungry. At this stage of her development, she grows like mad. She needs food."

Mihr proceeded to feed his cat what we had left. Jerky, sandwiches, and chili chips. Kasha didn't care, she gulped everything down he held out. Soon, we were out of snacks, but it didn't matter, as we neared the coast.

"You sure you can fly us across, straight to Nova Scotia?" I asked when we pulled into the small town of Cutler.

"Of course," Mihr said. "Just make sure that we hide the car well outside of town."

I wasn't convinced. He would have to carry me, Kasha, our suitcase, his sword, and the remaining metal. I had plans for it.

****

I realized my doubts had been unfounded as we glided through the sea of clouds half an hour later. Mihr's strong wings propelled us through the sky at breakneck speed, making my eyes water. Kasha had taken up to hanging from his neck, like always, and I felt like a baby kangaroo, as he clasped me around the middle with one arm, his torso to my back.

Being in the air was both frightening and awesome. The thought of plummeting into the sea was scary, but the rush of shooting through the sky was out of this world. Still, I clung to his arm holding me and was very tempted to turn around so I could wind my legs around him for extra safety.

He was fast though, and so I reverted to holding onto his arm with one hand, while clutching the two remaining metal ingots with my other. The metal in my hand was a small consolation, and to my surprise, it wasn't nearly as comforting as Mihr's arm holding me.

213

Over time, my unease shifted to stark fear, though. When Mihr beat his wings so we climbed higher, I knew he was heading for the portal, and my stomach sank, feeling like I left it somewhere beneath me, falling. Sure enough, I caught sights of the land mass far beneath us. We were above Nova Scotia now and dread trampled through my chest.

"How far?" I yelled through the wind howling past my ears.

"Not long now," came his answer. "You see that?" he lifted his arm carrying the suitcase, and pointed a finger at something above us.

I squinted my teary eyes and gasped when I saw what looked like a vertical slice of cloud. It was the exact same color as the clouds around it, and nearly vanished between them.

We reached it and Mihr took us around it a few times before hovering closer. Then we dove inside. Cold, wet, and swirling. Then a debilitating bout of nausea took hold of me and I gagged from it. Mihr's presence was the only thing grounding me as I was blinded by a stark light, losing all senses of my body and the surroundings.

I heard Kasha retch from somewhere behind me and felt Mihr hugging me closer. "It'll be over in a second," he promised.

The light faded slowly and my eyes adjusted, still, tears streamed from them as I tried to come to grips with what I saw.

Rolling hills of what looked like clouds, but couldn't be, as plants and trees grew from them, spanning everything as far as my eyes could see. The plants looked strange though, the trees were white as bone, and the rest a pale, beige color. The cloud-like ground beneath it was grayish-white and swirling. *Was it even ground?*

Mihr took us down. He landed and placed me on the weird surface gingerly. I immediately sank down into a crouch and touched a palm to the swirling ground.

"Uhhh," was all that escaped me.

"What does 'uhhh' mean, Fane?" Mihr asked.

"Fascinating. This... this is incredible," I said, ignoring his question. I dug my fingers into the ground and closed my eyes. It was sand, for I could feel it, but it was... "Alive. Your sand is alive."

"What are you talking about, Fane? These hills resemble the movement of clouds because we are in Heaven. The plane above, the holy, the divine."

I chuckled, feeling the sand tickle my palm inquisitively. "No, Mihr, this ground is alive. It moves."

"Yes, because that is what it does, Demon."

"Then why can I feel it searching my fingers to find out who and what I am? There is a consciousness here... Like the whisper of millions of tiny mouths, all saying the same thing." I was awestruck, then a sharp pain sliced into my palm. I jerked it back and watched in shock as my black blood dripped to the sand from a cut in the middle of my hand. The drop of blackness had a jaw-dropping effect. The sand changed from gray-white to a dark gray and swirled quicker. Within seconds, the whole atmosphere changed.

"It knows what I am," I said. The gray swirls grew closer, tightening around me in circles of storm-cloud waves. A tentacle-like extremity parted from the ground, swiping at me.

"Fane!" Mihr yelled. "Get back, I'll fly us away." He jumped to my side and slid his arm around me, but I gently pushed him away.

"No. Give me a moment." I grabbed the arm of sand with my injured palm and willed it to stop. Alive or not, it was sand, which meant it was rock. Rock was my domain, and I ruled over it.

The sand arm trembled and convulsed in my grasp, angrily ripping at my power. I fused warmth into it, tentatively, bit by bit. "Calm down," I whispered. "I mean no harm." After a few more tugs, the sand stopped fighting and I got the feeling of being appraised anew. The sand glided over my hand and up my arm, as though it searched me. I made my veins light up in welcome and the sand ran up my arm like a sleeve. It let go of the ground and zipped over my skin excitedly.

Smiling, I crouched down once more and pressed my palm to the ground. The remaining sand rushed back to its origin and the million little mouths rejoiced. It was the strangest thing. I had always been able to understand stone. The makeup of it, the inherent strengths and weaknesses, but this was different, it was almost a conversation. I understood that the material around me was... happy. Excited to have found someone who understood it.

I stood, feeling monumental wonder flash trough my entire being. "Heaven is made of living stone. Mihr... this is amazing."

"I'm not so sure about amazing," he said, eyeing the ground suspiciously. Swaths of sand broke free and raced up my legs and his, twisting around in flourishes of tickling grains.

Then they jarred to a stop. The grains fell from our legs as one and I quickly dug my fingers into it. Spiky and raw, prickling and stinging. A warning drummed against my hand. Sharp and urging.

"Uh, Mihr? The sand is saying that we are in danger."

"Excuse me?" my Angel asked, his face incredulous. A second later he cursed as his gaze locked onto something in the distance.

I turned my head to look in the same direction. On the horizon I saw wings. A squadron of Angels was barreling our way.

Chapter Nineteen
Mihr
Heaven,
The Walking Hills

How? They shouldn't know about us being here, they themselves shouldn't even be here. These hills were no man's land, and the portal was one of the long-forgotten ones. I knew for a fact that next to no one knew about it.

"Damnation," I uttered, patting a hissing Kasha softly to calm her. I handed my Demon the suitcase, pulled my sword from where I had tucked it into my belt, then snatched Fane with the other arm. She shrieked in surprise when I shot to the sky and beat wings. We sped off to the left and I prayed that I would be able to outfly my kin. At least until we exited at the portal I had chosen. They would know. Even if we made it out of Heaven, they would know where in the human plane we were.

I strained and worked my wings as fast as I was able. My back was fully healed by now, but there was a lingering stiffness between my shoulder blades, stemming from the scars of the Hellfire burn. With a look over my shoulder, I deduced that we wouldn't make it. They closed in steadily.

"Mihr, take us down!" Fane cried. "I can't help you in the air. The other Angels are too close already. We can't outrun them."

Pulling her squirming body closer, I said, "They'd cleave you in two before you even landed a blow. In the air or on the ground, it doesn't matter."

Doubling my efforts, I gnashed my teeth and ignored the stiffness that turned to a dull thrum as I forced my wings past it. "They won't even hit the ground themselves but snatch you up and rip you apart."

"Who said anything about me exchanging blows?" Fane pointed beneath us. "I'll use that to help us out."

I glanced at the ground and saw that the sand was following us. A wave of dark gray rumbled through the trees and plants, chasing us, matching our breakneck speed effortlessly.

"It doesn't look friendly," I said.

"Only one way to find out." Fane twisted out of my hold and plummeted down.

"No!" I dove after her, but we were too close to the ground and she fell straight into the dark gray mass, my outstretched fingers missing her by a hair's breadth.

The wave of sand caught the Demon and lowered her safely to her feet and Fane grinned at me. "See?"

"By all of Hell's disciples, you will be my end, Demon!" I shouted.

Fane dropped the suitcase and the steel ingots, then kicked off her shoes and dug her naked feet deeply into the cloudy ground. Her veins lit up, but not in their usual red. As the gray sand spread up her legs, until it engulfed her hips, her veins blazed to life in answer. White as lightning. Her hair whipped across her face in glowing white, her eyes shining with the same glaring light. The sand around her twisted into a moving, menacing maelstrom and tentacles erupted from the gray mass, swaying close to her body like dark arms.

"Holy mother of the Lord," I uttered at the sight, but there was no time to marvel at Fane and her living sand, for I heard the flapping of my approaching brethren.

Five warriors charged closer, and I gripped the hilt of my sword tightly, scanning their faces. I knew one of them, a born Angel like me, who had trained with me almost seven hundred years ago.

"Ezra, take your squadron and leave. No one has to die today," I addressed him.

The five Angels slowed until they hovered a few wingbeats from me, their weapons at the ready.

Ezra jerked his chin at me, his chocolate brown eyes melting away to mirror the angelic black of his wings. "You should not have come back, Mihr. You should have died with Rapha, or in Hell," he spat in my direction. "Instead, you enter the holy realm, with Hellspawn? Have you no shame, no pride?"

"Traitor," a black-haired woman with white wings said at his side. "To what end did you even come? To infiltrate or topple Cyrisas alone? With a kitten and… that?" she pointed her blade at Fane.

"Watch your potty-mouth, she-Angel," Fane shouted. "We are just passing through, so if you, feathered fiends, would kindly fuck off, no one will get hurt."

"It speaks, how nauseating," the she-Angel said with a sneer.

"Ezra, please. The Demon speaks the truth, we are only passing through, we want no conflict. Let us be and we will go in peace." I hoped that my words would find purchase, but did not have high hopes they would.

"You enter this holy place, a traitor, with not one, but two damned creatures, and demand I let you not only live, but leave?" his voice was as angry as his face, and I knew my hope had been in vain. "Hell must have taken you mind, Mihr. The only thing I can grant you is fair treatment until we reach Cyrisas, *if* you surrender now."

I bit my teeth together. This should not be happening. No one should have known… except Michael. I had shared all my knowledge with him, my brother of choice.

"Michael sent you, didn't he?" I asked.

Ezra inclined his head once. "He wants the both of you alive, that is more than many of us do."

"Right, I say we slay the lot," a large, brutish-looking Angel said. "They don't deserve to look at this divine place for a second longer."

"Hush, Arenth," Ezra chided. "We have our orders. If Mihr and his… creatures surrender, we will deliver them to Michael intact."

"We can't do that, Ezra," I said. "I accepted death as punishment for blessing a Demon, and I would have told him everything I knew about what I had witnessed in the underworld. But Michael wants me to be brought to the Seers." I shook my head, "I won't suffer the fate of the Empty. And I won't let the same happen to the Demon, or the Hellcat."

Ezra gaped at me, his eyes had widened at me mentioning the Seers.

"So, you have a choice," I continued. "You let us leave, or we fight. But none of us will come quietly."

"To Hell with this," Arenth hollered and twirled his sword in a circle once, then he beat his brown wings and soared straight at me. The tension was broken, and his peers followed suit, even Ezra.

I took a bracing breath and grabbed my new sword with both hands as Arenth reached me, hacking down at my head with a yell. I rolled to the side, his blade missing me narrowly. Kasha lunged from my back, soared with her little wings spread and landed on Arenth. She growled and bit him in the neck, her needlepoint claws slicing into the skin of his shoulder. The Angel swiped at her and I dove under him and let my sword flash up, opening his neck from ear to ear. As Arenth fell past me, I stretched out an arm and Kasha jumped, landing safely, before she bounded over my back and leapt off on my other side. She slammed her claws and fangs into the face of the she-Angel, who screamed and shook her off. Kasha fell, but her spread wings slowed her. I knew her fall wouldn't be hard and shot up, directing my sword at the distracted Angel, who was snarling at the falling cat. Her head reached the ground before Kasha did.

Ezra's sword clashed with mine as I barely got it up in time to ward off his blow. He was close to my age, and an experienced warrior. We exchanged swipes, countering each hit as we rolled, dove, and sped through the air at mind-numbing speed. We both used every maneuver known to us, no one getting the upper hand. His hits were hard, jarring my muscles when our swords met.

"Arken!" Fane yelled from below. "Say it, Mihr!"

I closed my wings and plummeted, gaining room from Ezra's swipes and chanced a look at my Demon.

She stood in her maelstrom, waving her arms around as if directing the tentacles to swipe at the two Angels circling her. Deep gashes littered her torso, and black blood ran over her red skin. Answering a twirl of her fingers, one tentacle changed its shape to a long spear and launched off, embedding itself into the chest of one of the Angels deeply. The Angel screamed as he was punched back, the spear driving him down and into the ground, pinning him there. Around him, the shifting waves lapped at him and over him as they and dragged the Angel under. Within two heartbeats, he was buried by the cloud-sand.

"The sword, Mihr!" Fane shouted. "Use the word. Arken!"

I turned away, avoiding a swipe from Ezra, who had caught up, and said the word Fane was yelling repeatedly now. My blade darkened in reply, blinking at me like polished onyx and when I swung it, it bit into Ezra's blade and melted it. Pulling it through with a yell, I swung it again. Ezra looked shocked, as my blade struck his neck. Like a knife through butter, my sword severed through skin, bone and sinew, parting Ezra's head from his body. Guilt slammed into me as I saw him fall, his wings fluttering uselessly.

A cry from below had me pivoting around. The one remaining Angel charged at Fane, swiping her sword, hacking through the sand tentacles until she was nose to nose with my Demon. The Angel pulled back and swung, embedding her sword deeply in Fane's side.

"No!" I cried and beat my wings to reach them.

A black blur shot up and landed on the Angel's back. Kasha scratched and bit, growling like the Hellspawn she was, and the Angel stumbled back, pulling her blade from Fane.

My Demon clasped a palm to the wound and fell to her knees, blood welled from between her fingers, dropping into the gray sand which reacted immediately. The maelstrom left Fane and encased the she-Angel. Spikes of sand shout out, pelting the Angel like bullets, tearing into her flesh with a vengeance.

The Angel screamed and tried to ward off the sand bullets and the cat at once, but she stumbled back, and the ground rose to meet her. Just like before, the ground swallowed her whole, then spat out Kasha, who shook out her fur and trotted over to Fane. I landed next to them both, just in time to catch Fane from falling over, planting her face into her magical, living, sand. Her glowing veins flickered out until she was her usual red.

"Fane?" I searched her skin, finding multiple wounds, before gently tugging her hand from the one in her side.

She gasped as blood flowed down freely. The wound was deep and right above her hip bone. I ripped off my shirt and held it to the wound. Pressing her fingers to it, I sat her down. "Keep pressure on it," I ordered.

"Yes, Theodora," Fane croaked. I hurried to the suitcase and opened it, rummaging through to find a towel. When I pulled it out and turned to Fane, I stopped short. The sand had built something close to a recliner, perching her up slightly and raising her to me. I cocked a brow and wound the towel around her waist and over my shirt.

"Nifty sand," Fane croaked. "Nice sand." She stroked her bloody fingers over the ground. "I like you," she cooed.

"Yeah, we have to get out of here, Fane," I said, scrutinizing the horizon. "More Angels are bound to come if these don't report back."

My Demon smiled mildly and patted my stomach, "Rock-hard abs, sexy beast."

"Stop it, Fane. Can you walk?"

"Walk? I will float on this sand like the queen I am." She coughed, blood speckling the palm she held in front of her mouth. With a sigh, she lay back. "Imma rest now, 'kay? Tired." Her lids slid shut.

I shook her and said her name, nothing. Her pulse was steady, but weak and I needed to really take care of her wound. Stem the bleeding and maybe even sew it shut.

Cursing, I went to close the suitcase, when movement at my feet caught my attention. The steel ingots plopped from the sand and inched closer. They were covered in the living sand, it didn't leave or fall off, even after I picked them up and swiped a palm over them. The sand stuck to the steel, like a rough skin. I shrugged and threw it into the suitcase.

"Kasha, let's go," I said, and my cat complied, clawing her way up my jeans. When she reached my hip, I picked her up and pressed my face to hers for a second. She purred like a little engine and snuggled closer.

"You did so well," I told her, then drew her around my neck. She purred on and licked over the nape of my neck once.

I tied Fane's feet together with a shirt from the suitcase and stepped in between her legs. Then I hiked her up, until her tied feet circled my hips. With one arm, I held her to me, with the other I picked up the suitcase.

I looked at the swirling sand once and felt utterly stupid when I nodded at it, "Thank you."

To my amazement, the grains of sand rustled audibly for a moment, then quieted down. "Unbelievable," I muttered, then launched us into the sky once more. It was time to leave this plane.

As we left behind the bodies of my kin and flew the rest of the distance to the portal that led to Europe, I fought off the thoughts bombarding me. Everything could wait. Me fighting my own kind, Fane finding living sand and using it like some sort of earthly squid, and me guilty at having killed Ezra. None of it mattered now.

I felt Fane's lagging heartbeat against my chest and increased our velocity. I needed to get us out of here and to a place where I could tend to her.

The urgency cutting into me was desperate and left my chest burning with it.

Finally, the portal came into view, a vertical swirl of white clouds. Without pause, I dove into it and glided through the light, that expelled us above Europe.

Fane had the information on where we were booked in and I had no idea where she kept it, so I had to improvise. I headed straight for the Black Forest, and the cabin I had used in the past.

Chapter Twenty
Fane
The Surface,
the Black Forest

Swaths of red and black was all I saw. Thick and sticky. There was no sense of time, or my body, as I drifted through nothingness. For a moment, my thoughts nudged at a strange question. If I died, would I go back to Hell? No, Demons didn't have a soul. Once dead, we were gone. Which meant I wasn't dead. Right?

Alive. The thought resounded through me and I clung to it. *I am alive.* Next was waking up. I fought my way through the thick fog permeating everything, time and reality lost to me. A strange vibration rattled my world and I concentrated on it. It was a warm rattle, something familiar, and it came from… my chest?

I found my breath and as my chest expanded, I felt it, the warm vibration seated on it. It wasn't heavy, but steady. Small touches repeatedly dabbed my collarbone. Gentle, grounding. Very slowly, I fought past the red and black clouds, heading straight for the familiar hum, feeling it, welcoming it.

My eyes blinked open and for a moment I thought I was still looking at black clouds, but then the black moved, and a sniffing snout came into view, crowned by glorious red eyes.

"Kasha," I croaked.

The cat mewled softly in answer, interrupting her purring for a second, then she reached out a paw and dabbed it on my collarbone. The Hellcat was sprawled over my chest like a sphinx, regal as ever. Her purring had woken me.

I smiled at her and tried to lift an arm to stroke her head. Sharp pain laced through my side at that endeavor, and I winced.

"Slowly, Demon," a dark voice drawled. "If you don't want to rip open the wound, keep still."

I turned my head to face the direction of the voice and there he was. My Angel sat next to me, his elbows perched on his knees, his chin resting on his knuckles. He looked strange, gaunt and strained.

"You look like shit," I rasped.

He smirked, but it looked strained as well. "Likewise."

"How long?"

Mihr lowered his folded hands and leaned forward in his chair. "One day and one night. You... nearly died. I had to resuscitate you more than once."

"You mean we kissed? And I wasn't present? That sucks."

This time his smile was a tad warmer and more natural.

"Explains the pain in my breast-bone, though." Apart from my left side, I felt multiple thrumming injuries, including my chest. Right below where Kasha lay, a dull agony throbbed, beating alongside my heart.

I shifted a bit and groaned. "Should be a fast recovery from now on," I said, my breath hitching with pain. "I don't heal as fast as you do, but much faster than an average Human."

Mihr nodded. "You want something to drink?"

"Please."

He got up and walked from my view. I heard glass clinking, then water running. The Angel came back carrying a glass filled with water. He bent over me and cradled the back of my head with his hand to help me rise a bit, then he tilted the glass to my lips.

I took a few gulps and groaned with a mixture of relief and discomfort. The water was cool and slid down my parched throat in welcome waves, but swallowing hurt in my chest. To distract myself, I locked gazes with Mihr, relishing the feel of his palm digging into my hair and his pretty face being so close. His storm-colored eyes were intense and filled with an array of emotions that confused me. I couldn't place exactly what I was looking at, but it hurt. It was like looking into an open wound and I gave him a slight nod.

Mihr pulled the glass back and placed my head down gingerly.

I let out a gasp and a sigh, even drinking had been draining. "You regret saving me?"

He placed the glass on the bedside table and frowned. "Why would you say that?"

"As I have said before, you look like shit and your eyes are filled with agony. Is it regret? Or something else?"

The Angel sat back down, resuming his position from earlier. "It is regret, but it has nothing to do with you. I could never regret saving you."

I bit the inside of my cheek when I understood. "It's because of the fight. You had to kill your own kind to protect Hellspawn. I can imagine that'd do your head in."

He didn't answer, but the way he looked at me was enough of an answer.

"If you want to leave, I understand," I said. "We are even now. You don't owe me a thing." I sucked in a shaky breath. "Would you have fought them if you were alone?"

Still there was no answer, only that tortured look.

"So that's a no."

"They shouldn't have been there."

"But they were, and you had to make a choice. It's okay if you regret that choice, and it's okay to hate me for it. A little."

He huffed out a dry chuckle. "I don't hate you, Fane. Not even a little. But I should." He leaned back and rubbed his eyes with his knuckles. "I should have given your whereabouts to Michael, I should have yielded to Ezra back in Heaven, I should have done a lot of things I didn't."

"Well, I should have let you die back in that desert. And I should have corrupted Dax and Cam the moment I was summoned to the surface. We both have decided not to do things we should have done."

He crossed his arms, making his muscles bulge. "Yes, but for me, you are the cause. I didn't do what is right, because of you. And I don't know why. It's eating away at me, yet I can't seem to help myself."

I raised a brow and lifted my right hand slowly, until I reached Kasha's black ears. Her purring doubled in volume, reverberating in my chest. "Letting yourself be emptied of all that makes you you, is the right thing? Having me meet the same fate to learn how to defeat Hell is right? Killing Kasha for bonding with you is right? Are you trying to tell me that?"

"It would have ended the war."

"And then, Mihr? What comes after victory over the underworld?"

"I don't know."

"Humans will always sin or live righteously, and their souls will always need a place to be reborn. Heaven will take those righteous ones, but what about the rest of them? Where will they go? Does your Lord even have a plan for them?"

"I don't know."

"What about the way Michael was so eager to have your insides turned out by the Seers? Don't you think that's a little strange?"

"I DON'T KNOW!" Mihr shouted. "I have no fucking idea. I used to know. I used to be sure and steadfast. I knew what was right and what was wrong. I *knew*. I don't anymore. You are fogging up my damned head and I have no idea what to do about it." He tugged at his curly hair with both fists. "You should not exist. Demons should not be able to love. Your kind is supposed to be evil to their very core. But you are not."

His words hurt, but seeing him fight himself to the very foundations of his belief, his existence, hurt even more.

"I have lived a lie, I have killed, suffered, seen loved ones die – for a lie." He bent over, his face in his palms, his big body trembling all over.

I sucked in a breath and pushed myself up. Gritting my teeth, I didn't let up until I was sitting upright. Kasha slumped down into my lap, never stopping her purring. Spreading out my hand, I leaned over and ran my palm over his hunched shoulders. My body pulsed with pain all over, my heart raced, and my breath was short after my little acrobatics, but I pushed all of it aside. "I'm pretty sure not many of my kind love anyone, so that mistake is easily made."

Mihr glared at me through a few locks tumbling over his face. "Don't laugh at me, Fane."

"I'm not. Hell is filled with assholes, scum, and bastards. Sinning Humans go there for a reason, but I don't think that makes any of us inherently evil. Just like being an Angel doesn't make you inherently good." I rolled my eyes. "Exhibit One, Michael."

"You don't know him."

"I know assholes, and he is one. Besides, anyone who tries to kill you is an asshole in my book."

I let my fingers run circles over his left shoulder, stopping here and there to squeeze softly. "I understand what you are feeling. It has to be confusing as shit. And if you want to leave, I really get it. But I'm also thankful that you are here. You saved my life, and Angel or Demon, saving a life is always the right thing to do."

"That would make killing always wrong," he said.

I let my palm run up to cup his face. "Why do you think we don't have an afterlife? None of us deserve it."

"You truly believe that?"

"Yes, I do." I stroked his cheekbone with my thumb. "We are all part of a war that has devoured both our kinds for millennia. How can any good come of it? All of it will end one day, and no one will survive it, not even this world."

Mihr reached up, covering my palm with his. "Maybe to fight each other is in our nature."

I laced my fingers with his. "I don't think so. But what I do know, is that this war has cost too many people too much."

The Angel pulled my hand from his face and held it with both of his. "That is true. Rest now, Demon. You need to heal." He placed my arm back on the bed and got up.

****

"This isn't the hut we booked, is it?" I asked hours later, hobbling from the bedroom into what looked like a kitchen, living room, and dining room all in one. The floor was wood, so I swayed more than I should have, but the walls were concrete and I steadied myself against one. The kitchen was on the far side, the cupboards were made of a dark wood, and the appliances looked old and well used. Between the kitchen and the couch in front of me was a dining table that seated four. The tablecloth was fabric shrink wrapped in plastic. The ends rolled up to either side of the table like pieces of glossy parchment.

Mihr sat on the huge leather couch that was coming apart at the seams. He had gotten a fire going in the hearth to my left and looked a little better than the last time I saw him.

Kasha, who exited the room behind me, mewled and trotted over to him. With a leap, she was on his lap and pressed her head into his chest.

Mihr scratched her behind the ears then pulled his fingers through the fur on her back. The cat trudged around in a circle, then plopped down in his lap.

"No, it isn't," Mihr said. "I had no address and no time to search you and find out where we should be heading. Besides, I think the people renting to us would have run for the hills if I had dropped down at their doorstep with you half dead. At the very least, they would have called an ambulance, or the cops. This was safer."

I let go of the wall and stumbled my way over to the couch, the floor creaking with each step I took. Holding a palm to the wound on my side, I eased down onto the leather.

"Well," I huffed, the pain robbing me of breath for a second. "As long as no one knows where 'here' is. Not even Michael, right?"

"No one," Mihr said. "I never told a soul when I came here."

"So, here is what I don't get." I leaned back until my back rested against the couch, hissing all the while. Once situated, I lounged there, very careful not to move a muscle. "Why did you feel like leaving your plane and coming here, alone? I mean, didn't you have a place to stay up there? Like a home?"

"I did. I have lodgings in Cyrisas, all to myself. It has a spectacular view over the holy city and the hills beyond. But sometimes, I liked to come here, where there are seasons, where I could lose myself in day-to-day labor. Like cutting firewood and keeping this hut from falling apart. The owners… they seemingly have all but forgotten about it."

"You come here to relax?"

"Mostly. Especially after battles. When I was a child, my parents took me to the coast of southern Africa, where we spent downtime after their battles. I learned early on, that getting away had a very calming effect. It has something to do with being totally alone, or feeling like it, anyway. After they died, I looked for a place to be alone somewhere else. I found this. It is nice to have a hideout." His eyes were drawn to the fire and he stared into it. "Having a place where I didn't have to look over my shoulder all the time."

I wiggled my nose, feeling an itch coming on. "Why would you have to, in Cyrisas, I mean?"

"I am a born Angel, decorated, a hero of many battles, yet, I have never achieved the status of Archangel. To become one, you have to be ambitious, be well regarded in the high society, and have good rapport with the other Archangels etc. Other than Michael, I never cared about becoming one. And I have never been ambitious when it comes to recognition. I know what I can do, and I am good at it. For me, that was enough. But in the past few hundred years, the politics have changed for the worse. There is a lot of intrigue and backstabbing going on. Because of my feats, I am regarded as a threat among the contenders for the position of Archangel. It means, I am constantly watched, bad-mouthed, and excluded." He shrugged, "One day, I just decided to remove myself from the equation. I come here to get away from all of it from time to time, and when I'm back, I don't socialize."

The itch got worse, and I scratched the top of my nose with an index finger. "That sucks. But it does explain your lack of knowledge."

He looked at me, a crease appearing between his brows. "What lack of knowledge?"

"To have fun. You're like a shriveled-up peach, Geraldine, sweet but dry."

The crease deepened. "I know how to have fun, and I am not... a shriveled-up peach."

I grinned at him. "I will test that at the nearest opportunity." With a sigh, I tilted my head back and closed my eyes for s few seconds.

"Why do you do that?"

"What?"

"Call me women's names?"

"Hmm." I chuckled and stopped short when pain laced through my side at the motion. "In the beginning, it was to take the scary out of you." I cracked a lid open and looked him over. "You are pretty intimidating, you know. In my head, it helped to make you a bit more harmless. Plus, I thought it would rile you up and annoy you."

"And now?"

I closed the lid once more. "Habit. It's turned into an endearment of sorts."

"You are full of shit, Fane."

Both my eyes popped open. "Why, Mihr, most incandescent of all Angels, your language leaves much to be desired. What's with all the swearing today?"

He made a curious sound, something between a chuckle and a grunt. "It's just been that kind of day."

I reached out and placed a hand on his lower arm. "You okay?"

He looked at my hand on his skin. Red on tanned white. "I will be. You?"

"This?" I waved up and down with my other hand, encompassing my whole body. "I'll be right as rain tomorrow. As I said, I need a bit longer to heal than you."

"You have never been trained to fight, have you?"

"Nope. Garbage kind of Demon, remember? Too weak to bother with training."

Mihr was still studying my hand on his arm and it felt a bit awkward, I had no idea if he wanted me to take it away or not. But as he didn't shrug me off, I decided to commit to it. I would sit here, feeling the glorious flutter in my lower belly that came with touching him until the sun came up if needed.

"It would have helped, though. Back in Heaven. Launching living sand at people may be a neat trick, but can you do it down here?"

I clicked my tongue. "Don't think so. Remember when I encased the Angels in Portsmythe? It took all of my energy. When I fought with the living sand, it was a symbiotic thing, much easier because the sand had the ability to move of its own accord. It still took the oomph from me, and being impaled didn't help."

"If you make a weapon for yourself, I can try to teach you the basics, just in case."

I blinked at him. "You… would teach me?"

"If you wish."

"Yeah, I fucking wish." I squeezed his arm repeatedly, excited. Had my body allowed it, I would have launched off the couch and done a little dance. I have never had the knowledge or the means to protect myself, other than with words and manipulation, the chance to learn made me giddy. And I would fashion my own weapons.

Mihr gave me one of his rare laughs, making a warm shiver run through me. "You have that demented goblin-look on your face again. It's about making your weapon, isn't it?"

My weapons would be the epitome of awesome, and Mihr – arguably one of the best warriors Heaven had to offer – would teach me.

"Hell yeah, it's about making my weapons, Cirilla. Would you be a dear and fetch my ingots?"

Mihr smiled mildly and covered my hand with his, making lighting shoot through my belly. Astounding how his touch alone had such an effect. "Tomorrow, Demon. You still need rest. Are you hungry? I did go out and got some stuff while you slept. Not that you need it, but I know how much you like to eat."

"Yes, I am always hungry."

"Gluttonous Demon," Mihr said and hiked Kasha from his lap to mine and got up.

"Wisecracking Angel."

Chapter Twenty-One
Fane
The Surface,
the Black Forest

I woke in the morning, giddiness making my bones sing. To my disappointment, Mihr had insisted on sleeping on the couch, deeming the bed too small for both of us. Personally, I thought he was trying to keep his distance in order to stave off the desire he felt for me, but I didn't tell him that. He had enough messing with his head as it was. But I wouldn't be myself if my good intention wasn't about to melt away the second I laid my eyes on him.

This time, the bed hadn't been as scary, or rather, I had been gone the moment my head hit the pillow. But maybe knowing that Mihr was only a door away had also made me feel safe. Maybe.

Stretching and yawning, I sat up and blinked at the ray of sunlight poking through the ripped curtains. The morning sun winked through a canopy of huge trees, whose branches swayed in a lazy breeze, welcoming me with tiny waves. At least, that was what it felt like. I smiled and got up, then took inventory of my body. My side had healed fine overnight, and the rest of the cuts and bruises were all but gone. Even the wooden floor was not throwing me off. I only had to steady myself once as I tip-toed to the door and stuck my nose into the living room.

The heap on the couch, consisting of wool blankets, messy dirty-blond curls and patches of naked skin was very inviting. But my conscience held out. I blew Kasha a kiss, who lay curled atop the Mihr-heap like a cherry on a sundae, and I silently braved the distance to the bathroom door.

I was helpless not to smirk at my reflection once I closed the door behind me. Today, I would fashion my own weapons. Mine. A thing that had been forbidden to me in Hell. What would an Ember even need weapons for? We were sculptors, sculptors who had to obey our Maester's every whim and wish. Weapons would have been too much of a temptation. It wasn't like the one or other lowly Demon had never attacked their Maester, but nonsense like that had always been swiftly crushed and ended with a severed head. And never the severed head of the Maester, no.

But weapons of my own? Infused with charms? By me? My smirk grew into a very cocky, self-assured, toothy grin. I wouldn't even have to be a great fighter to defend myself.

My belly felt like an ocean in a storm, I was so excited it nearly tilted into nausea territory. I blew out a breath through puffed-out cheeks and hurried through a very human morning routine.

When I slipped from the bathroom, the Mihr and Kasha sundae was gone from the couch. Instead, he stood in the kitchen, his back to me, while Kasha – I swear she had grown over night – sat on the counter and ate from a bowl.

I sauntered over, placing my steps with care the further away from the walls I ventured. Mihr was busy with something and I nearly lost my footing when I saw that he was only wearing jeans. Jeans that rode very low on his hips. He had the most scrumptious over-ass-dimples I had ever seen, and they prompted me to lick my lips. If I ever got him to lose control and jump my bones, I was going to bite those.

He rolled his head from side to side, the ends of his dark-blond-curls brushing the tops of his muscular shoulders.

"Coffee?" he rasped, nearly making me jump out of my skin.

I stumbled a little but steadied myself against the dining table. "Sure."

Mihr fiddled with what I guessed was the coffee machine for a few seconds, before mumbling beneath his breath. I took a few steps further and stroked Kasha, who didn't even look up, busy as she was gulping down her food.

"Hunk of human junk," Mihr said and knocked on the top of the machine that came into my view as I sidled up to him.

"This is the on button, right?" He pressed it without effect. "And I added water and coffee. Why isn't it working?"

I had to stifle a laugh when I spied the power cord lying beneath the outlet, useless and disconnected. With one step, I closed the gap to him and bumped him with my hip. As predicted, he shrank away fast. I reached for the power cord and plugged it in.

"Try it now. Most things work better with a little juice." I winked.

He glared at me. "You're kidding me, right?"

"Not at all. Juice and/or lube," I clicked my tongue and touched my thumb to my index finger, spreading the rest out straight, "does the job every time."

His nostrils flared and I wasn't sure if he was trying not to laugh or about to choke on a retort. I bent over and clicked the machine. It roared to life with the subtlety of a steam engine.

I bit my lip when my gaze swept to his very close, very naked abs, and the line of dark hair that vanished into those low-riding jeans. If I wanted to entice him to lose control, I was doing a bad job. At this rate and my wandering eye, I was going to decide to screw that, and him, sooner rather than later.

****

Mihr and Kasha watched me from the couch, the Angel sipping his well-earned coffee, while the cat was cleaning herself. Mihr had thrown on a shirt, depriving me from perusing him further. But I guessed it was a good thing that I wasn't too distracted for what came next.

I sat on the floor, next to the suitcase and rummaged through it for my ingots. When the phone fell into my hand, I pressed the 'on' button but nothing happened. Looked like the battery had given up between worlds. I pulled the cord, including the socket adapter, from the side of the suitcase and plugged the whole deal into the nearest wall outlet. I couldn't wait to call Cam and Dax, to tell them what had happened and gush about my new weapons.

Speaking of which. "What the...?" I pulled out the ingots and ogled them. A skin of gray-white sand covered them. It sang in my palms, tickling my skin, obviously happy to be held by me.

"Yeah. About that..." Mihr cleared his throat. "Looks like your living sand decided to follow you into this realm. At least a small part of it."

"This is… dope!" I scrutinized the sand and drew a finger over it. To my amazement, it followed and slid into my palm, where it pooled into an excited mass. Like sand on a subwoofer, it sprang around, vibrating with joy. "Un-fucking-believable."

This time, fashioning the steel and infusing it with pieces of meteor was almost done in a trance-like

244

state. The sand rushed over my hands and up my arms as I worked, adding itself to the metal in my hands at intervals. As the sand got less and less, I heard and felt the blades come to life in a mind-blowing way. It was like singing without sound, a feeling of tension and energy. An energy I understood because it spoke to my very instincts.

Eventually, I looked down at two curved scythes. Small and light, enough to allow fast and precise movement, but sharp enough to do major damage. The charms I scratched into them would need no words to work, I knew that. But these blades would only listen to me. Their magic would only come to life in my hands. It made a sensation of pride sweep me up, the likes of which I had never known. *Mine*. And infused with living sand from Heaven.

"You are positively glowing," Mihr announced from the couch.

I looked up. He had obviously not moved. His gray eyes a touch darker than the sand inhabiting my weapons.

"But just like in Heaven, the sand makes your veins white, instead of lava-like."

Grabbing one scythe, I looked at my fingers holding it and saw that my veins did light up in white, while my skin turned from red to oily black.

"Freaky. I like."

I placed the grip on the top of the scythe to measure and to my utter shock, the handle of my weapon slunk into the wood, expanding inside of its own accord. I blinked once, and my weapon was done. Quickly, I did the same for the other, flabbergasted as I got the exact same result. "Wow."

"You ready to try them out?" Mihr asked.

"Hell, yeah." I got up and followed him to the front door. As I stepped into the midday sun, I gasped at what I saw. A small clearing in front of the house extended into a dirt road, surrounded by large trees as far as my eyes could see. I smelled the pine and forest and filled my lungs with the slightly moist air. It smelled fresh, mixed with the smoke from the fire in our hearth inside. Countless sounds hovered through the forest. Birds sang and wind whistled as it rustled through the trees. From somewhere further down the hill we were situated on, came the gargling of a small creek. In the distance, hills and mountains rolled endlessly, all of them covered with vast mixes of greens. The atmosphere was one of utter solitude without a feeling of loneliness, and I knew exactly why Mihr loved coming here.

The ground was soft and almost bouncy. I stuck my naked feet in and realized that I had to dig in deep to even reach the earth. Leaves and pine needles covered a good portion of the ground, making it weird to walk and stand. It looked like earth, but I couldn't feel it easily.

Mihr cleared his throat at my side, pulling me from getting lost in our surroundings. "We will start with a few basics." He pointed at my scythes, "You won't need those yet."

I pouted, but placed them down on a wooden block that looked like it was used to cut firewood.

"Now, fighting Angels is different from fighting Demons, mostly because Angels will attack from above and not all Demons have wings. If fighting my kind, you will have to adapt a stance that makes it easier to protect from blows from above, as well as changing directions fast." He placed his right foot in front of the left, adapting a wide stance, then he bent his knees slightly and turned his torso sideways slightly.

I mimicked him.

With a quick shove, Mihr had me stumbling to the side. "Nope. Not there yet."

"Hey! I wasn't even ready," I sulked and dug my feet in once more.

"Okay, we'll try again. Let me know when you think you are ready." His gray eyes shone with mirth and I narrowed my gaze at him.

"Ready," I said, sure that this time he'd have a harder time of – my ass met the bouncy ground with a dull thud.

"I thought you were ready?"

I sprang back up and swiped some leaves off my butt. Not answering him, I silently readied myself then nodded at him once.

It was baffling how much thought went into the stance alone. After shoving me down a few times, Mihr explained what muscles to engage to be steadfast.

"You could have told me that before planting me on my ass," I said.

"True, but then you wouldn't know how fast a sloppy stance can kill you. Besides –"

"It was fun for you?"

He grinned. "A bit."

"Naughty Angel."

Mihr jerked his chin out, that grin still in place. "Again?"

"Hell, yeah."

Once he wasn't able to topple me as easily, he showed me how to switch positions fast, which was why the stance had to be wider than normal. Then we worked on blocking and warding off attacks from above.

My arms burned from holding them up over my head the whole time. It was a position they weren't used to. But I was confident that I would quickly get there, as my arms and hands were the strongest parts of me, due to my job as a sculptor.

Next, Mihr actually manifested his wings and swooped down at me, to show me how to drop down and out of reach at a moment's notice.

The first time, I didn't even move as I was staring at him in his complete stature, in awe. His wings were a tad darker than his eyes and there were four of them, two huge ones fanning out over his shoulders and two smaller ones beneath. When he spread them out and jumped into the air, I stood awestruck by his majestic appearance, my mouth hanging open stupidly.

Bam! He plowed into me, taking me clean off the ground and pulling me into the sky.

"You were supposed to duck," he chided mildly.

I wound my legs and arms around him. "Hmm? I was? Sorry." Shimmying against him a bit until I was perfectly positioned had him lose his own focus and we nearly hit a tree.

"Huh? Where is *your* concentration, Meredith?" I asked.

He groaned and hovered down. His feet touched the ground, but I was still hanging on like a sloth to a branch. Mihr unwound my legs and dropped me down. "Your tactics are unfair," his voice was a low rasp and sent the most amazing shivers through me.

I blinked, all innocence. "What tactics? You know I am afraid of heights."

He cocked a brow, but the corners of his lips twitched slightly. "Again. This time, duck."

I saluted, "Yessir."

My breath was ragged once we were done, and Mihr was somewhat happy with my dodging and steadfast stance skills. He did tell me I had a lot of work ahead of me, but I was not discouraged. At least I was learning.

"I think it best to teach you a few techniques to get out of danger when you have no weapons," Mihr said.

"You mean like if someone tries to grab me?" I waved him off. "I know those."

His dark eyes flashed once – all the warning I got – then he snatched me and turned my back to his chest. His large arm was around my neck and with the other he pinned my arms to either side of my body. "Get out of this, then," he rasped close to my ear.

Sheer panic overcame me within a heartbeat. I was back inside a memory, in a situation that I couldn't escape. Because he had ordered me to be still. Ordered…

I reacted purely on instinct. Instinct and a yearlong nourished fear of feeling this helpless. First, I slammed my heel down on his foot, then I bent forward slightly to surge back and hit the back of my head against his face. A dull crack told me I had met my target. His arms didn't let up though, and there was no way to turn and slam my knuckles to his nuts. My breath shortened and I started hyperventilating, a blood-curdling scream ripped from my chest and Mihr let go of me immediately.

I stumbled away and fell to the floor. Deep within my panic, I scrambled away from him as fast as I could. I dug my hands into the earth, ready to defend myself with any means at my disposal, but he hadn't followed. Instead, he walked backwards, his palms lifted in surrender.

My body shook and sweat broke from my skin as tremor after tremor raced over me and rattled my very bones. Dry sobs fought past my narrow throat as I tried to breathe and escape the panic clutching me.

"Fane. Fane, I'm sorry," his voice came from far away but it was level, not threatening. There was no aggression, no anger.

My throat opened and I sucked in a large breath. Slowly, my shaking subsided and I looked at Mihr. He stood far away, golden blood running from his nose and dripping down.

"I didn't mean to…" another breath, "I'm so –"

"You have nothing to apologize for, Fane. I do. I did not realize it would trigger this kind of reaction to grab you like that."

I stood on wobbly legs and dusted myself off. "It shouldn't have, not when it comes to you, at least. It's just…" I swallowed, trying to lock the memory of Lev down and out of sight.

Step by step, Mihr walked over, seeming to gauge my reaction with every stride. "You don't have to explain."

The tremors subsided and the fear dissipated as I looked at him. Nothing about him was aggressive. From the tips of his dirty-blond hair to his feet, there was nothing scary about him. He was not Lev.

I closed the distance to him and placed a palm on his cheek. "I'm really sorry about that. Let's go inside and I'll clean you up."

"It's nothing," he placed a hand over mine. "But you're right, we should go inside and call it a day."

As I got my blades and followed him, he turned to me. "We do have to work on this. You know that, right? I can show you how to escape, even someone as strong and used to pain as myself."

I swallowed once more. "I'd like that." A decision made my stomach plummet, but I bit my teeth together. "Maybe if you knew why… Would it help train me to overcome it?"

Mihr held the door open for me. "It can help. But as I said, there is no need to explain."

"If it helps, I will," I said and strode inside, going straight for the bathroom to wet a towel. I needed to clean up what I had done.

Chapter Twenty-Two
Mihr
*The Surface,
the Black Forest*

My Demon was quiet as she dabbed at the blood already drying on my face. The way her usually full lips were nary more than a tense line told me she was still dealing with the aftermath of her panic. Something I had done. It made me feel awful, but I couldn't have known. We were training. Still, I berated myself.

Fane wasn't angry at me though, and as much as I wanted to know why she had reacted the way she did – and kill the one responsible for it – I wrangled down my curiosity. And my wrath.

"I was in love once," she suddenly said. "He was a Demon prince, one of the rulers of the sixth ring. Our story isn't a happy one and I won't bore you with details, but it is important to know that I loved him. And he loved me." She swallowed and swiped the towel over my chin softly.

"The problem was that in order to be together, he had to buy me, which meant he owned me. Thanks to him, I was able to add many clauses to my ownership contract. Something that not many lowly Demons can say." Fane bit down on her lower lip and scrunched up her face. "The reasons why he let me add them were for my own protection, from him. He loved me, but he was a Demon prince, used to having his way, used to taking it if met with resistance. At first, our relationship was like any other, we couldn't get enough of each other, we

253

blossomed. But our love was an inferno, and we also fought a lot. He started to end the fights by ordering me to accept it, or to stop arguing. He would regret doing that later, but he couldn't stop himself in the moment."

Fane let the towel sink and wrung it in her hands. My reaction surprised me, as I envisioned the 'Demon prince' she was talking about to be the towel, but in *my* hands.

"I came up with the idea of adding clauses to my contract that would bind him from doing and ordering certain things. He denied me, telling me that he would work on himself, that we didn't need those because we loved each other. Surely, our love had to be enough?"

A sad smile played on her lips and she looked up, meeting my eyes. "You know, sometimes you meet someone you fall for, but you bring out the absolute worst in each other?"

I nodded, knowing relationships could be like that.

"That was me and Lev," she continued. "It got worse gradually. He didn't change for the better, and neither did I. I became a vindictive bitch, asserting my dominance over everything and everyone that was lower than me, while Lev's paranoia and possessiveness grew to new heights. It went so far that he physically restrained me from leaving an argument one day." Her skin bled to oily black within seconds, making her amber eyes stand out crassly. "He held me like you did just now, and he… he ordered me to stop fighting back. I had no choice, I was helpless not to obey his wishes." The towel in her fingers made a ripping sound as her knuckles whitened.

"He threw me down and ordered me to not move. When he was about to take me, I asked him to stop. I told him that I loved him and he wasn't himself. He stopped. I think it scared him half to death what he almost did to me, and he agreed to add the clauses for my protection." Fane proceeded to rip off tiny pieces of the towel, as if it was a paper napkin. "Still, to this day, it apparently triggers something in me if I am grabbed like that." She tilted her head looking at me, her oily skin shining in the light of the flickering fire. "It wasn't about the pain he caused me, or the betrayal I felt, it wasn't about almost being used against my will. It was the utter fucking helplessness I felt. The fact that I could do nothing to stop any of it." A bitter chuckle shook her. "Story of my life. I was never in control of my own fate, and in that moment, I felt it more than ever. There I was, helpless against the one person who was supposed to protect me from harm, like I would do for him. And I couldn't move a muscle. I had to resort to pleading and begging." A look of utter disgust flashed over her face, "Pathetic."

A scratching sound made us both jump and when I spun to face the door, Kasha sat before it, dabbing it with a paw. She proceeded to meow demandingly, then scratched the wood again.

Fane got up and opened the door for her. The Hellcat blinked at the outside but stayed in her sitting position. The Demon pushed her up and out with one foot gently. "Get out, you devil. See if there is something worth hunting outside." She closed the door and came back to the couch.

I gathered up the pieces of towel strewn all over the old leather and held it in one fist.

"Now you know," Fane said, plopping down next to me. "Will it help to teach me?"

"You sure he's dead?" I whispered, not trusting myself not to growl if I didn't.

"I am. He died in my arms." Fane's skin slowly lightened to its usual red, but her eyes now shimmered with tears.

I grunted in answer. It was hard to swallow what I thought. That it was his luck he was dead, because I felt like ending him. That I couldn't figure out why she had loved him in the first place. Did she still?

"Well?"

"Well, what?" I asked.

She lifted a brow at me. "Will knowing help you teach me?"

"I suppose." I got up and walked to the kitchen. No idea why, but I felt that I had to move around. Pacing back and forth a few times, I fought the urge to rip the fridge from its place and throw it across the room. The aggression inside me had grown over the course of her story and it was peaking now.

"Mihr, you're acting weird," Fane remarked from the couch, watching me.

"I am?"

"What is wrong?"

I threw the pieces of towel into the trash. "Wrong? Nothing is wrong." Truth be told, I seldomly got angry. The rage bounding through my entire being was like a fire I couldn't douse. Plus, I had no idea why her story had upset me so much. I resumed my pacing, clenching and unclenching my fists.

Fane got up and warily came my way. "Mihr?" She placed herself in my way and I stilled.

"What is it?"

"I can't…" White, hot wrath burned through me. "How could he even…" my voice was an unrecognizable growl.

Fane reached out and took one of my fists in her hands. She unclenched it and squeezed my palm. "You are angry on my behalf?"

"Of course, I'm fucking angry," I rasped. "No one has the right to do what he did. I can't believe…"

"What?"

"That he loved you. Has to be bullshit. No one in his right mind would –"

Her amber eyes flared when she pegged me with a hard stare. "He did. But that is not the issue here. I didn't tell you so you could get upset on my behalf. It is in the past. *He* is in the past. I told you so you could help me fight whatever makes me panic."

"You sure?"

Fane frowned. "About what?"

"About him being in the past."

"Wh… what does that have to do with anything?"

I shook my head. "Nothing. And you're right, you told me so I can help you." In that moment I wish she hadn't, as truth bombarded me with unwanted facts. I was angry because none of it should have ever happened to her. I was livid because that piece of shit had claimed to love her while abusing her, and I was jealous that she'd loved him despite all of it. *Jealous.* Yes, there it was. The root of the scalding wrath. Had I not still been fighting the urge to destroy the fridge, I probably would have laughed. Desiring her was one thing, but I felt something for her. Something I definitely shouldn't.

"It will help, though," I said. "Your panic seems to stem from losing control, from having choice and power taken away from you. I can show how to get out of any situation like that," I bent forward, so our faces were only inches apart, "and I will make sure you always have a choice. You will never be helpless again."

My Demon pressed her lids shut in response, in an expression I couldn't quite read. "I'm guessing you're wrong on the choice side, Angel," she whispered. "But I'm flattered that you got all dark and broody on my behalf." She stepped into me and drew my arm around her. Her head nestled to my chest, she pressed her entire body to mine and hugged me.

I wasn't sure how to react, but to reciprocate. We stood there for a while, just hugging, and it felt… right. Her being this close to me felt good. My heart hammered in my chest, now more in response to her proximity than the anger from before.

"Thank you for telling me, it couldn't have been easy."

"The only one besides you who knows is Cam," she mumbled against my chest. A tiny shrug made her shoulders rise. "I haven't thought of this instance in a while. The memory kinda surprised me, like you did."

"Well, I am sorry about that."

"And I am sorry for breaking your nose."

I sighed. "I'm sure you'll break it again, once we start to practice."

Her hands began to stroke up and down my back, squeezing my muscles here and there. A shiver danced over my skin, sprouting out from where she touched me. I inhaled her unique scent of smoky sandalwood and my head spun from it. I needed to get out of this hug now, away from her electrifying presence and her sensual scent.

Clearing my throat, I unwound myself from her hold, only to see her face, sporting a naughty grin. "Won't be long now, Angel," she said and winked.

"What won't be long?"

She eyed me up and down, then bit her bottom lip. "That's a surprise." She motioned turning a key in her lips and throwing it over her shoulder. "You hungry? I could eat the whole fridge."

"Good thing I didn't throw it through the room, then," I said. "And yeah, why not? I could eat something."

We ate the sandwiches Fane had made in a tense silence. My realizations concerning her and the hug that had turned… strange, heated the atmosphere. And without Kasha to distract either of us, our gazes met and wandered, then met again and held.

It was a kind of tension I hadn't known before, as my body felt drawn to her almost physically, while I tried hard to not act on it.

My eyes fell to her lips, moving as she chewed, tiny crumbs of bread sticking to them. Once done with her sandwich, she proceeded to lick her fingers clean, never breaking eye contact with me. It resulted in me nearly dropping what was left of my food.

"Do you think Kasha is okay on her own?" I asked to fill the silence and disperse the tension.

A small, knowing smirk tugged at the corners of her lips. "She's about the size of a big Jack Russel now, she will hunt things twice her size." Fane gathered the leftover crumbs from her plate with an index finger and stuck it into her mouth. She looked at me and pulled the finger free, giving it a cheeky lick when she did. I stifled a grunt at the sight.

"During this stage, she will do two things, eat and grow. She has to hunt. We won't be able to feed her all that she needs." Fane drew her brows together. "How far away are the next Humans?"

"About three kilometers, why? Would she attack them?"

"Don't think so, but she is too big for a house cat." Fane waved it off. "Worst that could happen is she scares the pants off some unsuspecting Human."

The Demon got up and gathered our plates, then walked into the kitchen and placed them in the sink. She stood still for a minute and gradually her shoulders bunched up.

"You okay?" I asked.

She mumbled something that I couldn't hear.

"Pardon?"

Fane turned, leaning her butt against the sink behind her, she crossed her arms. "I said you're a pain in my ass."

"Why?"

She huffed out a strange sound, somewhere between a chuckle and an annoyed groan. "Doesn't matter. You ready to try the grabbing thing again?"

I raised a brow at her. "No, I am not, and neither are you. We will do that tomorrow." I unfurled from my chair and prowled closer to her. "Why am I a pain in your ass, Demon?"

Fane uncrossed her arms and fiddled with the seam of her shirt, the red skin of her taut belly blinking through like a beacon. She tilted her head to one side and scrutinized me with a thoughtful look. "I'd like to fuck you."

I had to swallow once to hide my surprise. Careful to keep my face empty, I placed my elbows on the kitchen counter and leaned my body into them. "If you are trying to shock me, it's not working. I am used to your crudeness by now. Also, I have no idea why you would need to do so." The heat pooling to my lower body half made it hard to keep a straight face. Apparently, I liked her crude words.

Fane fiddled some more with her shirt, this time I spied her belly button. "I'm not aiming to shock you. You asked why you're being a pain?"

I nodded.

"This is why. You're just so damned… steadfast. Nothing makes you lose control. I was planning on goading and teasing you until you did and jumped me, but at this rate…" She blew out a breath, stopping her fiddling. "Will you ever be inclined to look past me being a Demon and find it somewhere," she glanced at my crotch, "in your body to do me? I just wanna know if there is even a chance, Mr. Stoic."

Very slowly, I straightened, rounded the kitchen island and came closer to her. I didn't stop until I loomed over her, our bodies a hair's breadth from touching. Reaching around her, I placed my hands on the sink on either side of her and bent forward until my mouth was close to her ear. "You know very well how much I am fighting for control, Demon," I whispered. "Since the moment I first saw you, there was desire, and in that motel room? I was this close," I let my nose barely graze her neck, "to carrying you from the bathroom and throwing you on the bed."

A tremor went through her. "W-why didn't you?" *Did her voice break?*

"Because it isn't right. We shouldn't complicate things by getting involved. You are a Demon, I am an Angel, what kind of future would there be?"

A snort came from her and she looked up, making me retreat a bit. "I'm trying to fuck you, not marry you. There is such a thing as sex purely for fun and to release some steam, you know that, right?"

"Yeah, I know. But I also know that if I go down that road with you, it will hurt us both."

She frowned, "What is that supposed to mean?"

"Means that neither of us would be able to simply 'fuck for a good time' as you'd no doubt put it. This," I wagged my index finger back and forth between us, "is dangerous. Think about it, Fane. You like being with me and apparently, I get jealous because of someone you used to be with. Granted, that guy was a… different story, but it doesn't change the facts."

She blinked at me. "Are you saying you think we'd develop feelings? That's why you're resisting so hard?"

I bent closer, so our foreheads almost touched. "Can you deny it? Could you make love to me and not feel a thing?"

Her nose crinkled when she grimaced. "Ugh, you are taking the heat right out of it. *Making love*. What a cringefest."

I gently took her chin into my hand and tilted her head up, so she had to look at me. "Can you deny it, Fane?"

Her grimace faded and those amber eyes seared into mine, catching me with their depth. I wanted to lose myself in them, in her, but I knew I was right. Yet, even as I tried to make her think on it, my own control slipped, and the thought of 'why am I fighting this' resounded through me.

She was too close, that was my fault. Why had I left my side of the kitchen? Almost touching her, feeling the heat of her skin through my shirt, it was nearly too much. I'd only have to lean closer, and she would be trapped between me and the sink. An overwhelming pull drew me to her, as if someone had slammed hooks into my chest that she reeled in.

Fane licked her lips, her chest heaved, and her pulse looked like it fluttered, as her veins became subtly visible. Fire entered her eyes and I fought to stop myself from surging down and kissing her.

But even as I struggled, thoughts shot through me like lightning. What would she taste like? How would she react to me? What wicked depths of passion would she take me to?

With more willpower than I knew I had, I straightened and let go of her chin and the sink.

Just when I wanted to step back, she closed in. "I can't deny it, no." The tips of her breasts brushed against my chest as she rose on tiptoes." But what if I didn't fucking care?" she whispered, inches from my lips.

I could almost hear my control snap.

Chapter Twenty-Three
Fane
The Surface,
the Black Forest

With a growl, he surged forward, taking my lips as if he were conquering them. I couldn't help a victorious smile when our lips clashed and I threw my arms around his neck, digging my fingers into his locks.

His kiss was heat, and as his arms came around me and he picked me up, I opened my legs and locked my feet behind his back. I groaned when I felt his hardness right at my center. Something crashed to the floor when he whirled me around and sat me on the counter opposite the sink.

His big hands dug into the muscles of my back and I marveled at the power they held. It felt desperate. Desperate for me.

I licked over his bottom lip then nipped at it, eliciting a coarse moan from both of us. His lips parted and with the first velvet swipe of his tongue against mine, I almost melted into a puddle right then and there. I undulated my hips against the bulge of his jeans, needing pressure.

Our kiss deepened even more, lighting my innards on fire, and then his hands skimmed over my lower back and sank into the curves of my ass. I squeaked in pleasure and pressed myself to him. He lifted me from the counter and stumbled across the living room, in the direction of the bedroom. But when I undulated my hips against him and sucked his lower lip into my mouth, he stopped, and a shiver raked over him.

I slid down his body, needing his skin on me with an urgency that was unusual for me. Grabbing his shirt, I tried to pull it over his head. He didn't lift his arms quick enough, so I ripped it apart with a growl. He tugged on my shirt with the same fervor, but I was quicker with lifting my arms and he pulled it over my head. For about a split-second he looked at me and I at him. Then our bodies met as if yanked together by an invisible force. My naked chest met his torso and tingles shot over my skin at the feel of him. I needed more hands. My palms roamed his torso, his back, his abs, his upper arms and chest.

Then I nestled at his pants. He pushed me back a bit and undid them within seconds, while I did the same to mine. A heartbeat later we were both completely naked.

He was mouthwatering. From head to toe. I would have liked to just stare at him, but he pulled me against him, wonder prominent in his eyes.

I hissed when nothing separated us and need, heavier than ever, sank into the pit of my stomach. So much so, that the craving for him was almost painful. We nearly missed the couch, but Mihr managed to plant his ass on it while I climbed onto his lap.

He groaned and his brows crinkled when I took hold of him and positioned myself over him to slide down. Right now, I needed to be joined with him, but I couldn't wait to explore him some more. With hands, tongue, and eyes. He was magnificent.

"Fane, are you sure?" he rasped, when my entrance met him.

"You're kidding me, right?" I gasped, out of breath. "You ask me this *now*?"

His palms cradled my face on both sides, his stormy eyes luminous as he searched mine. "I want you, Demon. All of you. And once we go on, I won't stop until we are both completely spent. Are you good with that?"

"Am I good… Hell, yes, I'm good with that."

"Good."

I kept watching his face as I sank down on him. His eyes widened and then snapped shut when he stretched me. Both his hands sank to my hips and he bobbed me up and down, until he filled me completely.

We gasped in unison when he was buried inside me to the hilt. For a moment, we stilled, our ragged breaths the only sounds in the hut.

Once more, his palms slid to my face and his fingers sank into my hair. He pulled me to him and kissed me with such tenderness and reined abandon, that I nearly lost it.

When I wanted to move, he held me still, making me receive his kiss. It conveyed what couldn't be put into words, and a heavy feeling took hold of my heart. It was a drowsy, sweet heaviness, expanding until my throat got tight. His lips slid over mine, and it felt like he wasn't so much kissing me, as branding my very essence. I felt tears breach my eyes as all I could do was receive the magnitude of what he was exposing me to. As if I had lived in the dark my entire life and was standing in the sun. That was what it felt like. Warmth seeped into every crack and crevice of my being, like warm and languid honey.

His thumbs stroked at my tears and when he started moving, I nearly screamed into his mouth from the overwhelming sensations shooting through me. My body seemed out of my control, as did everything inside of me. I was lost, clinging to him with feverish longing, trusting him to tether me.

Finally, he drew back, leaving both me and my lips devastated. My Angel leaned back, drawing his hands down my neck, over my collar bone and cupped my breasts. I arched my back, pressing my breasts to him, while slowly sliding up and down.

The slick feel of him inside me was divine and I rolled my hips slowly, savoring every minute sensation that came from being joined to him. All the while his gray eyes roamed me, my body, my movements. His huge chest heaved with heavy breaths and his muscles clenched in response to every snap of my hips.

Light as feathers, his fingers skimmed down my stomach and lower. One hand bit into the outside of my thigh, while the thumb of his other vanished in my folds, searching until… "Fuck! Right there," I rasped.

Changing my angle slightly so I rubbed myself against him had me almost seeing stars, while he groaned, his sinful voice deep and sexy. *How did an Angel get a voice that was made for sin?*

Every thought vanished from my mind and I cried out when he wrenched me down on him, moved his thumb and jerked his hips up. If he did that move only a few more times I was going to – a moan tumbled from my lips when he did it again. The feeling was so intense, my gaze lost focus, and a steady half-growl, half-cry vibrated from my throat.

Mihr lifted my ass up slightly and I tilted over, my hands grabbing hold of his pecs. His arm circled my lower back and sank into the flesh of my butt, then he powered into me. A yell tore from me when my body strained, every muscle clenching, then releasing all at once. I barreled into the most spectacular orgasm I have ever had, convulsing and shivering as my body shook with it. The feeling seemed to last forever and Mihr helped me stretch out the sensation until my body went slack. He stilled, cradling me to his chest, as aftershocks racked me. My breath was on fire, and my heart drummed against his chest. I nestled my face into the crook of his neck, happy to just be.

When my breath and heart steadied, I undulated my hips and smirked at his moan. Starting with small licks and nibbles, I worked my way up his neck, while moving on top of him. My hands sank into his hair and I tugged at it softly, letting my kisses wander to his jaw, then his groaning lips. I swallowed the sounds escaping him, stealing them from him. His fingers pressed into my thighs almost painfully when I mimicked the sliding of him with my tongue, mirroring the rhythm.

"Wicked Demon," he rasped between kisses.

I straightened with a giggle, scratching over his pecs, leaving red lines as I went. He hissed, his luminous eyes turning as dark as his wings were. His face was a work of art as it reacted to each move I made. There was heated abandon in his gaze, his lips swollen from my harsh kisses, his neck filled with my marks. I watched all of it with satisfaction. A primal feeling engulfed me at the sight. As though my love bites belonged on his body, as though he belonged to me. I had no time to analyze the feelings or the thoughts following it, as he suddenly grabbed my knees and turned us, so I was the one half sitting on the couch.

Mihr lifted my legs so my feet stuck out over his shoulders, then he curled his hips into mine. A surprised moan left me as he sank even deeper into me than before. His gaze turned dark with scorching lust and a shiver ran through me. He looked like a fallen god, his dark beauty overwhelming. And when his wings manifested, shadowing us both with their sheer size and grace, I gasped in awe of him. He truly was a Heavenly being. Too magnificent to comprehend.

He bent down low, stretching my legs until his mouth met mine. He ravaged my lips with a scalding, passionate kiss that made my head swim.

"More," I growled.

A chuckle, warped with lust answered my demand, "Hold on, Demon."

My nails clawed into his back when he let loose and took me with a rawness and power that left me with nothing than to lay there and receive. I had been right. Once unleashed, his passion was a blast of abandon. I met each thrust with wonder and equal need. A tingle rose in my belly, letting me know that a second orgasm was not far off.

"More," I demanded again.

****

Mihr

She was everything I'd dreamed about and more. Like a liquid flame, she singed me with each movement, with each slide and touch. My skin felt like it was doused with flames, burning over my entire being with a ferocity I had never known. She was heat around me, against me. Her scent a fire in my nose, her taste like a drug. In that moment I knew I'd never get enough of her.

Fane watched me through heavy lids, her amber eyes burning with Hellfire. Forbidden and enticing. Just like she was. Her red skin was slick with sweat, her full lips inviting, her breath fast. The way her veins subtly turned orange, pulsing with her inner fire, left her body with a roadmap of intricate beauty.

Her eyes glinted with need and a growl with a second demand of 'more' had me nearly hurtling over the edge. I pressed my lids shut for a second to regain control. But I was happy to oblige.

Shrugging her feet from my shoulders, I wound my arms under her lower back and lifted her up, then I bent forward until my fingers curled up to hold her shoulders.

Our faces only a breath apart, I slammed into her deeply. She bit her lower lip, her eyes losing focus for a moment. Her chin tilted up, her expression lost in the beautiful sensation of utter surrender, and I let loose.

Fane screamed my name as my movements grew frantic. I felt her clench me inside her, her nails scratching at my back with little bites of sharp pain, and a yell escaped me as I lost myself in her.

Spent and huffing, we both clung to each other. Our heartbeats synched, their rhythm fast and heavy before slowing again. I pushed myself up on my elbows and cupped her face with both my hands. I still was hungry for her and kissed her softly.

She moaned in response, reciprocating in kind. Languid, lazy, and deep. Our lips and tongues merged in a slow dance, her taste the most delicious thing I had ever experienced.

The pads of her fingers stroked over the dents her nails had left in my skin, impossibly soft and soothing. My wings folded together, and I pulled them in, making them disappear. The fact that they had shot out in the first place was a sign of how much I had lost control.

I slumped to my knees and picked her up, so her legs encircled me, and we were both upright, never breaking our kiss.

With one hand, I held the back of her head and she groaned, "That will kill me one day," she whispered hoarsely.

I smiled, adding a bit of pressure to my fingers, eliciting a sound close to purring.

A second later, it was my turn, as she sucked my lower lip into her mouth and stroked it with her tongue. Goosebumps erupted all over my skin and a shiver raked me in response.

"I could taste you forever," she rumbled.

"And I could stay inside you forever," I answered.

A sigh floated from her. "Wicked Angel."

"Hey, that's my saying."

A laugh shook her, and she hugged me close, nestling her face into the crook of my neck. Never in a million years would I have pegged her to be this affectionate and warm.

"And? Was I right?" I asked, knowing that – for me – I was. The stupid happiness bouncing around in my chest, a testimony of that. Holding her felt right, being joined with her had felt right, kissing her was… like a stab of joy straight into my heart. It shouldn't be. And it was unnerving. I couldn't feel what I clearly did, not for her, not for anyone. I should be numb to all of it by now. But I clearly wasn't, and I couldn't help but wonder if any of this would end well.

"Well, it was certainly something." Fane pulled back and fixated me. "Blew my mind. Twice."

"So, not again?"

The smile fell and a derailed, almost shocked expression grew on her features. "Are you crazy, Regina? Now that I know what's in store, you won't keep me off you."

"Where does that leave us?"

Fane tapped the tip of my nose with one finger. "Fucking each other to death, of course. Not a bad way to go, if you ask me. You have to admit, we are spectacular together."

"We are," I agreed. "But we can't just –"

"Shush, your tasty mouth," Fane said, lowering a finger to my lips. "Let's just… enjoy each other for the moment, okay? I'm not ready to dissect it. Not yet."

My eyes roamed her face and as much as I wanted to argue, to talk it out, what I saw had me hold my tongue. Fear. Fane was afraid of what she felt. It was in the subtle twinge around her lips and the way her gaze didn't linger on mine for long.

"Okay. Fucking each other to death it is," I said. I couldn't help myself and added, "But don't go falling for me while we do, Demon."

She snorted and smiled, but the corners of her mouth trembled, and her eyes stayed the same. Scared. "I'll do my best."

Fane pressed a palm to my chest and made me sink back. I let her push me until I lay on my back, the subtle heat of the fire behind me fanning over my shoulders while she crawled over me like a predator. "Now, hush, I have exploring to do."

"Me too," I protested.

The Demon smirked and littered my chest with kisses. "Later," she whispered in between licks and nips. "First, it's my turn."

Her hands and mouth skimmed over me as she explored me from top to bottom, making shivers dance beneath her touch, while my muscles clenched as if begging to meet her attention. Like tuning an instrument, Fane worked my body, eliciting hisses, groans and tremors as she went. In no time at all, I wanted her again and she smiled wickedly when she noticed.

"You are truly magnificent," she said, making her way down, down, until her nose grazed my hip bone.

"Every," a lick stroked up the V-shaped muscle between my hip and groin, "last," her breath cooled my wet skin making me twitch, "part." She held my gaze as her mouth closed around me.

I nearly jerked up in response, a deep moan breaking free of my chest.

"Mhhhh," her voice vibrated around me and I balled my fists to keep still. She let go of me and licked her lips. "We taste good together." A devilish smirk flashed across her face, then she went to work on me until I was sure I could hear the Cherubs sing her praise.

When I filled her sweet mouth, she watched me closely, Hellfire burning in her amber eyes.

Chapter Twenty-Four
Fane
The Surface,
the Black Forest

My entire body felt heavy and used in the most delicious way. My bones hummed with utter bliss and my skin – where it touched his – felt alive and tingly.

I had no idea how many times we had lost ourselves in each other, but flashes of his eyes meeting mine while his tongue burrowed into me, the sound of his moans, the way his body moved on me, danced through my inner eye and I shimmied closer to him. The constant need to touch him didn't subside, not even now, when the windows lit up with morning sun and the sounds of birds singing floated into our perfect little world.

"You okay?" his voice was coarse and warm, and his fingers stroked over my shoulders in soothing circles.

Draped across his chest, I took inventory of my very relaxed limbs. "Yeah. Dunno if I can walk, but yeah. I'm good. You?"

"I –"

A loud mewl and claws scratching the door interrupted him. Mihr groaned, hugged me once and moved out from under me. He got to his feet and stopped at his clothes for a second. To my dismay, he pulled on his boxer shorts. Then he took the wool blanket from the couch and draped it over me. I smiled, finding humor in his modesty. Kasha was after all a cat, she didn't care about our nakedness.

The Angel opened the door for her, and Kasha sped inside, proceeding to wind around his legs, purring happily as she went. She had grown again, reaching his knees by now, and small, black horns started growing over her ears.

"Had fun?" Mihr asked her.

He got a loud meow as answer, and I chuckled, sitting up. "That makes three of us," I mumbled.

"Huh?" Mihr turned to face me.

"Nothing."

The way his gaze snapped to my naked shoulder made me pull the blanket down lower until he swallowed visibly. "Cheeky Demon," he growled.

Kasha sat down, her red eyes lingering on me with an unreadable expression. I stuck my tongue out at her and she reacted by starting to clean herself.

With limbs like rubber, I struggled to my feet and dropped the blanket completely. I heard Mihr's breath hitch, and satisfaction radiated through me.

"I need a shower," I announced. "You are welcome to join me."

His fists clenched at his sides. "You know we'll never leave the bathroom if I do."

"True. Is that a 'yes'?"

He gave me one of his rare smiles. "No. One of us has to have a little self-control. I'll make breakfast. After this night, I feel like I need human food."

I winked and blew him a kiss, then stalked to the bathroom. While busy with my shower and brushing teeth, I avoided thinking about last night. I wasn't ready to analyze the feelings bounding through me, or what being close to him was doing to me.

"Not ready," I whispered to myself. Because he'd been right. There was no such thing as just fucking each other. Not for us.

"Damnation." I got dressed quickly and stopped to stare at my refection for a moment. "You are screwed," I told myself. "In more than one way."

Blowing out a breath to calm my tingling nerves, I exited the bathroom to the smell of coffee and eggs.

"Almost ready," Mihr called from the kitchen when he saw me, then he turned to the sink, presenting me with a mouthwatering view of his muscular back and spectacular ass. I nibbled at my bottom lip. I still hadn't bitten into those dimples. *Scrumptious.*

To keep myself from stalking over and doing just that, I glanced around the room and my eyes fell on the phone.

I tugged it away from the charger and tried the 'on' button again. This time, the screen lit up. Once the little bars told of a connection, pings went off in rapid succession. My eyes widened as messages came through. Twenty-four. All from Cam.

I opened the chat and cursed.

"What's wrong?" Mihr asked, carrying a steaming mug over to me.

"Cam," I said. "She…" I scrunched up my nose, reading her messages. "She got a message when we didn't turn up at the rented place. She tried calling and texting for a while. Then —" I gasped, "some weird woman came to their house asking about us." I glanced at him. "She freaked out, left Dax with a friend and bought a plane ticket."

I'm coming, Fane, read her last text. That had been last night.

"She is coming here, or rather… to where we were supposed to be."

"What?" Mihr's brows shot up. "Is she crazy? After someone asked about us?"

I frantically dialed her number, but it went straight to voicemail. "She has to be flying by now." I let the phone sink. "We have to go there, Mihr."

"Meeting her will put her in danger, you know that, right? If anyone followed her…"

"I know."

A loaded silence followed my words, and our eyes locked. Mihr nodded after a few seconds. "Let's go."

****

We hadn't taken much with us. Mihr's sword was fastened to his belt and my new scythes were tucked into my pants. I hung from Mihr's chest, his arms circling my torso, and I periodically felt the metal of my weapons. They sang at my touch, calming my frayed nerves somewhat.

The forest and small towns we passed didn't register with me as my frantic mind drummed up possibilities and scenarios.

Wind whistled past my face, stinging my cheeks with its chill and making my eyes water. Kasha's paws occasionally nudged my ears, as her limbs stuck out way past Mihr's neck by now. Soon, she'd be flying by his side.

I tried to envision her in all her grown Hellcat glory, mostly to steady my staccato heartbeat and spiky anxiety, but the image was soon swapped for another. A vision of Cam walking through these very woods, followed by a figure shrouded in shadow. Who had come to them? How did they find them? Mihr had made sure Angels couldn't trace us.

An ugly suspicion scratched at the back of my mind, but I pushed it aside. Firmly.

278

I pulled the phone from my pocket and studied the screen. "Has to be up past this hill. In the valley beyond," I yelled over the wind.

My belly lurched as Mihr dove down in the direction I pointed. Clenched as my innards were, it was a highly nauseating feeling, and I fought with the urge to gag for a moment.

"There," I said and gestured at a lone hut across the valley, halfway up the hill, surrounded by a thicket of trees. Clutching my stomach with one hand, I tucked the phone into my pocket with the other.

Mihr swooped down, landing in a tree to the side of the hut. I scrambled from his grip, my eyes searching the hut and its surroundings below us. All was quiet. No cars, no people. Nothing.

"It's too quiet," Mihr whispered.

I listened for any kind of sound and agreed. No birds, no other animals, not even a gust of wind made any sound at all. The silence was heavy with a tense foreboding and I tried swallowing past the knot in my throat.

A scent hit us, and I nearly fell off the branch as my body stiffened in shock. Sulfur, ash, and roast. The smell of Wanderers.

"They are here," I whispered.

Mihr gave me a nod, his nostrils flaring as he smelled them, too. "How?" he mouthed.

All I could do was shrug as I pulled my scythes from my belt.

"No," Mihr mouthed, his expression stricken. "Stay here." He gestured for us to wait and watch.

My entire body thrummed with fear, but it felt wrong to just sit here and wait. Somewhere down there was Cam, being held by a bunch of Demons, probably. I needed to know.

I started to climb down when Mihr's hand grabbed my upper arm. "Wait. We can't just rush in."

"I need to feel the earth," I told him. "I need to know where they are and how many."

His mouth a thin line, he picked me up and jumped from the branch. Silently, we floated down and as soon as my feet met the forest floor, I kicked off my shoes and sank into a crouch. Digging my hands and feet through the leafy and mossy surface, I felt for earth. Almost like an electric current, a zap went through me when my skin connected to my element. It felt like it had been a long time since I'd felt it.

Concentrating, I let my senses roam through the ground, searching the immediate surroundings and farther. To my right, hiding in a small underground tunnel, a group of mice had bundled together, shaking and fearful of the evil they felt lurking on the surface.

Feet walking. A group of them. Sharp claws and hooves, muffled by the leaves but still prominent.

"Fifteen Demons," I whispered. "Going down the hill. They are heading for the village in the valley."

"How many Humans are in the village?" he asked.

I closed my eyes and concentrated, but it was too far away. The river flowing through the village made it impossible to make out any movements from up here. "I don't know," I said.

"Then we have to go down there, now," Mihr whispered.

Fear gripped me. They were fifteen, we two and a half. We'd never make it out alive and if we did, I would be back in Hell and Cam was fair game. The woman who had asked her about me had to be a Demoness, since a herd of my kin was trampling through the valley as we spoke. They knew about her.

"No. I have to find Cam," I said. "Us going down there won't make a difference," I added when his incredulous eyes found mine.

"Are you serious, Fane? You are just going to let a group of Demons lay waste to a human village?"

My brows rose. "We are hopelessly outnumbered, and we both know I'm no real help in any fight yet. Also, we came here for Cam, and I will not rest until she is safe."

His face hardened as he stepped back, a look I had never seen before took up space on his features. Not even when he saw me for the first time, back in the Deep, had he ever looked at me like that. Disappointed, angry, sad. Spears of pain laced into me, and I felt all the air vanish from my chest as a result.

"You'd pick one life over many?" his voice was filled with acid.

"It's Cam. So, yeah," I pressed past my steadily closing throat. "What good would it do if we died for a few strangers? Cam would still be in danger, and these Humans would still die." I pointed to the valley. "There are too many, Mihr. Please understand."

"Oh, I understand, Demon." His knuckles whitened by how hard he grabbed the hilt of his sword. "No matter how much you tell yourself that you are different, you still can't do the right thing."

"Which is what? Dying? I am not about to put my life on the line for a couple of strangers, and neither should you."

His scalding glare felt like a physical punch.

"Mihr, I am a Demon. I never told you any different. You are the one who hasn't changed, you'd charge into certain death because a life of war has told you it's the right thing to do. It is not. Come with me. Please."

"I'm a fool," he rasped. "A fool for thinking... after everything, Fane."

My mouth opened and shut a few times, no words passing the monumental pressure in my throat, as I understood that he *couldn't* turn his back on those people in the valley. It was impossible for him.

His glare was a scalding mix of anger, sadness and disappointment. "I know right from wrong. And I hope one day, you will too." My Angel shook his head, then sprang into the air to barrel into the village below. Kasha looked from him to me, then bounded off with flapping wings, chasing her chosen warrior.

"Fuck," I mumbled, torn between going after him and walking to the hut and checking it out. Maybe Cam had hid in there. *Unlikely*, I thought. Still, I had to see for myself. I had to find her.

As quick as I could, I braved the distance, the leaves covering the ground rustling softly under my steps. I reached the hut and peeked into the window. It was small and looked absolutely empty. I got out my phone and tried her number once more, but it went straight to voicemail, again.

I cursed and hung up, glanced at the road leading into the valley and back at the phone.

A bloodcurdling cry echoed from the village, the sound zinging through me like an electric shock. Crippling fear zapped through me and my heart thrummed in my chest as though it was about to jump ship. My body acted on its own as my feet carried me past the hut and to the road. I had to force myself to stop, then I shook my head.

"The Hell am I doing?" I grumbled and felt for my scythes. "Bloody Angel." I was not about to let him die. Not alone. Springing into a jog, I began my descent of the hill, running toward my death as if I was keen to meet it. Over three hundred years of living would have to do. At least, I had found someone worthwhile to die for. As my heart swelled with heaviness and pulled at my body, I knew one thing to be true – there were no longer only two people I would die for. I had finally gone and done it. I was falling for a good guy.

Chapter Twenty-Five
Fane
The Surface,
the Black Forest

I hadn't made it halfway, when wingbeats sounded behind me and I was whisked off the ground. I screamed and glanced up. For a second, I froze completely – which was my mistake – as I met Maeve's eyes. She gave me a chilling look, threw me up and caught me so her arms circled around mine, pressing them to my sides in an almost bone-crushing way.

"What the hell, Maeve? Let me go!" I squirmed and tried to pry myself free.

"Be still, Fane. You are finally getting what is coming for you," she hissed past the wind as she leaned into a turn and sped away from the valley. Over the hill with our rented hut we went, hurtling away from Mihr and the village at breakneck speed.

"What is going on, Maeve?" I yelled.

"I'm taking you home, that's what's going on."

We passed two more valleys while I screamed bloody murder and fought for a way out. Unknown wrath consumed me, right next to stunning waves of panic. I had to get to Mihr. Now.

Without warning, Maeve let go of me, dropping me down over the pebbled ground of a riverbank. My knees buckled and the air got knocked from my lungs as I rolled over the stony ground. I wheezed, trying to get up while fighting to breathe.

Maeve glided down a few paces away and my wheezing grew frantic when I saw fifteen Demons exit the forest behind her. My naked feet on the pebbles confirmed my suspicion. These were the same Demons that had made their way to the village. But what were they doing here? Had they already killed Mihr? No, that couldn't be, not without him killing any of them.

I hacked and forced my body to straighten, grabbing hold of my scythes with each hand. They sang at my touch, a sizzling only perceivable to me. Welcoming me. Infusing me with a confidence I was nowhere near feeling the right to have.

I coughed. "Why, Maeve?" Without a doubt, I knew she had to have been the one asking Cam about me.

My former roommate scowled at me, before she spat on the ground, her red eyes shining like illuminated blood. "Why? Seriously? You tricked me into helping you free a fucking Angel from the Deep." She looked me over with absolute disgust. "You said you'd talk to it. Make it free you. But you freed it. If I had known, I'd never have helped you. Do you have any idea what *He* did to me?" She shook subtly and bared her fangs at me, "Of course not. Maybe you didn't know, maybe you didn't care. But none of it matters now, once I bring you back, He'll free me of this." She tugged at a metal band circling her neck and I gasped when I recognized it as a penance band. Lucifer only dealt those out to the ones who'd truly wronged him. They were excruciating to wear, and he could dial up the agony they dealt to the point of unprecedented suffering. Wearing one meant wishing for permanent death. What was more– similar to some of the cells that had kept me in the Deep – it was made from Lillithium. Even across the distance I could smell its bitter and acrid scent. Dead stone. Unnatural.

A mean smile spanned Maeve's cheeks as she drummed her nails against the hilt of her sword, pacing over the pebbles with crunching steps. "And once Lucifer is done with you for stealing his Angel, Lord Ragon will have you back." She shrugged, "What is left of you, at least." She snapped her fingers and the group of Demons she'd brought along began clearing a patch of ground from stones. A circular patch. Shock slammed into me as I understood. They were opening a portal to Hell.

"You know, Lord Ragon had your contract nullified while you were gone," Maeve said. "Once you are back, there will be nothing protecting you, not that you'll care, after Lucifer has had his fun with you." Her face twitched with stark panic. "Nothing will ever matter after that," she whispered, more to herself.

"I'm sorry for what happened after I left, Maeve. I never meant for you to be punished on my behalf."

"You just didn't care, right?"

"Would you have?" I asked in return.

I was met with a silent glare, answer enough for me.

I inclined my head once in understanding. "Where is Cam? And Mihr?"

Maeve frowned. "You are about to receive the ultimate punishment, yet you still ask about a Human and an Angel?"

"Some things are more important than the threat of immediate suffering. Tell me. It's not like I can do anything about either." Slowly, I dug my feet deeper into the pebbles, pulling at the stones the other Demons cleared. Subtly, the pebbles rolled back here and there, slowing them down.

Maeve gave me an evil smirk. "Your Human is probably still wondering where she misplaced this." Maeve got Cam's phone from her pocket and waved it back and forth before sticking it back. She clicked her tongue. "Regarding your Angel… We have had a squadron following us since Emerald Falls. I think I made out Michael amongst them. They didn't attack. Not even when we lay waste to the village back there. My guess is, they thought we'd bring them to their lost Angel. Which is right, of course. They are surely lying-in wait for him."

"How? We can't kill Humans."

Maeve glared at me. "The way you left Hell obviously gave Lucifer and idea." She waved a hand at the Demons behind her, "All of them have been blessed. We used an Angel I found behind a bar in Portsmythe. We were following up on a big energy surge – or the Ember with us was – and we stumbled upon an Angel encased in metal and sand. I knew it was your work immediately and that we were close to your Humans. All I had to do was search for a woman named Camille who had a son called Daxter. I obviously found them."

"But if you are blessed, that means you are free. You don't have to go back."

Maeve tugged on her Lillithium collar and I noticed that each of the Demons was wearing one. "Not likely," the Fury said. Then she continued drumming her nails on her hilt. "But back to the Archangel. We spied on their group a little and heard some things. Michael is quite pissed at your Angel. Something about him blaspheming the holy realm by taking you there. Is that true? Did he take you to Heaven?" Maeve kicked a pebble in my direction and it hit my shin.

"Thank you," I said, carefully opening the floodgates to the rage brimming on my mind. I'd need it.

"For what?"

"Telling me."

Maeve huffed. "I did it so you'd know just how much your actions screwed you over. You fucked up the minute you used me to escape. I will see to it that you'll live through Lucifer's torture, and through Ragon owning you." Her features morphed into a hateful mask, making any guilt I was tempted to feel evaporate. "You will live and know only pain, and that you failed, causing the death of the freaks you care about so much. Maybe I'll even make a trip back to Emerald Falls, who knows?"

It wasn't hard letting myself be swallowed whole by anger. The question was – would it be enough?

My skin erupted with fire, burning away my clothes that fluttered to the ground in bits of glowing fabric. Hissing where they touched the surface of the river behind me, they added to the melody of the gargling water and the sound of the stones scraping across the bank.

"You will not touch him," I growled.

The Fury laughed. "And what are you going to do about it? Ember? I could snap you in half with no effort at all."

"I invite you to try." Turning one foot, I sent a wave of power through the bank and the stones around the Demons clearing them flew up like a blanket of gray pebbles. Grunting with the effort it took, I concentrated on my anger, pulled them together and made them twist into a maelstrom.

The stones hit the bodies in their way like punches, making the Demons yell and roar, as the wave of rocks herded them closer together. I stomped my other foot and the twisting wave crashed over the whole group, burying them. Sinking into a crouch, I dug my hands – holding the scythes – deep into the bank. With an ear splintering crack, followed by a rumble that shook the ground, the earth cracked open beneath the Demons and they slid into the depth helped along by tons of gray pebbles.

Sweat ran down my forehead as the scythes in my hands sang with power, doubling the effect of what I did.

Cries, claws scraping over stone and rumbling earth, mixed into a melody of panic and pain as I buried them ever deeper.

One, two, three, and four bodies shot from the earth-maw I had created, all of them Demons who could fly.

By now, Maeve had recovered from her surprise and sprang up alongside the other four Demons, out of reach of my power.

Turning my hands as though I was screwing a lid shut, I twisted the very earth over the maw, closing it over the lamenting mouths and crunching bones.

I felt them being crushed, felt their skin rip, their hearts pop and their black blood flow, as I ground eleven of my kin into paste.

Agony laced through my entire being and dots of black danced along my vision as I shook my head to clear it and struggled to a stand. Swaying like a piece of straw in the wind, I set my eyes on the five Demons above me and fought to hold onto the grips of my scythes. I doubted very much that unleashing what I just had left me in any kind of fighting condition. To be honest, I felt close to vomiting and passing out. My stomach burned and clenched as though it was eating itself, every fiber of muscle I had seared with what felt like Hellfire, making it hard to even stand. I shook as tremors of pain raked me, tempted to succumb to the exhaustion I felt. But I could not. I needed to end this, I needed to get back to Mihr.

"Let's go, Maeve. Come at me you feathered bitch," I slurred, attempting the stance Mihr had shown me.

The Fury stared at me, her mouth slightly opened, as her wings kept her level. Two Ifrits, another Fury and a Wanderer hovered by her sides. They did look a bit worse for wear, but also pissed off beyond reasoning. Good, I clung to the rage I still felt pumping through my veins, willing it to ignite me once more.

"Get her!" Maeve yelled and her goons shot my way.

Wailing like a banshee, the Wanderer swooped down and my right hand lifted in a snap. The blade bent to my will as it elongated and softened until it whipped through the air, snapping right through the Demon. Blood rained down as the two halves of the Wanderer landed on either side of me, the sound a sickening combination of wet skin and crunching stones.

My scythe-turned-whip curled, moving my wrist as if it had a life of its own. With shaking arms, all I could hope was to hold onto the weapons long enough to finish this. I felt the live metal hum in my palms, and knew it would protect me as long as I was connected to it, as long as I was conscious.

The Ifrits – having seen the fate of their comrade – circled me carefully. In one move, they dove down, attacking me from both sides. I crouched down, but my hands moved up on their own, pulled by my weapons. I screamed when a claw tore through my shoulder, and another ripped open the skin on my back, but my scythes didn't let me pull away. Instead, my wrists snapped, making the metal sing through the air and before I knew it, two burning heads rolled over the bank. The rest of one of the Ifrits hissed and gargled as it hit the river, making steam erupt and glide over me.

Bile rose and I swallowed once, twice, to keep everything where it was supposed to be. Fighting my body into an upright position, I ignored the pain in my back and my left shoulder as best I could and looked up.

Maeve and her Fury companion stared at me from a distance.

"What are you waiting for?" I whispered. "I can do this all day."

My former roommate pulled her sword free and readied herself to dive at me, when her companion put a palm on her elbow. "Mistress Maeve, don't. Look at her, something is wrong."

I glanced down at myself and saw that my skin was pitch-black, streaked with white veins that pulsed in sync with my thrumming heart. This wasn't a color Embers took on, so seeing it would have to be a shock to anyone. It was the Heavenly sand in my weapons, something they couldn't know about.

"I have to get her back, or our Lord will have my head," Maeve snarled. But as much hate and drive as her face showed, there was fear in her red eyes. It was something I could use.

Pulling at every reserve I could muster, I straightened further and infused the metal in my hands with anger. Of its own accord, the whips coiled into the air like snakes, snapping at Maeve and her last Demon friend. With a sharp crack, one of the whips sliced into Maeve's chest, opening her armor and skin like it was butter.

Maeve yelled and nearly fell from the sky, but the other Fury caught her.

"I will kill you for that!" Maeve yelled, blood spurting from the gash in her chest.

"Let's go, Mistress. Please," the unfamiliar Fury begged, her fearful gaze glued to me.

Maeve screamed with rage and pointed her blade at me with a shaking hand. "This isn't over, Fane. I will find you. I will hunt you down. I will eradicate everything you love."

As she hollered and raged, the other Fury carried her off as fast as her wings would carry them both.

My legs shook and finally buckled, the changed weapons falling from my cramping fingers. I inhaled a rattling breath after the other, fighting for control. Losing consciousness wasn't far off, and I still needed to get back to the village.

Grunting, I wound the whips around my arms, to keep them there and started to crawl over the bank, back where we had come from. My skin had returned to its normal red and it took a while, but eventually the pads of my fingers grew black with blood as the skin ripped with my effort to crawl on. But I didn't care. I needed to get there.

My breath rattled and I felt like pieces of me were falling off and I was leaving a trail of flesh behind, but that was just my imagination, and the agony pounding through me like a group of Hellhounds on a hunt. The corpse of the Ifrit floated past me and I eyed the river. I remembered it flowed through the village, as well.

Cursing and grunting, I pulled myself down the bank and rolled my beaten body into the water. Immediately, my body became light as a feather and the current tugged at me gently. I floated and bounced along, deliriously happy with myself and the relief my body went through. If only the water ran faster.

For the first time in my life, I prayed and pleaded with anyone who'd listen that I wasn't too late. That I would make it back to him.

Chapter Twenty-Six
Mihr
The Surface,
the Black Forest

Ire raced through my veins, beat in my chest and thrummed in my ears. Part of me couldn't believe what had just happened. The other part chided, *Of course, it did, she is Hellspawn, after all. What did you think would happen?* I thought she cared, that was it. I thought that after… last night, things had changed.

I beat my wings faster and soared close to the treetops, my feet grazing leaves as I went. A scream from below had me speeding up even more. Swooping straight into the main street, I cast my eyes left and right, but all I saw was devastation.

Bodies piled up next to houses that had holes in their brick-walls as though wrecking balls had gone to town on them. Twisted faces, the horror of their last moments still starkly imprinted on their features staring into nothingness. Men, women, children, animals. All of them lay together in heaps of death.

How was I too late? And how had the Demons been able to kill them? They shouldn't be able to, besides, they had just taken off toward this village. The scream sounded once more and I ran in the direction. Skidding between two houses and vaulting over a small fence, I came to face an Ifrit crushing the life from a young woman.

"Let her go, vermin!" I yelled, brandishing my sword as I barreled closer. The fire-Demon snarled, its

295

pointed teeth of coals aflame. It dropped the woman, who sank into herself like a wet washcloth, then the Ifrit sprang into the sky and beat wings.

I sank down next to the woman and felt for her pulse, but there was nothing, she was already dead.

"Get back here and fight!" I roared at the Ifrit, but I saw it join the rest of the Demons, on their way into the woods. They seemed to follow... a Fury carrying a screaming and fighting Fane.

Without thinking, I spread my wings to follow them, my heart sinking straight into the pit of my stomach.

"She is on her way to where she belongs," a familiar voice said behind me. "And now, so will you."

My heart lurched and it felt like it was hitting my throat. I turned to face Michael and six other Angels. They were the ones who I had met in Portsmythe. Young, newly turned Angels. "This was a trap," I surmised, my eyes flitting around, analyzing. They were too close, I wouldn't get far, but I had to try, nonetheless. Before Fane was dragged back to Hell by her peers.

Michael smiled, looking as handsome and righteous as ever. The Angels around him didn't seem surprised at the death surrounding us. That was when I knew.

"You watched and waited, for me."

"Sometimes, one has to sacrifice a few for the good of the rest. Once you have divulged everything to the Seers, we will, no doubt, have the final victory." Michael and his warriors glided down a few feet.

"How could you? You waited and watched an entire village getting slaughtered, to get to me?"

"You are a rogue Angel. Capturing you takes precedence. Over everything."

I gaped at him. "Since when? Michael, you must see that what you are doing is wrong," I said, noticing Kasha sneaking up behind the Angels facing me. "We *never* sacrifice innocents. No matter what."

"It's a nice sentiment to believe in," Michael mused. "But really, all of this is your fault. Had you simply come with us, none of this would have ever happened."

"I would have told you everything I know," I said, my chest tightening with anger. "But you'd rather watch Demons level a village than trust me. Tell me, Michael, does *He* even know what you have been up to? Does He know of this?" I gestured around me.

Michael's eyes grew hard. "He said to catch you using any necessary means. You brought Hellspawn into the divine plane. How could you?"

I shook my head, ignoring his accusations. "There are lines we do not cross! I very much doubt the killing of these people was a necessary means. And He does not know, does he?"

"We didn't kill these people," Michael said.

"That is bullshit!" I grabbed my sword tighter and bent my knees slightly. "You lay in wait for me, so you saw everything happen. That makes you no better than the Demons you hold in such low regard." With a tremendous leap, I jumped up and shot into the air. Beating my wings backward before I turned, I headed for the forest, the hills where Fane had been carried off to.

As I had predicted, I didn't make it far. A hand closed around my foot and Michael swung me into the tower of the village church. My back collided with concrete and a dull gong vibrated through my body as I hit the bell, knocking it clean from the tower. The bell and I plummeted to the ground, but before I hit the bottom, I snapped open my wings. The bell pulverized the wall of a bakery below me with an ear splintering crash. Debris and dust rained down and coated my skin.

With a yell, I swung my sword and rose, coming up against one of Michael's Angels. "Arken!" I cried, turning my blade to black, before swiping the sword up. Just like with Ezra, it melted through the metal of the Angel's sword and bit into his skin. I tore my weapon free, decapitating my kin in the process. Unlike before, I felt no remorse as I watched the warrior fall.

One down, six to go. Speaking of which, I was surrounded within a few wingbeats. A circle of wings and swords formed around me, and I nodded at them. Right now, they were nothing but an obstacle, keeping me from Fane. Who I had left, who had begged me not to, who had known something wasn't right.

Swings rained down on me, but my superior blade made short work of theirs and before they knew what was happening, I had killed three of them.

Three to go. Something hard knocked into me from behind and I tumbled through the air, my wings straining to keep me flying. But just as I had caught myself, a body smashed into my side. Arms came around me and a foot connected with my jaw, making me see stars. In a heap of limbs and wings, I crashed to the pavement along with the other Angels. Before I could get up, my wrist was stomped into the concrete by Michael's foot. I heard my hand and wrist break and felt the blade being wrenched from my grasp.

"What is this? Huh?" Michael shouted, holding the sword to my face. "How did you get ahold of such a weapon?"

I spat out blood and heaved in a breath past at least four broken ribs. "I know the best weaponsmith in all three realms," I rasped. "And you just let her get carted off to Hell."

Michael stared at me, while the remaining two Angels held me down, their faces grim. "Doesn't matter now," the Archangel said, twirling my sword. "This is mine now."

Wrestling for control was about as successful as trying to lift a mountain. I was pinned down.

"Stop it, Mihr," Michael spat. "I am tempted to kill you on the spot as it is."

"Would be a shame if your plan to empty me was thwarted by your own hand, wouldn't it?"

A black blur tackled one of the Angels off me and I ripped myself free. The Angel Kasha had tackled screamed in agony and she slammed her claws and fangs into her face, ripping into skin and flesh. The she-Angel tugged at the Hellcat, resulting in chunks of her face coming off alongside Kasha, who was propelled through the air. My demonic feline stopped midair, her leathery wings keeping her airborne. She spat out a bloody muzzleful and roared as she dove at the Angel once more.

Using the surprise, I grabbed the laughable rest of a sword that I had demolished earlier and took a stance. Half of the blade was melted clean off, but it would have to do. My right hand was unusable, but I had lived and fought long enough to be equally good with my left.

Michael raised a brow at Kasha and the warrior she fought. "You got that, Pheydra?"

Pheydra screamed, but a 'yes' sounded through.

Turning their backs on Pheydra and Kasha, Michael and his last remaining warrior faced me. The Archangel smirked as he swung my blade – which was its normal color again – and prowled closer. "I don't want to do this, Mihr. Just give up and come with us."

"You will have to pry me from this plane, dead as a doornail."

His face hardened. "So be it."

The Angel to his right plucked two daggers from his boots and closed in on me, as well.

A gurgle and a feeble moan sounded from Pheydra and Kasha sprang up as the she-Angel slumped in on herself. Her eyes frantic, but her body lax. Looked like Kasha's venom had developed since Hell. She shot past Michael and his last warrior to crouch at my side. Her rattling growl had both Angels glance back.

"Looks like Pheydra didn't have it," Michael said.

Kasha snarled and hissed at him, her red eyes focused like laser pointers.

I breathed past the pain littering my body and the panic making my heart thrum like the wings of a hummingbird. The panic would have to go, but it was nearly impossible as images of Fane back in Hell tortured my inner eye. What if I was already too late? How was I supposed to get her back once she left this plane? *I'll find a way*, I thought. No matter where she was, I'd find my Demon.

I'd have to survive first, so I stomped on the panic and the pain, focusing absolutely on the task before me. *Two to go.*

"We got this, Kasha," I murmured.

The sound of wings had us all look up and my heart nearly stopped when another Angel swooped in, dropping Fane to Michael's feet.

I wanted to go to her, but stopped short when Michael held my weapon to her throat and shook his head. "What have we here?" he asked. "You should be in Hell by now."

My Demon was naked, drenched with both blood and water, her face gaunt and she looked near fainting, but her amber eyes found me. "It's a trap, Regina," she whispered.

Despite the situation and the horror creeping in on me I had to smile. "Using Regina twice? You're getting lazy, Demon."

Fane grunted and flipped me off weakly.

"She did something really strange," the Angel who had brought Fane said and hovered down until her feet touched the ground. "I watched, as you ordered, and she somehow opened the earth and killed most of the other Demons with it. Then she turned these," she held up what looked like whips at Michael, "into whips and sliced most of the rest into pieces."

Michael's brows shot up. "What kind of a Demon are you?"

Fane's head bobbed when he shook her. "Someone very special, blondie."

"You made this?" he asked, holding my blade to her face.

"Mihr, you gave over your sword? Rude. I made it for you."

"It wasn't exactly a choice, Fane," I said mildly.

Her eyes wandered to my crushed hand and her face darkened.

Michael shook Fane once more, his features irritated and pissy. "Answer me, Demon! What are you and how did you make this weapon? Does Hell have more of your kind?"

I surged forward but Michael clicked his tongue and held the blade to her neck once more.

"You really are a nasty piece of work, Archangel," Fane muttered. "And you can go right ahead and kill me, cause there is no way I am telling you anything."

He pulled her up, winding one arm around her neck, choking her from behind. "Don't worry, where the two of you are going, all secrets will be emptied from you.

301

And nothing will be left of you but the shell of your bodies."

My heart broke when Fane's eyes widened in panic. I had never shown her how to get out of that hold.

"Let her go, you, big, winged freak!"

I groaned when I recognized the voice. This wouldn't end well.

Cam strutted from behind the broken wall of the bakery, a gun pointing at Michael.

"What the hell are you doing here, Cam?" Fane cried, the panic on her features doubling. She pulled and wriggled in Michael's grip, but he didn't budge.

"I came for you, of course," Cam said, her aim still trained on Michael, unblinking.

"Who are you, Human? And why can you see us?" Michael asked.

"Let. Go. Of. Fane." Cam cocked the gun, her hands steady.

"What? This?" Michael shook Fane a bit. "What is this abomination to you anyway?"

Fane – pale with fear – nodded at Cam while snaking her fingers between the blade and her throat. The Human inclined her head once, some unheard message passing between them.

"She is my best friend, asshole," Cam said and pulled the trigger.

Chapter Twenty-Seven
Fane
The Surface,
the Black Forest

A shot rang through the valley, echoing off the hills and rolling through the village. The scent of gunpowder was subtle but there, and it tickled my nose with its sharpness. My overwhelmed senses clung to the scent, able to focus for a moment.

Next was Michael's laugh, shaking me as I was pressed against him. "You really thought that would do something?" the Archangel asked, then swiped the bullet from where it had hit his shoulder. With a soft *plink*, the metal hit the pavement and Cam's eyes widened. She pulled the trigger again, and again. The shots pierced through Michael's continuous chuckles, which rose to a roaring laugh, until Cam had no bullets left. None of them even nicked his skin and I watched with horror as my friend blanched, still pointing the empty gun at Michael.

"My turn," Michael said and pulled at the blade he held to my neck.

I grunted as my fingers sank into the metal and tore through it, pain ratcheted up my spine and nailed itself to the base of my skull. Had Michael not held me in an iron grip, I would have fallen to my knees from the agony. There was hardly anything left for me to give, but the blade that had rested on my neck tumbled to the ground, severed from both the tip and the hilt by my hands.

My world swayed and danced, losing focus as Michael's grip loosened a fraction. I heard his surprised gasp, then everything tilted off kilter as something rammed into the both of us and tackled us down. Blinded by pain and exhaustion, I found my nose suddenly pressed to skin I knew.

Mihr.

"Kill them!" Michael screamed beneath me, then the sound of punches erupted around me and I was jostled between the two fighting Angels. Being the cheese in the sandwich, I rolled with them as they grappled and fought, until Mihr wrenched Michael's arms to the side and gave me a shove.

I landed on a paved sidewalk, my nose crunching as it caught my fall. With what little was left of my strength, I flopped onto my back and groaned when the first thing I saw, after blinking tears from my eyes, where the two other Angels, looming over me with their weapons at the ready.

This had turned out to be a shitty day. But my beaten body was glad it would be over soon. I had nothing left in me and doubted I could even raise an arm in defense.

The hateful faces of the Angels came closer and they raised their swords, but before they could strike, something stepped over me, obscuring my view of oncoming death.

"No," I croaked, when I saw Cam's unmistakable curls as she faced the Angels.

"Leave her alone," my friend snapped.

With herculean effort, I managed to push my torso into a semi upright position as panic flooded me. My breath wheezed from me in laughable gasps and my heartbeat banged and fluttered behind my ears, letting my veins pulse inside my skull, feeling like they would burst at any second. "Cam, run," I rattled.

"No way, sleaze. I got you. No matter what."

Leaning on my left elbow I spied around her at the Angels, who looked a tad unsure receiving Cam's glare.

"Move to the side, Human," the male said. "She is Hellspawn. Dangerous. Let us end her."

"Listen, featherboy," Cam snarled. "Fane is my friend. She saved my life and the life of my son. I am going nowhere. If you want to kill her, you will have to go through me."

The two Angels shared a look, surprise written plainly on their faces. "What do you mean, she saved you?" the she-Angel asked. "She is a Demon. They corrupt, they don't save."

Cam widened her stance over me a tad. "This woman has been my friend for a year now and she threw my ex out on his ass when he threatened my son and me with a knife one night. He would have killed both of us, but Fane… she beat him up and threw him out. So, know that I am not moving. If you won't go through me, then I suggest you flap off to where you came from."

My heart swelled with both love for Cam and fear for her life.

"What are you idiots waiting for?" Michael yelled as he and Mihr rolled over us, their fight obviously having taken to the sky. Kasha swoped around them and swiped at Michael with her small paws where she could. The Archangel kicked at her, making the Hellcat swerve off and hit a couple of bushes. Then he punched Mihr straight in the chin, rammed his knee into his stomach and pushed him off to turn to our little group.

"Kill the Human if you must, but do it now," Michael hollered.

"Don't," Mihr ground out when he tackled Michael from the side and they both spiraled past us. "Remember what you are," he shouted as they both rose higher, their fight picking up speed. They dove at each other now, trading one or two punches and kicks, before parting and picking up velocity for the next attack. High up as they were, the sounds of them meeting grew louder each time, until their clashes echoed over the valley, the same as Cam's gunshots had before.

The two Angels facing Cam and me seemed even more unsure than before. Undecided and unmoving, they stood and traded glances with each other, before looking at Cam.

Behind them, Kasha emerged from the bush and spat out a leaf that had lodged itself in her snout. She glared at Mihr and Michael, then her head swiveled to us.

The booms from above grew ever louder, the distance from which Michael and Mihr now attacked further than before.

The Hellcat hopped from the bush and slunk over to us, sneaking up on the Angels. I desperately looked around for something that could help in this situation. If Kasha surprised the Angels, Cam and I would have to move fast to use it. Or Cam would. I wasn't sure if I was up to doing anything helpful. My eyes fell onto my scythe-turned-whips that the she-Angel had taken from me. They lay, curled up and shiny, a few pawsteps to Kasha's left. I pointed to them and looked at Kasha directly, hoping she would understand.

The Hellcat did not, as her gaze was trained on the Angels in front of her.

"Cam," I murmured softly. "Get me the whips."

A very subtle nod from my friend told me that she had heard and we both waited with bated breath.

"Kill them already!" Michael screamed from way up in the sky. His hollering was followed by an ear splintering boom when he and Mihr collided once again. I dimly wondered how much more both of them could take.

Still hesitant, the Angels grabbed their weapons tighter and stepped closer. Just when the male opened his mouth, Kasha leapt off the ground and landed on his back. She sliced her claws into his cheek and bit in the side of his neck. The man screamed and bent over, trying to grab hold of Kasha and shake her off. The she-Angel sprang into action and raised her blade to hack at Kasha.

"Now, Cam!" I yelled and my friend sprinted off.

The Angel hopped, cried, and turned with Kasha on his back giving the she-Angel a hard time to strike.

Cam slid over the patch of grass next to the pavement, snatched up my whips and threw them my way. They clattered down next to me with a metallic sound and my palm closed around the hilt of one. The whip came to life in my hand, making my overused power wake with the agony of someone taking a baseball bat to the back of my head. I screamed when my arm was raised and the whip curled through the air. With a deafening crack, it sliced open the wrist of the she-Angel who had finally found an angle on Kasha. With a yelp, she let go of her sword and the blade swished past Kasha by a hair's breadth.

The whip curled in once more before snapping around the she-Angel's neck. I pulled, wrenching the woman from her feet. Cam sped over, snatched the Angel's sword from the ground and pointed it at her chest.

Kasha was launched through the air, as the Angel had managed to shake her off, and landed to my right. She spat out a bit of flesh, her muzzle golden with blood.

The male Angel swerved to face us, but before he could take a step, he slumped to his knees, then keeled over, his face hitting the concrete with a dull crack.

"Good job, little one," I gasped at Kasha. The cat gave me a mewl and crouched next to me, her red eyes trained on the she-Angel.

The she-Angel who struggled in the hold of my whip, making me grunt and sending stabs of pain shooting up my arm from the movement. I gnashed my teeth to ignore it.

"Stop squirming, Angel," Cam said. "It's over."

"What did you do to him?" the Angel asked, eyeing her companion.

"Kasha is a Hellcat," I said.

"What does that mean?" she choked past the whip. Her voice was thick with panic and she started squirming again.

"Seriously?" I huffed out, spots dancing in my vision.

"This is my first time outside the compound, Michael hasn't taught us everything yet."

"Compound?" My confusion dampened the pain somewhat. My eyes met Cam's and my friend flitted in and out of focus as my body finally failed me.

"Hold still," Cam ordered and pressed down on the sword a little. "Fane, will her companion die from Kasha's bite?"

I forced my head to nod once. "Needs help now, or he's gone," I croaked.

"You heard it, Angel," Cam said. "If we let you go, you can take your friend and get him help."

Her struggling stopped. "You'd do that?"

I slumped onto my back and let go of my whip. "Go."

Cam kept the sword pointing at her as the Angel got up. She unwound the whip from her neck and stroked over her reddened skin. The she-Angel hobbled to her fallen comrade and dragged him to a stand, draping one of his arms over her shoulder. The man gasped, his face and neck mangled and torn up.

A whooshing from above had us all looking up. Michael and Mihr came plummeting down, the Archangel had pinned Mihr's wings with his hands and aimed him at the ground. I struggled to heave my torso onto one elbow, fear slicing into me like a razorblade.

"No!" I cried, knowing that even Mihr wouldn't hold out if stomped into the ground like this.

My Angel fought tooth and nail, but his punches and kicks didn't deter Michael, whose face was dark with rage and determination.

Kasha leapt from next to me, flapping her small wings to get to her warrior. She would never be able to help him. I winced when I grabbed both hilts of my weapons, bile rising steadily within me. I gagged as my head swam, my body feeling like it was crumbling apart. My whips snapped backwards, coiling around the top-loop of the church bell in the wall to my left side. With a roar I flung my arms forward and up. Feeling the connection racing through my whips to the bell, I infused it with what was left in me.

The last thing I saw was the bell launching from the wall – spraying bricks and dust everywhere – and sailing toward Michael's head. Then my hands opened and I felt my head hit concrete. Darkness bled into my field of view from all sides, until all I saw was black. Pain and darkness enveloped me and carried me off as I sank ever deeper into both. Until I became it, until it was all I was.

Chapter Twenty-Eight
Mihr
The Surface,
the Black Forest

No matter where or how hard I punched, Michael didn't budge, his six wings drove us toward the ground at hair-raising speed and I knew I'd never walk away from it.

A whistling sound was all the warning I got, then Michael's stare left my face, zeroing in on something over my right shoulder. I turned to the left, wrenching from his hold. *Gong!* Something huge and made of metal grazed my shoulder and slammed into Michael's chest. The Archangel was ripped off me, taking a good portion of my wings with him. Feathers tore free where he gripped them, and I heard one of my wingspines breaking when he was punched back. I turned, opening what was left of my wings and felt my plummet slow. Still, I barreled past Kasha who had flown up to help, no doubt, and saw the ground coming closer at an alarming rate. Trying to steer my body, I aimed for the field of grass next to the pavement.

A loud boom sounded from somewhere behind me, telling me that Michael had already reached the ground. But it barely registered due to my own imminent crash-landing.

This was going to hurt. My body connected with the field. The impact reverberating through my entire being. I felt bones crack, then break as I vaulted off the ground to reconnect once more in a mess of limbs and

311

pain. I rolled across the grass a few times, then finally came to a stop. I hacked and coughed to get some air down my throat, but for a few heartbeats nothing happened, and panic mixed with the pain radiating across my entire body. Then a searing breath passed down my windpipe and inflated my lungs. It felt like fire racing down my throat, to singe my chest from the inside out.

"Mihr!" Cam's voice reached me, and I struggled to stand. One leg was broken and useless, the other seemed to be intact, but my ankle pounded something fierce as I hopped toward Cam and Fane. The Human waved me over, her expression panic-stricken. Off to one side, stood the she-Angel, holding her companion up, looking unsure as to what to do.

Kasha sailed down, landing in the small crater I had made with my body when it had hit the ground. She bounded through the grass to be at my side, and I strained to pat her head when she reached me.

"Come quick!" Cam yelled and pointed behind her.

The breath burning in my lungs left me in a rush when I saw Fane lying next to the bakery, unmoving.

Cam sank down at her side and shook her shoulders, then felt for a pulse. *What happened?*

I hobbled on as fast as I could, when arms came around me and I was whisked off the ground. Michael threw me across the field and onto the concrete pavement. I caught the fall, rolling over and straightening on my half-good leg. I barely felt the added bruises my fall had caused, and hopped on, my gaze trained on Fane's unmoving body.

Shortly before I reached her, Michael grabbed me from behind and wrenched me back. I hit the concrete and slid across it, small stones and dirt scraping at my skin and embedding themselves into the open wounds on my back. Still, I didn't allow my eyes to leave Fane. *Had she moved?* Nothing I felt could counter the ice-cold fear holding my heart in a firm grip.

"Kill them already," Michael huffed, pointing at Fane and Cam.

The she-Angel looked at him, then at Cam, and finally at her comrade. "He will die. I need to get him back to so he can get help."

"I don't fucking care," Michael fumed. "You let him go and finish your job! Now!"

"No regard for the life of your own?" I heaved out, trying to get up and failing.

"They serve a purpose, like we all do," Michael said. "Nothing more, nothing less. Now, do as I command, Karina."

Karina stared at him, then she hiked her companion up and spread her wings. "No." She leapt into the air and flew away, the male Angel dangling at her side.

"Karina! Get back here!"

I spat out a mouthful of blood and chuckled, my chest hurting from the vibration. "You lost, Michael. She will tell her peers what happened here today. You lost control over her."

The Archangel snorted and walked over, his face bruised and beaten from our fight and whatever had bitchslapped him from the sky. His nose was busted, and blood dripped from a cut on his lower lip.

He placed his foot on my chest, pressing me down and I grunted as his weight crushed my broken ribs further.

"Looks like you lost," he said. "I'll make sure your Demon is dead, then I will take you with me. To the Seers. And once this mess is cleaned up and I go to Him with my findings, I will be the one in highest regard. And Hell will fall."

A gurgling hiss sounded, and Kasha sprang up to slice and bite at his leg, attached to the foot stepping on me.

Michael backhanded her and she was flung away with a yowl, the sound piercing me like a dagger. My former friend stomped on me once, sending the burning air from my lungs. And I wheezed and tried to suck in rattling wet breaths as he turned from me.

"I have had enough of this Demon and this Human interfering," he said and stalked toward Cam, who was still perched over Fane, trying to wake her up. I rolled onto my stomach and pulled my body over the ground, crawling to try and stop Michael. Somehow. My hands scraped through the sand and dirt and I knew I'd never reach them in time. And even if I did, there was no way I could best him.

My finger sliced along something sharp, and I glanced at it. What was left of my sword poked out from a pile of rubble. Fane had torn the blade apart when Michael had tried to kill her. I grabbed hold and pulled the middle part from the rubble and tucked it against my side.

"He will never stand for what you did, Michael," I rasped, crawling closer. "If you kill that Human, he will cast you out. Just like he did with Lucifer."

Michael slowed, but didn't stop. He bent down, pulling Cam from Fane.

The Human yelled, slapped and kicked at him, but he just picked her up by her throat. If he squeezed, Cam was done for.

"You'll be just like him. A fallen Angel. Is that what you want?" My arms shook as I pushed my torso up. Coughing up blood, I made it to my knees. "You will never be good enough, Michael. Because you are lacking the most important thing."

Cam's feet kicked the air and her face was turning red, her eyes budging in their sockets.

I stumbled to my good leg and hopped a step closer. "You are made, not born. He will never see more in you than something taken from the Earth. He will never call you kin. Not truly."

Michael pivoted to face me, swinging Cam with him. His jaw clenched and a muscle in his cheek twitched. His eyes were as white as his wings, his divine face a mask of hate and rage.

"You want me to shut up? Then finish me, you unworthy piece of shit. I am closer to Him than you'll ever be. Even cast out and shunned, I am still something you'll never be – born of His blood."

With a sharp yell, Michael threw Cam away, who landed on her ass, gasping for air but alive. Then the Archangel strode my way. His palms both closed around *my* neck now and I was the one being lifted into the air.

"You have no idea what you are talking about," he snarled. "I have killed more Demons than anyone. I have built up an army that will overtake Hell. What have you done?"

"I haven't changed so much for the worse that I'm unrecognizable to those that love me. And I didn't almost kill a Human just for protecting her Demon friend."

He glared at me, his fists squeezing around my throat. "I know He will understand once I explain. And I will always be better than you."

"Maybe," I squeezed past his hands, readying the blade in my left hand. "But you'll also be dead."

"Arken." He frowned at me as I said the word and brought my blade to his neck. The metal bled to black, searing my flesh, and I roared with pain as I clutched it with both hands and drew it through Michael's neck, from his throat to his spine. It was like slicing butter with a heated knife. The surprise on his face stayed put, even as his hands let go of me and his head tumbled off his shoulders. I let go of the blade and landed hard. Turning flat on my stomach, my hands blistered and burned, I used my underarms to crawl to Fane.

As soon as I reached her, Cam knelt down at her other side, still wheezing.

"Fane," I rasped, cradling her face in my shaking hands. The blood from my palms colored her red skin and our touch hurt my burned skin, but I didn't care. "Wake up, wicked Demon." I slid my finger to her neck and felt for a pulse. Holding my breath, I waited. There. Her pulse tickled my finger.

"She's alive," I said. Relief flooded me like a warm wave, drowning the terror I'd felt at seeing her this still.

Cam sobbed and tucked a strand of Fane's brown hair behind her ear. "I didn't feel any pulse," she said with a thin voice.

"It's very weak. What happened?"

Cam's green eyes found mine, brimming with tears. "She threw the church bell at that… thing," she pointed at Michael.

"She did what?"

"When you both came barreling down, she threw it, and punched him away from you. Then she just… passed out."

I gaped at Cam, then at Fane. Scooting closer, I searched her face. "Why the hell would you do that, reckless Demon?"

A soft mewl preceded Kasha, who stumbled our way. One of her wings was bent at a weird angle and she didn't use her front left paw. I stretched out an arm and she ducked under it, pressing her body to my chest. "You did so well, Kasha," I told her.

"That she did," Cam said. "She saved us. If she hadn't attacked the one Angel from behind, Fane and I would be toast now."

"And you," I raised a brow at Cam. "Why did you come? I mean, I'm grateful that you tried to shoot Michael, but you kind of lead them and us here."

Camille frowned. "What are you talking about? My phone vanished, the same day that strange woman came, asking about Fane. Dax somehow tracked it and where did it surface? Right where you guys were supposed to be."

I blinked. "B-but then how… How did you get here?"

Her face reddened a bit, and she bit her lower lip. "The same way we will get away from here. And I think we should move sooner rather than later." She indicated around us, "We did leave a bit of a mess, and soon, either your or Fane's kind is bound to show up for some cleaning action."

"You're right. We have to move."

"Right." Cam got to her feet and offered a hand to me. "Can you walk?"

I glanced at my ruined leg, then at Fane. "How far?"

"To the hut we rented." The Human let her gaze swivel around. "Got an idea, wait here." She dashed off, leaving me to stare after her. How in the name of all saints had she gotten here?

I willed my healing to speed up, wanting to get away from here as soon as possible. With the back of my hand, I stroked Fane's face. "You hold on now, you hear?" Seeing her lying there, unresponsive and spent, it twisted my heart painfully. "Stubborn Demon," I whispered. She had to hold on, had to make it, or I would break. To keep my thoughts from closing in on the possibility of losing her, I scooted closer, so Kasha, Fane and I lay touching, almost in a heap. Feeling them both close was comforting. My gaze fell on Michael's body, the emptiness taking hold of me at the sight should have been alarming, but I couldn't bring myself to feel anything. The Michael I had known hadn't been here. The man I killed hadn't been my brother for a long while. His comment about building an army himself was something I had to contemplate. Later.

The roar of an engine pulled me from my thoughts and sure enough, Cam appeared, driving a minivan that looked a bit worse for wear. The windows were smashed, and one side looked like a Demon had ripped it open with a claw. Which was probably what happened.

Cam stopped and sprang from the car. She helped me up and we both carried Fane over to the car – me hopping and having to rest every few feet, while Kasha limped behind us. We reached the car and got in.

As soon as I heaved my body onto the seat next to Fane, and pulled Kasha on my lap, Cam got inside and we sped off.

The drive was silent and didn't take long, but the evidence of what had happened in this town lined the streets and the silence grew to a grim tenseness. Too much death. Too much destruction.

Cam's face was a mask of horror as she focused on the road, her lips thinning each time she had to round a corpse in our way. It happened too often during our short drive.

Once outside the town, she steered the van up the hill at a brisk pace and we reached the hut, she had originally rented for us, in no time.

I picked up Kasha and placed her down on the forest ground, then got out and helped Cam to carry Fane inside.

The hut was empty, and a gasp left me when I saw the furniture tilted over and strewn to the edges of the room. In the very middle was a collection of circles and shapes that looked like they had been burned into the wooden floor.

"That is… those are magical runes, demonic ones," I said.

"Yup."

Cam pulled us onward until we stood in the middle of the runes. "Put her down here and don't exit the circle," Cam instructed, while taking a small piece of paper and a bit of chalk from her jacket.

I gently placed Fane down, my leg shaking from the effort of our short trip. Kasha mewled at my knee and pressed her face to my good leg.

The Human studied the paper, then sank into a crouch and scraped a small rune into one of the outer circles. "Now hold still. It's a tad unpleasant."

"Cam, stop, this is dark magic."

She smirked softly over her shoulder, as if to say sorry, then shrugged and finished her rune with a last stroke.

The ground was ripped from beneath us and we fell into nothingness. Next, I saw Cam, Kasha and Fane vanish like smoke in the wind. My own body dissolved, the strangest sensation I had ever felt raced across my limbs as they simply turned to smoke in front of my eyes. A prickling explosion, not painful, but extremely uncomfortable.

In no time at all – not unlike a rubber band – my body snapped back together, and I felt my body touch solid stone. My legs didn't hold me and I fell on my butt. I blinked and perceived a room I knew. Cam's living-room. I grabbed Kasha, who appeared at my side, and hugged her close, then looked around. We had landed in an exact copy of the runes back in the hut.

Cam was already busy hoisting Fane up on the couch and Dax jumped from where he had sat on the far side when he saw us arrive. He quickly helped his mother, then they both turned to me and helped me up me so I could sit down next to Fane.

"How?"

Dax grinned at me. "The tome. I found a spell that allows travel."

"The tome?"

He nodded at me.

"So, you are able to use those spells," I surmised. "I did wonder about it. It means you are one of the few Humans who can."

Cam sighed. "Seems like my son is a magician then."

"But it's dark magic and you have to be very –"

"Mihr?" Fane croaked.

I bent over her. "I'm here, Demon."

She slowly opened her eyes and looked at me. "You 'kay. Cam?"

"All of us are okay. We are back at Cam's."

"Back?"

"Yeah, apparently Dax can do a bit more magic than summon you from the underworld."

Fane's mouth twitched into a small smile. "Warlock Dax. Fits."

Cam took one of Fane's hands and squeezed it softly. "We can't stay here," she said. "Not after they learned where to find us. Do you know a place where we would be safe? Where no one would look for us?"

"Not really," Fane said.

I let my gaze sweep from Fane to Cam, then to Dax. "I do. It's remote. I don't think they'll look for us there."

The boy smirked and held up a piece of chalk. "Tell me where."

Chapter Twenty-Nine
Mihr
The Surface,
a village along the Coast,
Namibia - Two days later

"This is nice," Fane said, grinning in her goblin-like way, a glass of gin and tonic in her hand.

"This is epic," Cam added, taking a sip from her own drink.

We sat on the balcony of a beautiful house, on the edge of a small town. The tiled space had a round table and a set of chairs one could recline. From our perch, we saw the fair sand of the beach and the grey-green waves of the ocean. A breeze carried forth the smell of salt, sea, and freshness.

"Oceanview, hardly any people..." Fane sighed happily. "Sunshine. This is the life!"

I smiled at her blatant joy, taking a swig of my beer.

"A good thing you are a diamond-printing machine, Sleaze," Cam said, crossing her long, brown, legs.

My Demon smirked and raised her glass. "One house on the beach? How many rocks ya need?" The two giggled and toasted.

Then Cam turned to me, "How did you find this place?"

"My parents used to take me here when I was a kid."

"You used to be a kid?" Cam asked, making Fane spit out her mouthful.

"What? You thought Angels just poofed into existence?" my Demon cackled.

Cam smiled and shrugged, "No idea, that's why I asked."

"Made Angels do, in a way," I said. "But I was born, like you. My parents wanted me to see and appreciate the world we fought in and protected, and they chose this country for many trips."

"To your parents," Fane said and raised her glass.

I raised my own glass and took another sip. "Never thought I'd ever toast to the memory of my parents with a Demon and a Human," I said.

"Things happen," Fane said and winked at me.

"Are you sure we are safe here?" Cam asked. "I mean, they will be looking for us, won't they?"

Fane's smile faded as her expression sobered up. "Yeah. They'll all be after us now."

"The spell Dax wove over this house is solid," I said. *Even if it is dark magic*, I added in my thoughts, still not okay with using it. But right now, we had no choice but to use what we had. I was set on getting safe spells for Dax, though. There was no telling what using this devil magic would do to him in the long run. "As long as none of us go outside and cause a ruckus, we should be able to hide for a while."

Cam nodded. "But we can't stay in here forever."

"Speak for yourself," Fane said. "I'm never leaving."

"On that note, I'll go and get dinner ready," Cam announced and got up. She walked through the sliding glass doors and vanished inside the house.

"You know we can't stay here forever," I said. "And if what that Fury told you is true, *He* won't stop looking. What is more, they'll need more Angels to be able to roam this realm. When I blessed you and Kasha, it was excruciating. I'm not sure how much a newly born Angel is capable of enduring."

Fane sighed. "Not to mention Michael being all, 'I built my own army, blah, blah, blah.' That shit is scary." The ice-cubes in Fane's hand clinked as she slurped the remainder of her drink.

"The Angels with him were young, and you say one of them spoke of a compound. There is no such thing in Cyrisas. We have training facilities, but not a compound. I have a feeling they were part of his new – so-called – army. It would explain why they didn't care watching an entire village of Humans being slaughtered." I frowned at my beer. "But if that is true, he would have been stealing souls. How? The process of ascending Humans is a closely monitored and sacred occurrence. You can't just steal souls from it."

"I agree, it's shady what he's been up to." Fane said. "But it's not like we can fly up and find out." She looked at me. "Right? We're not gonna go looking for trouble, are we?"

"Maybe we should," I said.

Fane straightened and glared at me. "No way. Absolutely not. We are safe here. You said it yourself, no one can find us here. I'll be damned if we go looking for trouble."

"You are damned anyway, aren't you?" I asked with a grin.

Fane stuck out her tongue at me. "Smartass."

"But jokes aside, what if we are right?" I asked. "We have to help. We can't stand by while they steal innocent souls."

"And we can't let Demons who are visible and able to kill roam the Earth," Fane said, her tone defeated.

"But we could… plan and rest for a bit beforehand? I mean, I nearly died two days ago. I think that warrants a bit of relaxing time." Fane reached out and took my hand. The skin contact was like an electric sizzle and when our eyes met, I had to swallow. We hadn't truly been alone since the fight. And there were many things left unsaid between us. Her presence was still like a magnet, but after what happened, I wasn't sure she felt the same.

"I'm sorry I left you," I rasped. "If I hadn't, the Fury wouldn't have caught you."

Fane squeezed my hand softly, sending a tingle through my body. "You wouldn't be you if you hadn't tried to save those people. And you wouldn't be you if you weren't adamant on getting out there again as soon as possible. It's one of the things I like about you."

"Still, you almost… I couldn't have —"

"Shhhh." Fane scooted her chair closer. "It was a trap. For both of us. They were ready. Neither of us had a choice." She leaned closer, bringing her face to mine, her amber eyes searching mine. I balled my fist to stop from pulling her into a kiss. I had no idea if it was what she wanted.

"Are we really gonna do this again?" she asked, the corners of her mouth twitching.

"What?"

"You making me lose it until I tell you exactly what I want?" Her breath fanned over my skin and her gaze dipped to my lips.

"What do you want?"

"Stoic Angel. I want what I have wanted ever since laying my eyes on your fine behind. You. Didn't we have a deal that went along the lines of 'fucking each other to death'?"

I groaned at her words and lifted her from her chair and onto my lap. She gasped when I ground my hips into her. "Stoic, huh?" I asked, my voice guttural.

"Naughty," she whispered and straddled me. Cupping my face with both hands, she dipped down and kissed me. Our lips met with held back lust, our moans ones of abandon as our kiss deepened. My hands squeezed her ass and I had to steady her movements on top of me, lest I lost control right then and there.

"Wicked Demon," I rasped against her lips. "Admit it, you are already half in love with me."

She nipped my lower lip in answer, then sucked it into her mouth and licked it.

"Dream on, Angel," she whispered. Her soft body molded to mine just like I remembered, and I was of half a mind to carry her off into my room and –

"Dinner!" Cam yelled through the house.

Fane stopped moving and rose a bit, the Hellfire in her eyes still blazed and her chest rose and fell with ragged breaths. "Cockblocker Cam," she said. My Demon groaned and stood from my lap. "To be continued, Bianca," she said and winked, turning to leave.

I blew out a breath, watching her saunter away. I drew both hands through my hair and stood up.

After getting my body in order, I followed Fane and found her, Cam, Dax and Kasha in the dining room.

Kasha bounded through the room to greet me and I gave her a good scratch behind the ears and around her horns. I didn't have to kneel to do so anymore, as she already almost reached my hip.

Dax and Fane were busy helping Cam set the table. I joined in and soon we sat around the table, enjoying our meal.

As I looked around, laughing at something Dax said, then at Cam's retort, I felt good. My eyes met Fane's across the table, and I smiled at her. No matter how short or long this time would last, I was set on living every minute of it.

Chapter Thirty
The Compound, Heaven,
The Burned Valleys

He looked up from the parchment on his table containing the listing of the souls in transit from last week. A good haul. Many righteous men and women. They would make a fine addition to their numbers. Yes, these twenty would do fine. He marked their names and mentally went through the checklist of things needed to be done before he and Michael could go and get them.

"Five Lillitium rocks for Raegis, fix the —" his whispers were interrupted when the door flew open, and Chase barged in.

"Commander Shamal, Karina is back. She carried Thomas with her, she says…" the young Angel trailed off.

"She says what? Out with it, Chase!" Shamal commanded, standing to his full imposing height and rounding the table.

Chase swallowed and stood straighter. "Commander, she says that she fled the scene, leaving Michael alone."

"What?" Shamal strode through the stonewalled room, heading for the door himself. "Where is she now?"

Chase, who stumbled to catch up with him, nearly jogged at his side as they exited the room. "In the infirmary, with Thomas. She won't leave his side."

They braved the courtyard of the stronghold, their feet swiftly moving over the blocks of stone making up the ground. Blocks whose inner stone seemed to move as it swirled and twisted like clouds caught in a rectangular shape.

"Where is Michael?" Shamal thundered once entering the infirmary and glimpsing Karina in the hall. The she-Angel sat, her back against the wall, her face buried in her hands. She glanced at her commander, but didn't move.

Shamal stomped over, anger and anxiety twisting his chest painfully. "On your feet, soldier."

Karina stood slowly, her expression unreadable. Her face was smudged with golden blood, dirty and pale.

"Where is Michael?" Shamal repeated.

"I don't know. Probably back in the that village on Earth." Her gaze turned hard. "He wanted me to let Thomas die. I disagreed and came back here to save him."

"You will take me there. Now."

"But, Thomas –"

"Now!" Shamal yelled.

The she-Angel jumped and saluted, then she led him outside and they both took to the sky.

The descent didn't take long and Shamal – hardened through years of war – felt sick to his stomach when he saw the destruction. "Necessary," he whispered to himself.

Karina landed ahead of him and he nearly plummeted when he recognized Michael's unmistakably huge form, crumpled on the pavement.

Shamal's feet hit the ground, then his knees did as he slumped down next to Michael. The Archangel's head was missing and Shamal reached out with a shaking hand, his fingers gliding over Michael's polished armor. "How? How could this happen?" Agony and deep sorrow sliced into him and tears blurred his vision. This couldn't be. It had to be a bad dream. Michael was one of their best, their strongest. He was…

"You left him to die," he rumbled, his watering eyes finding Karina.

The she-Angel shook her head, shock plain on her features as she beheld Michael's dead body. "But he is unbeatable."

"You did this, Karina," Shamal hissed and stood up. He prowled toward the she-Angel. "And you will spend the short rest of your miserable life telling me *everything* you saw and heard." His palm closed around her throat and he pulled her up and close, so their faces almost touched. "You will make this right. And then you will die."

****

The Ninth Ring, Hell

Ragon snarled as he watched Maeve's unconscious body being carried past him. He should have doled out the punishment. It had been his property she had been tasked with bringing back, after all. But one didn't argue with Lucifer. Pity.

Black anger ate at him. If only he could go up and look for her. If only – a bloodcurdling cry interrupted his thoughts and he looked at the door it had come from. The same one Maeve had been carried out of. The very same one he was waiting to be called into.

The black, stone door opened, and a Succubus stuck out her lovely face. "Lord Ragon? He commands that you leave immediately. He has a quest for you."

"What? Why? I have an audience with Him. My property is running amok up there and –"

She slunk from the room and closed the door behind her, then sashayed her way over. Her movements were magnificent and entrancing, she was temptation from the tips of her horns to the hook of her tail, swishing from side to side.

The Lustdemon sat down next to him and stroked one long finger over his cheek. "You would dare have Him hear you arguing His wish?" she rasped in a sultry voice. "I don't recommend it. Especially not now, where Maeve has failed, and His little Angel has cried for last time."

"The Angel is dead?" Ragon asked, remembering the cry from before. That had to have been him. "Why would He kill it? Doesn't He need it to bless more of us?"

"Yes," the Succubus purred and shimmied closer, her perfect breasts wiggling softly as she did. "And Lucifer has decreed that a squadron ascend to look for more Angels. We will need quite a few to put His plans into motion." She threw her golden hair over one shoulder and placed a palm into his lap, stroking him to hardness. "He wants you to lead the squadron. And I am to accompany you." A throaty chuckle tumbled from her succulent lips, leaving Ragon a heartbeat away from pulling her on top of him. Succubi were dangerous, but danger had a way of spicing things up to unknown heights.

"I am to go?" Ragon asked, excitement mixing with lust.

"Yes," the Succubus purred. "But you are to look for Angels, not her. Someone else will take care of her."

"Who?"

"Why should we care? She is one small Ember, we have bigger targets." She stroked him up and down, then dipped her hand into his pants.

Ragon hissed when her silky skin met his hardness. "He sent you to watch over me, so I wouldn't go and look for her, didn't He?"

The Succubus smiled and bit her lower lip. "Maybe. But that doesn't mean we can't have some fun along the way. Now, will you feed me? I am so hungry. I need a bit of... sustenance before we embark on our mission up top." She straddled him and fed him into herself in one smooth movement.

Ragon closed his eyes at the feel of her and groaned with abandon. Nothing felt like a Succubus. He thrust into her when a thought hit him, and he smiled. Lucifer sent him to get Angels. Without a penance band. If he were to find an Angel and get it to bless him... He grabbed hold of the Succubus' butt and thrust again, making her convulse and moan. He could be as free as Fane – free to find her, wherever she was hiding.

****

The Surface, a house on the beach, Namibia

She listened to the waves breaking, rolling, and thundering. It was a nice sound. Agreeable. A door opened and she hopped from the bed, landing on her soft paws without making a sound. It was time for her to leave her warrior behind for now.

Sure enough, almost silent footsteps reached her ears. The Demon. She was coming to mate with her Angel. Kasha would leave them their privacy.

The door to Mihr's room opened and Kasha dashed through the gap, unseen by Fane. With a click, it closed behind her and she sat, listening to whispers and giggles of the two in the room behind her. When the sounds turned to kisses and moans, Kasha snuck off. She knew of one who would still be awake at this hour, other than the lovebirds.

She walked up a flight of stairs, passed Camille's room and stood on her hind legs to paw the handle of the next room. The door opened and she squeezed inside.

Just like she predicted, the boy was lying on his stomach, the book he always read opened before him, the soft glow of his bedside lamp making shadows fall across his face. He had grown gaunt. It was almost invisible, but Kasha had noticed. He snuck food to her underneath the table, instead of eating it.

"Kasha?" Daxter asked and scrambled from the bed. He walked over, closed the door and gave her ears a scratch. "Can't sleep either?"

She mewled in answer. Together they climbed onto the bed and lay side by side.

Daxter was soon immersed in his book once more, while he absentmindedly stroked her back. Kasha stretched and purred. So good.

A strange smell hit her sensitive nose and she sniffed. Rot and blood. It came from the arm of the boy. She pawed his arm and he sucked in a breath.

"Ouch." He pulled back and looked at her.

Confused, Kasha looked from him to his arm. Her claws had been retracted, how had she hurt him?

He smiled softly, his eyes sad. "It wasn't you." He leaned closer. "Can you keep a secret Kasha?" Daxter drew the sleeve of his shirt up, revealing long gashes on his flesh. The origin of the smell. Kasha licked over his wounds once. They were dry, not bleeding, but the taste of rot made her sneeze. It was wrong.

"They have gotten worse," Daxter murmured. "When I summoned Fane, they were small and I could hide them easily. Now? Since the portal and the protection spell… They grow bigger every night."

The boy pulled the sleeve back down and bit his lip. "There has to be something in here to help me. Something that tells me what I can do to make it better."

He flicked through the pages. "If only I could read all of it. But see here? All of this is in some weird language I can't decipher. Neither Fane nor Mihr can read it, so I have no idea what it is." A frustrated grunt left him and Kasha snuggled closer, purring a bit more.

He was agitated and in pain, and she couldn't help him.

Daxter drew and arm around her and buried his face in her fur. "Thank you for being here. I have no idea what to do." She felt tears drop onto her fur and licked his hands to try and help.

"I can't tell anyone. They need me to keep them safe. If I told them… Mom would never allow me to use magic again." He sniffled and pulled his face free, then he wiped his eyes with a palm and opened the book with a grim expression.

"There *has* to be something in here."

Continue with Angel Falling (Embers Duology Book Two) to find out what happens.

Acknowledgements

Writing Demon Rising was a new experience for me and I have many people to thank for making it a such an amazing one.

Thank you, special friend, for believing in me and always telling me that I have what it takes. You make my days better and my work more colorful.

To the team at Butterdragons Publishing, thank you for trusting in me and my work. Here's to many more projects together.

To Dazed Designs. Are you kidding me? The covers are gorgeous! You did stellar work, and I am deeply in love with your art.

MJ and Joshua… You rocked my socks off. Thank you for lending Fane and Mihr your voices.

My readers, always, my readers. I look forward to you enjoying this story.

About Victoria Larque

Victoria Larque writes Paranormal Romance and Urban Fantasy. Her love for the genre is rooted in the fact that she has rules to go by, but they can be bent and even broken if need be. She was born and raised in the wonderful country of Namibia and is now residing and working in Germany where she lives in the woods with her adorable, grumpy husband. She has learned the amazing craft of being a car-mechanic, but her passion is writing, telling stories and dreaming up impossibilities. When she gets home from work, she writes. On the weekends she writes. Her goal is to, one day, be able to do nothing but indulge in her passion.

Other BDP books by Victoria Larque

Terrifying Love - A Halloween Anthology
Beautiful Tragedy - A Halloween Anthology
Angel Falling (Embers Duology Book Two)
Lakeborn
Princess of Stone (Fractured Queendom Trilogy Book One)
Golden Tattoo A Halloween Anthology

www.ingramcontent.com/pod-product-compliance
Lightning Source LLC
Chambersburg PA
CBHW010427120726
47992CB00010B/3346